THE VALLEY OF DECISION

THE VALLEY OF DECISION

A NOVEL

BY

EDITH WHARTON

VOLUME I

Multitudes, multitudes in the valley of decision

AMS PRESS, INC.
NEW YORK

Reprinted from the edition of 1902, New York
First AMS EDITION published 1970
Manufactured in the United States of America

International Standard Book Number:
Complete Set . . . 0-404-06914-2
Volume 1 0-404-06915-0

Library of Congress Catalog Card Number: 79-126661

AMS PRESS, INC.
NEW YORK, N.Y. 10003

TO MY FRIENDS
PAUL AND MINNIE BOURGET,
IN REMEMBRANCE OF
ITALIAN DAYS TOGETHER.

CONTENTS
OF VOLUME FIRST

BOOK I

BOOK II

BOOK I

THE OLD ORDER

Prima che incontro alla festosa fronte
I lúgubri suoi lampi il ver baleni.

THE
VALLEY OF DECISION

BOOK I
THE OLD ORDER

I

IT was very still in the small neglected chapel. The noises of the farm came faintly through closed doors—voices shouting at the oxen in the lower fields, the querulous bark of the old house-dog, and Filomena's angry calls to the little white-faced foundling in the kitchen.

The February day was closing, and a ray of sunshine, slanting through a slit in the chapel-wall, brought out the vision of a pale haloed head floating against the dusky background of the chancel like a water-lily on its leaf. The face was that of the saint of Assisi—a sunken ravaged countenance, lit with an ecstasy of suffering that seemed not so much to reflect the anguish of the Christ at whose feet the saint knelt as the mute pain of all poor downtrodden folk on earth.

When the small Odo Valsecca—the only frequenter of the chapel—had been taunted by the farmer's wife for being a beggar's brat, or when his ears were tingling from the heavy hand of the farmer's son, he found a melancholy kinship in that suffering face; but, since he had fighting blood in him too, coming on the mother's side of the rude Piedmontese stock of the Marquesses di Donnaz, there were other moods when he turned instead to the stout Saint George in gold armor just discernible through the grime and dust of the opposite wall.

The chapel of Pontesordo was indeed as wonderful a story-book as fate ever unrolled before the eyes of a neglected and solitary child. For a hundred years or more Pontesordo, an old fortified manor of the Dukes of Pianura, had been used as a farm-house; and the chapel was never opened save when, on Easter Sunday, a priest came from the town to say mass. At other times it stood abandoned, cobwebs curtaining the narrow windows, farm-tools leaning against the walls and the dust deep on the sea-gods and acanthus volutes of the altar. The manor of Pontesordo was very old. The country-people said that the great warlock, Virgil, whose dwelling-place was at Mantua, had once shut himself up for a year in the topmost chamber of the keep, engaged in unholy researches; and another legend related that Alda, wife of an early lord of Pianura, had thrown herself from its battlements to escape the pursuit of the terrible Ezzelino. The chapel adjoined this keep, and Filomena, the farmer's wife, told Odo that it was even older than the tower and that the

walls had been painted by early martyrs who had concealed themselves there from the persecutions of the
pagan Emperors.

On such questions a child of Odo's age could ob-
viously have no pronounced opinion, the less so as Filomena's facts varied according to the seasons or her
mood, so that on a day of east wind or when the worms
were not hatching well she had been known to affirm
that the pagans had painted the chapel under Virgil's
instruction, to commemorate the Christians they had
tortured. In spite of the distance to which these conflicting statements seemed to relegate them, Odo somehow felt as though these pale strange people—youths
with ardent faces under their small round caps, damsels
with wheat-colored hair, and boys no bigger than himself, holding spotted dogs in leashes—were younger and
nearer to him than the dwellers on the farm: Jacopone
the farmer, the shrill Filomena, who was Odo's foster-
mother, the hulking bully their son, and the abate who
once a week came out from Pianura to give Odo religious instruction, and who dismissed his questions with
the invariable exhortation not to pry into matters that
were beyond his years. Odo had loved the pictures in
the chapel all the better since the abate, with a shrug,
had told him they were nothing but old rubbish, the
work of the barbarians.

Life at Pontesordo was in truth not very pleasant

for an ardent and sensitive little boy of nine, whose remote connection with the reigning line of Pianura did not preserve him from wearing torn clothes and eating black bread and beans out of an earthen bowl on the kitchen door-step. "Go ask your mother for new clothes!" Filomena would snap at him, when his toes came through his shoes and the rents in his jacket-sleeves had spread beyond darning. "These you are wearing are my Giannozzo's, as you well know, and every rag on your back is mine, if there were any law for poor folk, for not a copper of pay for your keep nor a stitch of clothing for your body have we had these two years come Assumption.—What's that? You can't ask your mother, you say, because she never comes here? True enough—fine ladies let their brats live in cow-dung, but they must have Indian carpets under their own feet. Well, ask the abate, then—he has lace ruffles to his coat and a naked woman painted on his snuff-box.—What? He only holds his hands up when you ask? Well, then, go ask your friends on the chapel-walls—maybe they 'll give you a pair of shoes—though Saint Francis, for that matter, was the father of the discalced, and would doubtless tell you to go without!" And she would add with a coarse laugh—"Don't you know that the discalced are shod with gold?"

It was after such a scene that the beggar-noble, as they called him at Pontesordo, would steal away to the chapel and, seating himself on an upturned basket or a heap of pumpkins, gaze long into the face of the mournful saint.

There was nothing unusual in Odo's lot. It was that of many children in the eighteenth century, especially those whose parents were cadets of noble houses, with an apanage barely sufficient to keep their wives and themselves in court finery, much less to pay their debts and clothe and educate their children. All over Italy at that moment, had Odo Valsecca but known it, were lads whose ancestors, like his own, had been Dukes and crusaders, but who, none the less, were faring, as he fared, on black bread and hard blows and the half-comprehended taunts of unpaid foster-parents. Many, doubtless, there were who cared little enough as long as they might play morro with the farmer's lads and ride the colt bare-back through the pasture and go bird-netting and frog-hunting with the village children; but some, perhaps, like Odo, suffered in a dumb animal way, without understanding why life was so hard on little boys.

Odo, for his part, had small taste for the sports in which Giannozzo and the village lads took pleasure. He shrank from any amusement associated with the frightening or hurting of animals; and his bosom swelled with the fine gentleman's scorn of the clowns who got their fun in so coarse a way. Now and then

[7]

he found a moment's glee in a sharp tussle with one of the younger children who had been tormenting a frog or a beetle; but he was still too young for real fighting and could only hang on the outskirts when the bigger boys closed, and think how some day he would be at them and break their lubberly heads. There were thus many hours when he turned to the silent consolations of the chapel. So familiar had he grown with the images on its walls that he had a name for every one: the King, the Knight, the Lady, the children with guinea-pigs, basilisks and leopards, and lastly the Friend, as he called Saint Francis. An almond-faced lady on a white palfrey with gold trappings represented his mother, whom he had seen too seldom for any distinct image to interfere with the illusion; a knight in damascened armor and scarlet cloak was the valiant captain, his father, who held a commission in the ducal army; and a proud young man in diadem and ermine, attended by a retinue of pages, stood for his cousin, the reigning Duke of Pianura.

A mist, as usual at that hour, was rising from the marshes between Pontesordo and Pianura, and the light soon ebbed from the saint's face, leaving the chapel in obscurity. Odo had crept there that afternoon with a keener sense than usual of the fact that life was hard on little boys; and though he was cold and hungry and half afraid, the solitude in which he cowered seemed more endurable than the noisy kitchen where, at that hour, the farm-hands were gathering for their polenta and Filomena was screaming at the frightened orphan who carried the dishes to the table. He knew, of course, that life at Pontesordo would not last forever; that in time he would grow up and be mysteriously transformed into a young gentleman with a sword and laced coat, who would go to court and perhaps be an officer in the Duke's army or in that of some neighboring prince; but, viewed from the lowliness of his nine years, that dazzling prospect was too remote to yield much solace for the cuffs and sneers, the ragged shoes and sour bread of the present. The fog outside had thickened and the face of Odo's friend was now discernible only as a spot of pallor in the surrounding dimness. Even he seemed farther away than usual, withdrawn into the fog as into that mist of indifference which lay all about Odo's hot and eager spirit. The child sat down among the gourds and medlars on the muddy floor and hid his face against his knees.

He had sat there a long time when the noise of wheels and the crack of a postilion's whip roused the dogs chained in the stable. Odo's heart began to beat. What could the sounds mean? It was as though the flood-tide of the unknown were rising about him and bursting open the chapel-door to pour in on his loneliness. It was in fact Filomena who opened the door, crying out to him in an odd Easter Sunday voice, the voice she used when she had on her silk neckerchief and gold chain, or when she was talking to the bailiff.

Odo sprang up and hid his face in her lap. She seemed, of a sudden, nearer to him than any one else, a last barrier between himself and the mystery that awaited him outside.

"Come, you poor sparrow," she said, dragging him across the threshold of the chapel, "the abate is here asking for you;" and she crossed herself as though she had named a saint.

Odo pulled away from her, with a last wistful glance at Saint Francis, who looked back at him in an ecstasy of commiseration.

"Come, come," Filomena repeated, dropping to her ordinary key as she felt the resistance of the little boy's hand. "Have you no heart, you wicked child? But, to be sure, the poor innocent doesn't know! Come, cavaliere, your illustrious mother waits."

"My mother?" The blood rushed to his face; and she had called him *cavaliere!*

"Not here, my poor lamb. The abate is here; don't you see the lights of the carriage? There, there—go to him. I haven't told him, your reverence; it's my silly tender-heartedness that won't let me. He's always been like one of my own creatures to me—" and she confounded Odo by bursting into tears.

The abate stood on the door-step. He was a tall stout man with a hooked nose and lace ruffles. His nostrils were stained with snuff and he took a pinch from a tortoiseshell box set with the miniature of a lady; then he looked down at Odo and shrugged his shoulders.

Odo was growing sick with apprehension. It was two days before the appointed time for his weekly instruction and he had not prepared his catechism. He had not even thought of it—and the abate could use the cane. Odo stood silent and envied girls, who are not disgraced by crying. The tears were in his throat, but he had fixed principles about crying. It was his opinion that a little boy who was a cavaliere might weep when he was angry or sorry, but never when he was afraid; so he held his head high and put his hand to his side, as though to rest it on his sword.

The abate sneezed and tapped his snuff-box. "Come, come, cavaliere, you must be brave; you must be a man; you have duties, you have responsibilities. It's your duty to console your mother—the poor lady is plunged in despair. Eh? What's that? You have n't told him? Cavaliere, your illustrious father is no more."

Odo stared a moment without understanding; then his grief burst from him in a great sob and he hid himself against Filomena's apron, weeping for the father in damascened armor and scarlet cloak.

[11]

"Come, come," said the abate impatiently. "Is supper laid? for we must be gone as soon as the mist rises." He took the little boy by the hand. "Would it not distract your mind to recite the catechism?" he enquired.

"No, no," cried Odo with redoubled sobs.

"Well, then, as you will. What a madman!" he exclaimed to Filomena. "I warrant it has n't seen its father three times in its life.—Come in, cavaliere, come to supper."

Filomena had laid a table in the stone chamber known as the bailiff's parlor; and thither the abate dragged his charge and set him down before the coarse tablecloth covered with earthen platters. A tallow dip threw its flare on the abate's big aquiline face as he sat opposite Odo, gulping the hastily prepared *frittura* and the thick purple wine in its wicker flask. Odo could eat nothing. The tears still ran down his cheeks and his whole soul was possessed by the longing to steal back and see whether the figure of the knight in the scarlet cloak had vanished from the chapel-wall. The abate ate in silence, gobbling his food like the old black pig in the yard; when he had finished he stood up, exclaiming, "Death comes to us all, as the hawk said to the chicken! You must be a man, cavaliere;" then he stepped into the kitchen and called out for the horses to be put to. The farm-hands had slunk away to one of the outhouses and Filomena and Jacopone stood bowing and curtsying as the carriage drew up at the kitchen-door. In a corner of the big vaulted room the little foundling was washing the dishes, heaping the scraps in a bowl for herself and the fowls. Odo ran back and touched her arm. She gave a start and looked at him with frightened eyes. He had nothing to give her, but he said, "Good-bye, Momola," and he thought to himself that when he was grown-up and had a sword he would surely come back and bring her a pair of shoes and a *panettone*. The abate was calling him and the next moment he found himself lifted into the carriage, amid the blessings and lamentations of his foster-parents; and with a great baying of dogs and clacking of whip-cord the horses clattered out of the farm-yard and turned their heads toward Pianura.

The mist had rolled back and fields and vineyards lay bare to the winter moon. The way was lonely, for it skirted the marsh, where no one lived; and only here and there the tall black shadow of a crucifix ate into the whiteness of the road. Shreds of vapor still hung about the hollows, but beyond these fold on fold of translucent hills melted into a sky dewy with stars. Odo cowered in his corner, staring out awestruck at the unrolling of the strange white landscape. He had seldom been out at night and never in a carriage; and there was something terrifying to him in this flight through the silent moon-washed fields, where no oxen moved in

the furrows, no peasants pruned the mulberries and not
a goat's bell tinkled among the oaks. He felt himself
alone in a ghostly world from which even the animals
had vanished, and at last he averted his eyes from the
dreadful scene and sat watching the abate, who had
fixed a reading-lamp at his back, and whose hooked-
nosed shadow, as the springs jolted him up and down,
danced overhead like the huge threatening Pulcinella
at the fair of Pontesordo.

II

THE gleam of a lantern woke Odo. The horses had
stopped at the gates of Pianura, and the abate
giving the pass-word, the carriage rolled under the
gate-house and continued its way over the loud cobblestones of the ducal streets. These streets were so dark,
being lit but by some lantern projecting here and there
from the angle of a wall, or by the flare of an oil-lamp
under a shrine, that Odo, leaning eagerly out, could
only now and then catch a sculptured palace-window,
the grinning mask on the keystone of an archway, or
the gleaming yellowish façade of a church inlaid with
marbles. Once or twice an uncurtained window showed
a group of men drinking about a wine-shop table, or an
artisan bending over his work by the light of a tallow-
dip; but for the most part doors and windows were

[14]

barred and the streets disturbed only by the watch-
man's cry or by a flash of light and noise as a sedan-
chair passed with its escort of link-men and servants.
All this was amazing enough to the sleepy eyes of the
little boy so unexpectedly translated from the solitude
of Pontesordo; but when the carriage turned under another arch and drew up before the doorway of a great
building ablaze with lights, the pressure of accumulated
emotions made him fling his arms about his preceptor's
neck.

"Courage, cavaliere, courage! You have duties, you
have responsibilities," the abate admonished him; and
Odo, choking back his fright, suffered himself to be
lifted out by one of the lacqueys grouped about the
door. The abate, who carried a much lower crest than
at Pontesordo, and seemed far more anxious to please
the servants than they to oblige him, led the way up a
shining marble staircase, where beggars whined on the
landings and powdered footmen in the ducal livery
were running to and fro with trays of refreshments.
Odo, who knew that his mother lived in the Duke's
palace, had vaguely imagined that his father's death
must have plunged its huge precincts into silence and
mourning; but as he followed the abate up successive
flights of stairs and down long corridors full of shadow
he heard a sound of dance-music below and caught the
flash of girandoles through the antechamber doors.

The thought that his father's death had made no difference to any one in the palace was to the child so much more astonishing than any of the other impressions crowding his brain that these were scarcely felt, and he passed as in a dream through rooms where servants were quarrelling over cards, and waiting-women rummaged in wardrobes full of perfumed finery, to a bed-chamber in which a lady dressed in weeds sat disconsolately at supper.

"Mamma! Mamma!" he cried springing forward in a passion of tears.

The lady, who was young, pale and handsome, pushed back her chair with a warning hand.

"Child," she exclaimed, "your shoes are covered with mud; and, good heavens, how you smell of the stable! Abate, is it thus you teach your pupil to approach me?"

"Madam, I am abashed by the cavaliere's temerity. But in truth I believe excessive grief has clouded his wits—'t is inconceivable how he mourns his father!"

Donna Laura's eyebrows rose in a faint smile. "May he never have worse to grieve for!" said she in French; then, extending her scented hand to the little boy, she added solemnly, "My son, we have suffered an irreparable loss."

Odo, abashed by her rebuke and the abate's apology, had drawn his heels together in a rustic version of the

[16]

low bow with which the children of that day were taught to approach their parents.

"Holy Virgin!" said his mother with a laugh, "I perceive they have no dancing-master at Pontesordo. Cavaliere, you may kiss my hand. So—that's better; we shall make a gentleman of you yet. But what makes your face so wet? Ah, crying, to be sure. Mother of God! as for crying, there's enough to cry about." She put the child aside and turned to the preceptor. "The Duke refuses to pay," she said with a shrug of despair.

"Good heavens!" lamented the abate, raising his hands. "And Don Lelio—?" he faltered.

She shrugged again, impatiently. "As great a gambler as my husband. They're all alike, abate; six times since last Easter has the bill been sent to me for that trifle of a turquoise buckle he made such a to-do about giving me." She rose and began to pace the room in disorder. "I'm a ruined woman," she cried, "and it's a disgrace for the Duke to refuse me."

The abate raised an admonishing finger. "Excellency . . . excellency. . ."

She glanced over her shoulder. "Eh? You're right. Everything is heard here. But who's to pay for my mourning the saints alone know! I sent an express this morning to my father, but you know my brothers bleed him like leeches. I could have got this easily enough from the Duke a year ago — it's his marriage has made him so stiff. That little white-faced fool—she hates me because Lelio won't look at her and she thinks it's my fault. As if I cared whom he looks at! Sometimes I think he has money put away. . . All I want is two hundred ducats . . . a woman of my rank!" She turned suddenly on Odo, who stood, very small and frightened, in the corner to which she had pushed him. "What are you staring at, child? Eh, the monkey is dropping with sleep—look at his eyes, abate! Here, Vanna, Tonina, to bed with him; he may sleep with you in my dressing-closet, Tonina; go with her, child, go; but for God's sake wake him if he snores. I'm too ill to have my rest disturbed—" and she lifted a pomander to her nostrils.

The next few days dwelt in Odo's memory as a blur of strange sights and sounds. The super-acute state of his perceptions was succeeded after a night's sleep by the natural passivity with which children accept the improbable, so that he passed from one novel impression to another as easily and with the same exhilaration as if he had been listening to a fairy tale. Solitude and neglect had no surprises for him, and it seemed natural enough that his mother and her maids should be too busy to remember his presence. For the first day or two he sat unnoticed on his little stool in a corner of his mother's room, while packing-chests were dragged in, wardrobes emptied, mantua-makers and milliners

consulted, and troublesome creditors dismissed with
abuse, or even blows, by the servants lounging in the
antechamber. Donna Laura continued to show the
liveliest symptoms of concern, but the child perceived
her distress to be but indirectly connected with the loss
she had suffered, and he had seen enough of poverty at
the farm to guess that the need of money was somehow
at the bottom of her troubles. How any one could be
in want who slept between damask curtains and lived
on sweet cakes and chocolate it exceeded his fancy to
conceive; yet there were times when his mother's voice
had the same frightened angry sound as Filomena's
on the days when the bailiff went over the accounts at
Pontesordo. Her excellency's rooms, during these days,
were always crowded; for besides the dressmakers and
other merchants, there was the hair-dresser, or French
Monsù, a loud important figure with a bag full of cos-
metics and curling-irons, the abate, always running in
and out with messages and letters, and taking no more
notice of Odo than if he had never seen him, and a succession of ladies brimming with condolences, and each
followed by a servant who swelled the noisy crowd of
card-playing lacqueys in the antechamber. Through
all these figures came and went another, to Odo the
most noticeable, that of a handsome young man with a
high manner, dressed always in black, but with an excess of lace ruffles and jewels, a clouded amber head to

his cane and red heels to his shoes. This young gentleman, whose age could not have been more than twenty,
and who had the coldest insolent air, was treated with
profound respect by all but Donna Laura, who was forever quarrelling with him when he was present, yet
could not support his absence without lamentations
and alarm. The abate appeared to act as messenger
between the two, and when he came to say that the
Count rode with the court, or was engaged to sup with
the prime-minister, or had business on his father's estate
in the country, the lady would openly yield to her distress, crying out that she knew well enough what his excuses meant, that she was the most cruelly outraged of
women and that he treated her no better than a husband.

For two days Odo languished in his corner, whisked
by the women's skirts, smothered under the hoops and
falbalas which the dressmakers unpacked from their
cases, fed at irregular hours, and faring on the whole
no better than at Pontesordo. The third morning
Vanna, who seemed the most good-natured of the
women, cried out on his pale looks when she brought
him his cup of chocolate.

"I declare," she exclaimed, "the child has had no air
since he came in from the farm. What does your excellency say? Shall the hunchback take him for a walk in
the gardens?"

To this her excellency, who sat at her toilet under

[20]

the hair-dresser's hands, irritably replied that she had not slept all night and was in no state to be tormented about such trifles, but that the child might go where he pleased.

Odo, who was very weary of his corner, sprang up readily enough when Vanna, at this, beckoned him to the inner antechamber. Here, where persons of a certain condition waited (the outer being given over to servants and tradesmen), they found a lean hump-backed boy, shabbily dressed in darned stockings and a faded coat, but with an extraordinary keen pale face that at once attracted and frightened the child.

"There, go with him; he won't eat you," said Vanna, giving him a push as she hurried away; and Odo, trembling a little, laid his hand in the boy's.

"Where do you come from?" he faltered, looking up into his companion's face.

The boy laughed and the blood rose to his high cheek-bones. "I?— From the Innocenti, if your excellency knows where that is," said he.

Odo's face lit up. "Of course I do," he cried, reassured. "I know a girl who comes from there—the Momola at Pontesordo."

"Ah, indeed?" said the boy with a queer look. "Well, she's my sister, then. Give her my compliments when you see her, cavaliere. Oh, we're a large family, we are!"

Odo's perplexity was returning. "Are you really Momola's brother?" he asked.

"Eh, in a way—we're children of the same house."

"But you live in the palace, don't you?" Odo persisted, his curiosity surmounting his fear. "Are you a servant of my mother's?"

"I'm the servant of your illustrious mother's servants; the *abatino* of the waiting-women. I write their love-letters, do you see, cavaliere, I carry their rubbish to the pawnbroker's when their sweethearts have bled them of their savings; I clean the bird-cages and feed the monkeys, and do the steward's accounts when he's drunk, and sleep on a bench in the portico and steal my food from the pantry . . . and my father very likely goes in velvet and carries a sword at his side."

The boy's voice had grown shrill and his eyes blazed like an owl's in the dark. Odo would have given the world to be back in his corner, but he was ashamed to betray his lack of heart, and to give himself courage he asked haughtily: "And what is your name, boy?"

The hunchback gave him a gleaming look. "Call me Brutus," he cried, "for Brutus killed a tyrant." He gave Odo's hand a pull. "Come along," said he, "and I'll show you his statue in the garden—Brutus's statue in a prince's garden, mind you!" and as the little boy trotted at his side down the long corridors he kept repeating under his breath in a kind of angry sing-song, "For Brutus killed a tyrant—killed a tyrant. . ."

The sense of strangeness inspired by his odd companion soon gave way in Odo's mind to emotions of delight and wonder. He was, even at that age, unusually sensitive to external impressions, and when the hunchback, after descending many stairs and twisting through endless back-passages, at length led him out on a terrace above the gardens, the beauty of the sight swelled his little heart to bursting.

A Duke of Pianura had, some hundred years earlier, caused a great wing to be added to his palace by the eminent architect Carlo Borromini; and this accomplished designer had at the same time replanted and enlarged the ducal gardens. To Odo, who had never seen plantations more artful than the vineyards and mulberry orchards about Pontesordo, these perspectives of clipped beech and yew, these knots of box filled in with multi-colored sand, appeared, with the fountains, colonnades and trellised arbors surmounted by globes of glass, to represent the very pattern and Paradise of gardens. It seemed indeed too beautiful to be real, and he trembled, as he sometimes did at the music of the Easter mass, when the hunchback, laughing at his amazement, led him down the terrace steps.

It was Odo's lot in after years to walk the alleys of many a splendid garden, and to pace, often wearily enough, the paths along which he was now led; but never after did he renew the first enchanted impression of mystery and brightness that remained with him as the most vivid emotion of his childhood.

Though it was February the season was so soft that the orange and lemon trees had been put out in their earthen vases before the lemon-house, and the beds in the parterres were full of violets, daffodils and auriculas; but the scent of the orange-blossoms and the bright colors of the flowers moved Odo less than the noble ordonnance of the pleached alleys, each terminated by a statue or a marble seat; and when he came to the grotto where, amid rearing sea-horses and Tritons, a cascade poured from the grove above, his wonder passed into such delicious awe as hung him speechless on the hunchback's hand.

"Eh," said the latter with a sneer, "it's a finer garden than we have at our family-palace. Do you know what's planted there?" he asked turning suddenly on the little boy. "Dead bodies, cavaliere; rows and rows of them; the bodies of my brothers and sisters, the Innocents who die like flies every year of the cholera and the measles and the putrid fever." He saw the terror in Odo's face and added in a gentler tone, "Eh, don't cry, cavaliere; they sleep better in those beds than in any others they're like to lie on. — Come, come, and I'll show your excellency the aviaries."

From the aviaries they passed to the Chinese pavilion, where the Duke supped on summer evenings, and
thence to the bowling-alley, the fish-stew and the fruit-
garden. At every step some fresh surprise arrested Odo,
but the terrible vision of that other garden planted
with the dead bodies of the Innocents robbed the spectacle of its brightness, dulled the plumage of the birds
behind their gilt wires and cast a deeper shade over
the beech-grove where figures of goat-faced men lurked
balefully in the twilight. Odo was glad when they left
the blackness of this grove for the open walks, where
gardeners were working and he had the reassurance of
the sky. The hunchback, who seemed sorry that he had
frightened him, told him many curious stories about
the marble images that adorned the walks, and pausing
suddenly before one of a naked man with a knife in his
hand, cried out in a frenzy, "This is my namesake,
Brutus!"—but when Odo would have asked if the
naked man was a kinsman, the boy hurried him on,
saying only: "You'll read of him some day in Plutarch."

III

ODO, next morning, under the hunchback's guidance, continued his exploration of the palace. His
mother seemed glad to be rid of him, and Vanna pack-
ing him off early, with the warning that he was not to

fall into the fish-ponds or get himself trampled by the horses, he guessed, with a thrill, that he had leave to visit the stables. Here, in fact, the two boys were soon making their way among the crowd of grooms and strappers in the yard, seeing the Duke's carriage-horses groomed and the Duchess's cream-colored hackney saddled for her ride in the chase; and at length, after much lingering and gazing, going on to the harness-rooms and coach-house. The state-carriages with their carved and gilt wheels, their panels gay with flushed divinities and their stupendous velvet hammer-cloths edged with bullion, held Odo spell-bound. He had a born taste for splendor, and the thought that he might one day sit in one of these glittering vehicles puffed his breast with pride and made him address the hunchback with sudden condescension. "When I'm a man I shall ride in these carriages," he said; whereat the other laughed and returned good-humoredly, "Eh, that's not so much to boast of, cavaliere; I shall ride in a carriage one of these days myself." Odo stared, not over-pleased; and the boy added, "When I'm carried to the church-yard, I mean," with a chuckle of relish at the joke.

From the stables they passed to the riding-school with its open galleries supported on twisted columns, where the Duke's gentlemen managed their horses and took their exercise in bad weather. Several rode there that morning; and among them, on a fine Arab, Odo recognized the young man in black velvet who was so often in Donna Laura's apartments.

"Who's that?" he whispered, pulling the hunchback's sleeve as the gentleman, just below them, made his horse execute a brilliant *balotade*.

"That? Bless the innocent! Why, the Count Lelio Trescorre, your illustrious mother's cavaliere servente."

Odo was puzzled, but some instinct of reserve withheld him from farther questions. The hunchback, however, had no such scruples. "They do say, though," he went on, "that her Highness has her eye on him, and in that case, I'll wager, your illustrious Mamma has no more chance than a sparrow against a hawk."

The boy's words were incomprehensible, but the vague sense that some danger might be threatening his mother's friend made Odo ask in a whisper, "What would her Highness do to him?"

"Make him a prime-minister, cavaliere," the hunchback laughed.

Odo's guide, it appeared, was not privileged to conduct him through the state-apartments of the palace, and the little boy had now been four days under the ducal roof without catching so much as a glimpse of his sovereign and cousin. The very next morning, however, Vanna swept him from his trundle-bed with the

[27]

announcement that he was to be received by the Duke that day, and that the tailor was now waiting to try on his court-dress. He found his mother propped against her pillows, drinking chocolate, feeding her pet monkey and giving agitated directions to the maid-servants on their knees before the open carriage-trunks. Her excellency informed Odo that she had that moment received an express from his grandfather, the old Marquess di Donnaz; that they were to start next morning for the castle of Donnaz, and that he was to be presented to the Duke as soon as his Highness had risen from dinner. A plump purse lay on the coverlet, and her countenance wore an air of kindness and animation which, together with the prospect of wearing a court-dress and travelling to his grandfather's castle in the mountains, so worked on Odo's spirits that, forgetting the abate's instructions, he sprang to her with an eager caress.

"Child, child," was her only rebuke; and she added, with a tap on his cheek, "It is lucky I shall have a sword to protect me."

Long before the hour Odo was buttoned into his embroidered coat and waistcoat. He would have on the sword at once, and when they sat down to dinner, though his mother pressed him to eat with more concern than she had before shown, it went hard with him to put his weapon aside and he cast longing eyes at the

corner where it lay. At length a chamberlain summoned
them, and they set out down the corridors, attended by
two servants. Odo held his head high, with one hand
leading Donna Laura (for he would not appear to be
led by her) while the other fingered his sword. The de-
formed beggars who always lurked about the great
staircase fawned on them as they passed, and on a landing they crossed the humpbacked boy, who grinned
mockingly at Odo; but the latter, with his chin up,
would not so much as glance at him.

A master of ceremonies in short black cloak and
gold chain received them in the antechamber of the
Duchess's apartments, where the court played lansque-
net after dinner; the doors of her Highness's closet
were thrown open, and Odo, now glad enough to cling
to his mother's hand, found himself in a tall room,
with gods and goddesses in the clouds overhead and
personages as supra-terrestrial seated in gilt armchairs
about a smoking brazier. Before one of these, to whom
Donna Laura swept successive curtsies in advancing,
the frightened cavaliere found himself dragged with his
sword between his legs. He ducked his head like the old
drake diving for worms in the puddle at the farm, and
when at last he dared look up, it was to see an odd
sallow face, half smothered in an immense wig, bowing
back at him with infinite ceremony—and Odo's heart
sank to think that this was his sovereign.

The Duke was, in fact, a sickly narrow-faced young man with thick obstinate lips and a slight lameness that made his walk ungainly; but though no way resembling the ermine-cloaked King of the chapel at Pontesordo, he yet knew how to put on a certain majesty with his state-wig and his orders. As for the newly-married Duchess, who sat at the other end of the cabinet, caressing a toy spaniel, she was scant fourteen and looked a mere child in her great hoop and jewelled stomacher. Her wonderful fair hair, drawn over a cushion and lightly powdered, was twisted with pearls and roses, and her cheeks excessively rouged, in the French fashion; so that, as she rose on the approach of the visitors, she looked to Odo for all the world like the wooden Virgin hung with votive offerings in the parish church at Pontesordo. Though they were but three months married, the Duke, it was rumored, was never with her, preferring the company of the young Marquess of Cerveno, his cousin and heir-presumptive, a pale boy scented with musk and painted like a comedian, whom his Highness would never suffer away from him, and who now leaned with an impertinent air against the back of the ducal armchair. On the other side of the brazier sat the dowager Duchess, the Duke's grandmother, an old lady so high and forbidding of aspect that Odo cast but one look at her face, which was yellow and wrinkled as a medlar, and surmounted, in the Spanish style, with black veils and a high coif. What these alarming personages said and did the child could never recall; nor were his own actions clear to him, except for a furtive caress that he remembered giving the spaniel as he kissed the Duchess's hand; whereupon her Highness snatched up the pampered animal and walked away with a pout of anger. Odo noticed that her angry look followed him as he and Donna Laura withdrew; but the next moment he heard the Duke's voice and saw his Highness limping after them.

"You must have a furred cloak for your journey, cousin," said he awkwardly, pressing something in the hand of Odo's mother; who broke into fresh compliments and curtsies, while the Duke, with a finger on his thick lip, withdrew hastily into the closet.

The next morning early they set out on their journey. There had been frost in the night and a cold sun sparkled on the palace-windows and on the marble church-fronts as their carriage lumbered through the streets, now full of noise and animation. It was Odo's first glimpse of the town by daylight, and he clapped his hands with delight at sight of the people picking their way across the reeking gutters, the asses laden with milk and vegetables, the servant-girls bargaining at the provision-stalls, the shopkeepers' wives going to mass in pattens and hoods, with scaldini in their muffs, the dark recessed openings in the palace-basements, where fruit-sellers, wine-merchants and coppersmiths displayed their wares, the pedlars hawking books and toys, and here and there a gentleman in a sedan-chair, returning flushed and disordered from a night at bassett or pharaoh. The travelling-carriage was escorted by half-a-dozen of the Duke's troopers and Don Lelio rode at the door followed by two grooms. He wore a furred coat and boots, and never, to Odo, had he appeared more proud and splendid; but Donna Laura had hardly a word for him and he rode with the set air of a man who acquits himself of a troublesome duty.

Outside the gates the spectacle seemed tame in comparison; for the road bent toward Pontesordo, and Odo was familiar enough with the look of the bare fields set here and there with oak-copses to which the leaves still clung. As the carriage skirted the marsh, his mother raised the windows, exclaiming that they must not expose themselves to the pestilent air; and though Odo was not yet addicted to general reflections he could not but wonder that she should display such dread of an atmosphere she had let him breathe since his birth. He knew, of course, that the sunset vapors on the marsh were unhealthy: everybody on the farm had a touch of the ague, and it was a saying in the village that no one lived at Pontesordo who could buy an ass to carry him away; but that Donna Laura, in skirting the place on a clear morning of frost, should show such fear of infection, gave a sinister emphasis to the ill-repute of the region. The thought, he knew not why, turned his mind to Momola, who often on damp evenings sat shaking and burning in the kitchen-corner. He reflected with a pang that he might never see her again, and leaning forward he strained his eyes for a glimpse of Pontesordo. They were passing through a patch of oaks; but where these ended the country opened, and beyond a belt of osiers and the mottled faded stretches of the marsh the keep stood up like a beckoning finger. Odo cried out as though in answer to its call; but that moment the road turned a knoll and bent across rising ground toward an unfamiliar region.

"Thank God," cried his mother lowering the window, "we're rid of that poison and can breathe the air."

As the keep vanished Odo reproached himself for not having begged a pair of shoes for Momola. He had felt very sorry for her since the hunchback had spoken so strangely of life at the foundling hospital; and he had a sudden vision of her bare feet, pinched with cold and cut with the pebbles of the yard, perpetually running across the damp stone floors, with Filomena crying after her: "Hasten then, child of iniquity! You are slower than a day without bread!" He had almost resolved to speak of the foundling to his mother, who

still seemed in a condescending humor; but his attention was unexpectedly distracted by a troop of Egyp-
tians, who came along the road leading a dancing bear;
and hardly had these passed when the chariot of an
itinerant dentist engaged him. The whole way, indeed,
was alive with such surprises; and at Valsecca, where
they dined, they found the yard of the inn crowded
with the sumpter-mules and servants of a cardinal
travelling to Rome, who was to lie there that night
and whose bedstead and saucepans had preceded him.

Here, after dinner, Don Lelio took leave of Odo's
mother, with small show of regret on either side; the
lady high and sarcastic, the gentleman sullen and po-
lite; and both, as it seemed, easier when the business
was despatched and the Count's foot in the stirrup.
He had so far taken little notice of Odo, but he now
bent from the saddle and tapped the boy's cheek, saying in his cold way: "In a few years I shall see you at
court—" and with that rode away toward Pianura.

IV

LYING that night at Pavia, the travellers set forward next morning for the city of Vercelli. The
road, though it ran for the most part through flat mulberry-orchards, and rice-fields reflecting the pale blue
sky in their sodden channels, would yet have appeared

diverting enough to Odo had his mother been in the mood to reply to his questions; for whether their carriage overtook a party of strolling jugglers, travelling in a roofed-in wagon, with the younger children of the company running alongside in threadbare tights and trunk-hose decked with tinsel; or whether they drove through a village market-place, where yellow earthen crocks and gaudy Indian cottons, brass pails and braziers, and platters of bluish pewter, filled the stalls with a medley of color—at every turn was something that excited the boy's wonder; but Donna Laura, who had fallen into a depression of spirits, lamenting the cold, her misfortunes and the discomfort of the journey, was at no more pains than the abate to satisfy the promptings of his curiosity. Odo had indeed met but one person who cared to listen to him, and that was the strange hunchback who had called himself Brutus. Remembering how entertainingly this odd guide had explained all the wonders of the ducal grounds, Odo began to regret that he had not asked his mother to let him have Brutus for a body-servant. Meanwhile no one attended to his questions, and the hours were beginning to seem long when, on the third day, they set out from Vercelli toward the hills.

The cold increased as they rose; and Odo, though he had often wished to see the mountains, was yet dismayed at the gloomy and menacing aspect of the re-

gion on which they were entering. Leafless woods, prodigious boulders and white torrents foaming and roaring seemed a poor exchange for the pleasantly-ordered
gardens of Pianura. Here were no violets and cowslips in
bloom; hardly a green blade pierced the sodden roadside; and snow-drifts lingered in the shaded hollows.
Donna Laura's loudly-expressed fear of robbers seemed
to increase the loneliness of the way, which now traversed tracts of naked moorland, now plunged again into
forest; with no sign of habitation but here and there
a cow-herd's hut under the trees or a chapel standing
apart on some grassy eminence. When night fell the
waters grew louder, a stinging wind swept the woods,
and the carriage, staggering from rut to rut, seemed
every moment about to land them in some invisible
ravine.

Fear and cold at last benumbed the little boy, and
when he woke he was being lifted from his seat and
torches were flashing on a high escutcheoned doorway
set in battlemented walls. He was carried into a hall lit
with smoky oil-lamps, and hung with armor and torn
banners. Here, among a group of rough-looking servants, a tall old man in a nightcap and furred gown
was giving orders in a loud passionate voice. This personage, who was of a choleric complexion, with a face
like mottled red marble, seized Odo by the wrist and
led him up a flight of stairs so worn and slippery that

he tripped at every step; thence down a corridor and
into a gloomy apartment where three ladies shivered
about a table set with candles. Bidden by the old gentleman to salute his grandmother and great-aunts, Odo
bowed over three wrinkled hands, one fat and soft as
a toad's stomach, the others yellow and dry as lemon-
skins. His mother embraced the ladies in the same
humble manner, and the Marquess, first furiously calling for supper, thrust Odo down on a stool in the
ingle. From this point of observation the child, now
vividly awake, noted the hangings of faded tapestry
that heaved in the draught, the ceiling of beams and
the stone floor strewn with rushes. The candle-light,
flickering on the faces of his aged relatives, showed
his grandmother to be a pale heavy-cheeked person
with little watchful black eyes, which she dropped at
her husband's approach; while the two great-aunts,
seated side by side in high-backed chairs, with their
feet on braziers, reminded Odo of the narrow elon-
gated saints squeezed into the niches of a church-door.
The old Marchioness wore the high coif and veil of
the previous century; the aunts, who, as Odo afterward learned, were canonesses of a noble order, were
habited in a semi-conventual dress, with crosses hanging on their bosoms; and none spoke but when the
Marquess addressed them. Their timidity appeared to
infect Odo's mother who, from her habitual volubility

of temper, sank to a mood of like submissiveness. A supper of venison and goat's cheese was not designed to restore her spirits, and when at length she and Odo had withdrawn to their cavernous bedchamber she flung herself weeping on the bed and declared she must die if she remained long in this prison.

Falling asleep under such influences, it was the more wonderful to Odo to wake with the sun on his counter-pane, a sweet noise of streams through the casement, and the joyous barking of hounds in the castle court. From the window-seat he looked out on a scene extraordinarily novel to his lowland eyes. The chamber commanded the wooded steep below the castle, with a stream looping its base; beyond, the pastures sloped pleasantly under walnut-trees, with here and there a clearing ploughed for the spring crops and a sunny ledge or two planted with vines. Above this pastoral landscape, bare crags upheld a snow-peak; and, as if to lend a human interest to the scene, the old Marquess, his flintlock on his shoulder, his dogs and beaters at his heels, now rode across the valley.

Wonder succeeded to wonder that first morning; for there was the castle to be seen, with the kennels and stables, roughly-kept, but full of dogs and horses; and Odo in the Marquess's absence was left free to visit every nook of his new home. Pontesordo, though perhaps as ancient as Donnaz, was but a fortified manor

in the plain; but here was the turreted border castle,
bristling at the head of the gorge like the fangs in a
boar's throat; its walls overhung by machicolations,
its portcullis still dropped at nightfall, and the loud
stream forming a natural moat at its base. Through
the desert spaces of this great structure Odo wandered
at will, losing himself in its network of bare chambers, some now put to domestic uses, with smoked
meats hanging from the rafters, cheeses ranged on
shelves and farmer's implements stacked on the floor;
others abandoned to bats and spiders, with slit-like
openings choked by a growth of wild cherries, and
little animals scurrying into their holes as Odo opened
the unused doors. At the next turn, he mounted by
a winding stair to the platform behind the battlements, whence he could look down on the inner court,
where horses were being groomed, dogs fed, harnesses
mended and platters of smoking food carried from the
kitchen to the pantry; or, leaning another way, discovered, between the cliff and the rampart, a tiny walled
garden with fruit-trees and a sun-dial.

The ladies kept to themselves in a corner of the
castle where the rooms were hung with tapestry and a
few straight-backed chairs stood about the hearth; but
even here no fires were suffered till nightfall, nor was
there so much as a carpet in the castle. Odo's grandmother, the old Marchioness, a heavy woman who

would doubtless have enjoyed her ease in a cushioned seat, was afoot all day attending to her household; for, besides the dairy and the bake-house, and the still-room where fruits were stewed and pastes prepared, there was the great spinning-room full of distaffs and looms, where the women spun and wove all the linen used in the castle and the coarse stuffs worn by its inmates; with workshops for the cobbler and tailor who clothed and shod the Marquess and his household. All these the Marchioness must visit, and attend to her devotions between; the ladies being governed by a dark-faced priest, their chaplain and director, who kept them perpetually running along the cold stone corridors to the chapel in a distant wing, where they knelt without so much as a brazier to warm them or a cushion to their knees. As to the chapel, though larger and loftier than that of Pontesordo, with a fine carved and painted tabernacle and many silver candlesticks, it seemed to Odo, by reason of its bare walls, much less beautiful than that deserted oratory; nor did he, amid all the novelty of his surroundings, cease to regret the companionship of his familiar images.

His delight was the greater, therefore, when, exploring a part of the castle now quite abandoned, he came one day on a vaulted chamber used as a kind of granary, where, under layers of dirt and cobwebs, lovely countenances flowered from the walls. The scenes de-

picted differed indeed from those at Pontesordo, being
less animated and homely, and more difficult for a child
to interpret; for here were naked laurel-crowned knights
on prancing horses, nimble goat-faced creatures grouped
in adoration round a smoking altar, and youths piping
to saffron-haired damsels on grass-banks set with poplars. The very strangeness of the fable set forth perhaps
engaged the child's fancy; or the benignant mildness of
the countenances, so unlike the eager individual faces of
the earlier artist; for he returned again and again to
gaze unweariedly on the inhabitants of that tranquil
grassy world, studying every inch of the walls, and with
much awe and fruitless speculation deciphering on the
hem of a floating drapery the inscription *Bernardinus
Lovinus pinxit.*

His impatience to know more of the history of these
paintings led him to question an old man, half house-
servant, half huntsman, now too infirm for service and
often to be found sunning himself in the court with an
old hound's chin on his knee. The old man, whose name
was Bruno, told him the room in question had been
painted for the Marquess Gualberto di Donnaz, who
had fought under the Duke of Milan hundreds of years
before: a splendid and hospitable noble, patron of learning and the arts, who had brought the great Milanese
painter to Donnaz and kept him there a whole summer
adorning the banqueting-room. "But I advise you, little

master," Bruno added, "not to talk too loudly of your discovery; for we live in changed days, do you see, and it seems those are pagan sorcerers and witches painted on the wall, and because of that and their nakedness the chaplain has forbidden all the young boys and wenches about the place to set foot there; and the Marchioness herself, I'm told, does n't enter without leave."

This was the more puzzling to Odo that he had seen so many naked pagans, in colors and marble, at his cousin's palace of Pianura, where they were praised as the chief ornament of that sumptuous fabric; but he kept Bruno's warning in mind and so timed his visits that they escaped the chaplain's observation. Whether this touch of mystery added charm to the paintings; or whether there was already forming in him what afterward became an instinctive resistance to many of the dictates of his age; certain it is that, even after he had been privileged to admire the stupendous works of the Caracci at Parma and of the immortal Giulio Romano at Mantua, Odo's fancy always turned with peculiar fondness to the clear-limbed youths moving in that world of untroubled beauty.

Odo, the day after his arrival at Donnaz, learned that the chaplain was to be his governor; and he was not long in discovering that the system of that ecclesiastic bore no resemblance to the desultory methods of his former pedagogue. It was not that Don Gervaso was a man of superior acquirements: in writing, ciphering and the rudiments of Latin he seemed little likely to carry Odo farther than the other; but in religious instruction he suffered no negligence or inattention. His piety was of a stamp so different from the abate's that it vivified the theological abstractions over which Odo had formerly languished, infusing a passionate meaning into the formulas of the text-books. His discourse breathed the same spirit, and had his religion been warmed by imagination or tempered by charity the child had been a ductile substance in his hands; but the shadow of the Council of Trent still hung over the Church in Savoy, making its approach almost as sombre and forbidding as that of the Calvinist heresy. As it was, the fascination that drew Odo to the divine teachings was counteracted by a depressing awe: he trembled in God's presence almost as much as in his grandfather's, and with the same despair of discovering what course of action was most likely to call down the impending wrath. The beauty of the Church's offices, now for the first time revealed to him in the well-ordered services of the chapel, was doubly moving in contrast with the rude life at Donnaz; but his confessions tortured him and the penances which the chaplain inflicted abased without reforming his spirit.

[43]

Next to the mass the books Don Gervaso lent him were his chief pleasure: the Lives of the Saints, Cardinal Bellarmine's Fables and The Mirror of True Penitence. The Lives of the Saints fed at once his imagination and his heart, and over the story of Saint Francis, now first made known to him, he trembled with delicious sympathy. The longing to found a hermitage like the Portiuncula among the savage rocks of Donnaz, and live there in gentle communion with plants and animals, alternated in him with the martial ambition to ride forth against the Church's enemies, as his ancestors had ridden against the bloody and pestilent Waldenses; but whether his piety took the passive or the aggressive form it always shrank from the subtleties of doctrine. To live like the saints, rather than to reason like the fathers, was his ideal of Christian conduct; if indeed a vague pity for suffering creatures and animals was not the source of his monastic yearnings, and a desire to see strange countries the secret of his zeal against the infidel.

The chaplain, though reproving his lukewarmness in matters of dogma, could not but commend his devotion to the saints; and one day his grandmother, to reward him for some act of piety, informed him with tears of joy that he was destined for holy orders and that she had good hopes of living to see him a bishop. This news had hardly the intended effect, for Odo's dream was of the saint's halo rather than the bishop's mitre; and throwing himself on his knees before the old Marquess, who was present, he besought that he might be allowed to join the Franciscan order. The Marquess at this flew into so furious a rage, cursing the meddlesomeness of women and the chaplain's bigotry, that the ladies burst into tears and Odo's swelling zeal turned small. There was indeed but one person in the castle who seemed not to regard its master's violences, and that was the dark-faced chaplain, who, when the Marquess had paused out of breath, tranquilly returned that nothing could make him repent of having brought a soul to Christ, and that, as to the cavaliere Odo, if his Maker designed him for a religious, the Pope himself could not cross his vocation.

"Ay, ay! vocation—" snarled the Marquess. "You and the women here shut the child up between you and stuff his ears full of monkish stories and miracles and the Lord knows what, and then talk of the simpleton's vocation. His vocation, *nom de Dieu,* is to be an abbot first, and then a monsignore, and then a bishop, if he can—and to the devil with your cowls and cloisters!" And he gave orders that Odo should hunt with him next morning.

The chaplain smiled. "Hubert was a huntsman," said he, "and yet he died a saint."

From that time forth the old Marquess kept Odo

oftener at his side, making his grandson ride with him about his estates and on such hunting-parties as were not beyond the boy's strength. The domain of Donnaz included many a mile of vine and forest, over which, till the fifteenth century, its lords had ruled as sovereign marquesses. They still retained a part of their feudal privileges, and Odo's grandfather, tenacious of these dwindling rights, was forever engaged in vain contests with his peasantry. To see these poor creatures cursed and brow-beaten, their least offences punished, their few claims disputed, must have turned Odo's fear of his grandfather to hatred, had he not observed that the old man gave with one hand what he took with the other, so that, in his dealings with his people, he resembled one of those torrents which now devastate and now enrich their banks. The Marquess, in fact, while he held obstinately to his fishing rights, prosecuted poachers, enforced the *corvée* and took toll at every ford, yet labored to improve his lands, exterminated the wild beasts that preyed on them, helped his peasants in sickness, nourished them in old age and governed them with a paternal tyranny doubtless less insufferable than the negligence of the great landowners who lived at court.

To Odo, however, these rides among the tenantry were less agreeable than the hunting-expeditions which carried them up the mountain in the solitude of morning. Here the wild freshness of the scene and the exhilaration of pursuit roused the fighting strain in the boy's blood, and so stirred his memory with tales of prowess that sometimes, as they climbed the stony defiles in the clear shadow before sunrise, he fancied himself riding forth to exterminate the Waldenses who, according to the chaplain, still lurked like basilisks and dragons in the recesses of the mountains. Certain it is that his rides with the old Marquess, if they inflamed his zeal against heresy, cooled the ardor of his monastic vocation; and if he pondered on his future, it was to reflect that doubtless he would some day be a bishop, and that bishops were territorial lords, who might hunt the wolf and boar in their own domains.

V

RELUCTANTLY, every year about the Epiphany, the old Marquess rode down from Donnaz to spend two months in Turin. It was a service exacted by King Charles Emmanuel, who viewed with a jealous eye those of his nobles inclined to absent themselves from court and rewarded their presence with privileges and preferments. At the same time the two canonesses descended to their abbey in the plain, and thus with the closing in of winter the old Marchioness, Odo and his mother were left alone in the castle.

To the Marchioness this was an agreeable period of spiritual compunction and bodily repose; but to Donna Laura a season of despair. The poor lady, who had been early removed from the rough life at Donnaz to the luxurious court of Pianura, and was yet in the fulness of youth and vivacity, could not resign herself to an existence no better, as she declared, than that of any herdsman's wife upon the mountains. Here was neither music nor cards, scandal nor love-making; no news of the fashions, no visits from silk-mercers or jewellers, no Monsù to curl her hair and tempt her with new lotions, or so much as a strolling soothsayer or juggler to lighten the dulness of the long afternoons. The only visitors to the castle were the mendicant friars drawn thither by the Marchioness's pious repute; and though Donna Laura disdained not to call these to her chamber and question them for news, yet their country-side scandals were no more to her fancy than the two-penny wares of the chapmen who unpacked their baubles on the kitchen-hearth. She pined for some word of Pianura; but when a young abate, who had touched there on his way from Tuscany, called for a night at the castle to pay his duty to Don Gervaso, the word he brought with him of the birth of an heir to the Duchy was so little to Donna Laura's humor that she sprang up from the supper-table, and crying out to the astonished Odo, "Ah, now you are for the Church indeed," withdrew in disorder to her chamber.

The abate, who ascribed her commotion to a sudden seizure, continued to retail the news of Pianura, and Odo, listening with his elders, learned that Count Lelio Trescorre had been appointed Master of the Horse, to the indignation of the Bishop, who designed the place for his nephew, Don Serafino; that the Duke and Duchess were never together; that the Duchess was suspected of being in secret correspondence with the Austrians, and that the young Marquess of Cerveno was gone to the baths of Lucca to recover from an attack of tertian fever contracted the previous autumn at the Duke's hunting-lodge near Pontesordo. Odo listened for some mention of his humpbacked friend, or of Momola the foundling; but the abate's talk kept a higher level and no one less than a cavaliere figured on his lips.

He was the only visitor of quality who came that winter to Donnaz and after his departure a fixed gloom settled on Donna Laura's spirits. Dusk at that season fell early in the gorge, fierce winds blew off the glaciers, and Donna Laura sat shivering and lamenting on one side of the hearth, while the old Marchioness, on the other, strained her eyes over an embroidery in which the pattern repeated itself like the invocations of a litany, and Don Gervaso, near the smoking oil-lamp,

[49]

read aloud from the Glories of Mary or the Way of Perfection of Saint Theresa. On such evenings Odo, stealing from the tapestry parlor, would seek out Bruno, who sat by the kitchen hearth with the old hound's nose at his feet. The kitchen indeed on winter nights was the pleasantest place in the castle. The firelight from its great stone chimney shone on the strings of maize and bunches of dried vegetables that hung from the roof and on the copper kettles and saucepans ranged along the wall. The wind raged against the shutters of the unglazed windows, and the maid-servants, distaff in hand, crowded closer to the blaze, listening to the songs of some wandering fiddler or to the stories of a ruddy-nosed Capuchin, who was being regaled, by the steward's orders, on a supper of tripe and mulled wine.

The Capuchin's tales, told in the Piedmontese jargon, and seasoned with strange allusions and boisterous laughter, were of little interest to Odo, who would creep into the ingle beside Bruno and beg for some story of his ancestors. The old man was never weary of rehearsing the feats and gestures of the lords of Donnaz, and Odo heard again and again how they had fought the savage Switzers north of the Alps and the Dauphin's men in the west; how they had marched with Savoy against Montferrat and with France against the republic of Genoa. Better still he liked to hear of the Marquess Gualberto, who had been the Duke of Milan's ally and had brought home the great Milanese painter to adorn his banqueting-room at Donnaz. The lords of Donnaz had never been noted for learning, and Odo's grandfather was fond of declaring that a nobleman need not be a scholar; but the great Marquess Gualberto, if himself unlettered, had been the patron of poets and painters and had kept learned clerks to write down the annals of his house on parchment painted by the monks. These annals were locked in the archives, under Don Gervaso's care; but Odo learned from the old servant that some of the great Marquess's books had lain for years on an upper shelf in the vestry off the chapel; and here one day, with Bruno's aid, the little boy dislodged from a corner behind the missals and altar-books certain sheepskin volumes clasped in blackened silver. The comeliest of these, which bore on their title-page a dolphin curled about an anchor, were printed in unknown characters; but on opening the smaller volumes Odo felt the same joyous catching of the breath as when he had stepped out on the garden-terrace at Pianura. For here indeed were gates leading to a land of delectation: the country of the giant Morgante, the enchanted island of Avilion, the court of the Soldan and the King's palace at Camelot.

In this region Odo spent many blissful hours. His fancy ranged in the wake of heroes and adventurers who, for all he knew, might still be feasting and fight-

ing north of the Alps, or might any day with a blast
of their magic horns summon the porter to the gates
of Donnaz. Foremost among them, a figure towering
above even Rinaldo, Arthur and the Emperor Frederic,
was that Conrad, father of Conradin, whose sayings are
set down in the old story-book of the Cento Novelle,
"the flower of gentle speech." There was one tale of
King Conrad that the boy never forgot: how the King,
in his youth, had always about him a company of
twelve lads of his own age; how, when Conrad did
wrong, his governors, instead of punishing him, beat
his twelve companions; and how, on the young King's
asking what the lads were being punished for, the peda-
gogues replied, "For your Highness's offences."

"And why do you punish my companions instead
of me?"

"Because you are our lord and master," he was told.

At this the King fell to thinking; and thereafter, it
is said, in pity for those who must suffer in his stead he
set close watch on himself, lest his sinning should work
harm to others. This was the story of King Conrad;
and much as Odo loved the clash of arms and joyous
feats of paladins championing fair damsels, yet Conrad's seemed to him, even then, a braver deed than
these.

In March of the second year the old Marquess, returning from Turin, was accompanied, to the surprise

of all, by the fantastical figure of an elderly gentleman in the richest travelling dress, with one of the new French toupets, a thin wrinkled painted face, and emitting with every movement a prodigious odor of millefleurs. This visitor, who was attended by his French barber and two or three liveried servants, the Marquess introduced as the lord of Valdù, a neighboring seigneurie of no great account. Though his lands marched with the Marquess's it was years since the Count had visited Donnaz, being one of the King's chamberlains and always in attendance on his Majesty; and it was amazing to see with what smirks and grimaces, and ejaculations in Piedmontese French, he complimented the Marchioness on her appearance, and exclaimed at the magnificence of the castle, which must doubtless have appeared to him little better than a cattle-grange. His talk was unintelligible to Odo, but there was no mistaking the nature of the glances he fixed on Donna Laura, who, having fled to her room on his approach, presently descended in a ravishing new sacque, with an air of extreme surprise, and her hair curled (as Odo afterward learned) by the Count's own barber.

Odo had never seen his mother look handsomer. She sparkled at the Count's compliments, embraced her father, playfully readjusted her mother's coif, and in the prettiest way made their excuses to the Count for the cold draughts and bare floors of the castle. "For having lived at court myself," said she, "I know to what your excellency is accustomed, and can the better value your condescension in exposing yourself, at this rigorous season, to the hardships of our mountain-top."

The Marquess at this began to look black, but seeing the Count's pleasure in the compliment, contented himself with calling out for dinner, which, said he, with all respect to their visitor, would stay his stomach better than the French kick-shaws at his Majesty's table. Whether the Count was of the same mind it was impossible to say, though Odo could not help observing that the stewed venison and spiced boar's flesh seemed to present certain obstacles either to his jaws or his palate, and that his appetite lingered on the fried chicken-livers and tunny-fish in oil; but he cast such looks at Donna Laura as seemed to declare that for her sake he would willingly have risked his teeth on the very cobblestones of the court. Knowing how she pined for company, Odo was not surprised at his mother's complaisance; yet wondered to see the smile with which she presently received the Count's half-bantering disparagement of Pianura. For the duchy, by his showing, was a place of small consequence, an asylum of superannuated fashions; whereas no Frenchman of quality ever visited Turin without exclaiming

on its resemblance to Paris and vowing that none who
had the *entrée* of Stupinigi need cross the Alps to see
Versailles. As to the Marquess's depriving the court of
Donna Laura's presence, their guest protested against
it as an act of overt disloyalty to the sovereign; and
what most surprised Odo, who had often heard his
grandfather declaim against the Count as a cheap jackanapes that hung about the court for what he could
make at play, was the indulgence with which the Marquess received his visitor's sallies. Father and daughter
in fact vied in amenities to the Count. The fire was
kept alight all day in his rooms, his Monsù waited
on with singular civility by the steward, and Donna
Laura's own woman sent down by her mistress to
prepare his morning chocolate.

Next day it was agreed that the gentlemen should
ride to Valdù; but its lord being as stiff-jointed as a
marionette, Donna Laura, with charming tact, begged
to be of the party, and thus enabled him to attend her
in her litter. The Marquess thereupon called on Odo
to ride with him; and setting forth across the mountain
they descended by a long defile to the half-ruined village of Valdù. Here for the first time Odo saw the spectacle of a neglected estate, its last penny wrung from
it for the absent master's pleasure by a bailiff who was
expected to extract his pay from the sale of clandestine
concessions to the tenants. Riding beside the Marquess,

who swore under his breath at the ravages of the un-
dyked stream and the sight of good arable land run
wild and choked with underbrush, the little boy obtained a precocious insight into the evils of a system
which had long outlived its purpose; and the idea of
feudalism was ever afterward embodied for him in his
glimpse of the peasants of Valdù looking up sullenly
from their work as their suzerain and protector thrust
an unfamiliar painted smile between the curtains of his
litter.

What his grandfather thought of Valdù (to which
the Count on the way home referred with smirking
apologies as the mountain-lair of his barbarous ancestors) was patent enough even to Odo's undeveloped
perceptions; but it would have required a more experienced understanding to detect the motive that led the
Marquess, scarce two days after their visit, to accord
his daughter's hand to the Count. Odo felt a shock
of dismay on learning that his beautiful mother was
to become the property of an old gentleman whom
he guessed to be of his grandfather's age, and whose
enamoured grimaces recalled the antics of her favorite
monkey, and the boy's face reflected the blush of embarrassment with which Donna Laura imparted the
news; but the children of that day were trained to a
passive acquiescence, and had she informed him that she
was to be chained in the keep on bread and water Odo

would have accepted the fact with equal philosophy. Three weeks afterward his mother and the old Count were married in the chapel of Donnaz, and Donna Laura, with many tears and embraces, set out for Turin, taking her monkey but leaving her son behind. It was not till later that Odo learned of the social usage which compelled young widows to choose between remarriage and the cloister; and his subsequent views were unconsciously tinged by the remembrance of his mother's melancholy bridal.

Her departure left no traces but were speedily repaired by the coming of spring. The sun growing warmer, and the close season putting an end to the Marquess's hunting, it was now Odo's chief pleasure to carry his books to the walled garden between the castle and the southern face of the cliff. This small enclosure, probably a survival of mediæval horticulture, had along the upper ledge of its wall a grass-walk commanding the flow of the stream, and an angle-turret that turned one slit to the valley, the other to the garden lying below like a tranquil well of scent and brightness; its box-trees clipped to the shape of peacocks and lions, its clove-pinks and simples set in a border of thrift, and a pear-tree basking on its sunny wall. These pleasant spaces, which Odo had to himself save when the canonesses walked there to recite their rosary, he peopled with the knights and ladies of the Novelle, and the fan-

tastic beings of Pulci's epic: there walked the fay Morgana, Regulus the loyal knight, the giant Morgante, Trajan the just Emperor, and the proud figure of King Conrad; so that, escaping thither from the after-dinner dulness of the tapestry parlor, the boy seemed to pass from the most oppressive solitude to a world of warmth and fellowship.

VI

ODO, who, like all neglected children, was quick to note in the demeanor of his elders any hint of a change in his own condition, had been keenly conscious of the effect produced at Donnaz by the news of the Duchess of Pianura's deliverance. Guided perhaps by his mother's exclamation, he noticed an added zeal in Don Gervaso's teachings, and an unction in the manner of his aunts and grandmother, who embraced him as though they were handling a relic; while the old Marquess, though he took his grandson seldomer on his rides, would sit staring at him with a frowning tenderness that once found vent in the growl—"Morbleu, but he's too good for the tonsure!" All this made it clear to Odo that he was indeed meant for the Church, and he learned without surprise that the following spring he was to be sent to the seminary at Asti.

With a view to prepare him for this change the

canonesses suggested his attending them that year on
their annual pilgrimage to the sanctuary of Oropa.
Thither, for every feast of the Assumption, these pious
ladies travelled in their litter; and Odo had heard from
them many tales of the miraculous Black Virgin who
drew thousands to her shrine among the mountains.
They set forth in August, two days before the feast,
ascending through chestnut groves to the region of
bare rocks; thence downward across torrents hung with
white acacia, and along park-like grassy levels deep in
shade. The lively air, the murmur of verdure, the perfume of mown grass in the meadows, and the sweet call
of cuckoos from every thicket, made an enchantment of
the way; but Odo's pleasure redoubled when, gaining
the high-road to Oropa, they mingled with the long
train of devotees ascending from the plain. Here were
pilgrims of every condition, from the noble lady of
Turin or Asti (for it was the favorite pilgrimage of the
Sardinian court), attended by her physician and her
cicisbeo, to the half-naked goat-herd of Val Sesia or
Salluzzo; the cheerful farmers of the Milanese, with
their wives, in silver necklaces and hairpins, riding
pillion on plump white asses; sick persons travelling
in closed litters or carried on hand-stretchers; crippled
beggars obtruding their deformities; confraternities of
hooded penitents, Franciscans, Capuchins and Poor
Clares in dusty companies; jugglers, pedlars, Egyp-

tians and sellers of drugs and amulets. From among these, as the canonesses' litter jogged along, an odd figure advanced toward Odo, who had obtained leave to do the last mile of the journey on foot. This was a plump abate in tattered ecclesiastical dress, his shoes white as a miller's and the perspiration streaking his face as he labored along in the dust. He accosted Odo in a soft shrill voice, begging leave to walk beside the young cavaliere, whom he had more than once had the honor of seeing at Pianura; and, in reply to the boy's surprised glance, added, with a swelling of the chest and an absurd gesture of self-introduction, "But perhaps the cavaliere is not too young to have heard of the illustrious Cantapresto, late primo soprano of the ducal theatre of Pianura?"

Odo being obliged to avow his ignorance, the fat creature mopped his brow and continued with a gasp —"Ah, your excellency, what is fame? From glory to obscurity is no farther than from one mile-stone to another! Not eight years ago, cavaliere, I was followed through the streets of Pianura by a greater crowd than the Duke ever drew after him! But what then? The voice goes—it lasts no longer than the bloom of a flower—and with it goes everything: fortune, credit, consideration, friends and parasites! Not eight years ago, sir—would you believe me?—I was supping nightly in private with the Bishop, who had

nearly quarrelled with his late Highness for carrying me off by force one evening to his casino; I was
heaped with dignities and favors; all the poets in the
town composed sonnets in my honor; the Marquess of
Trescorre fought a duel about me with the Bishop's
nephew, Don Serafino; I attended his lordship to
Rome; I spent the villeggiatura at his villa, where I
sat at play with the highest nobles in the land; yet
when my voice went, cavaliere, it was on my knees I
had to beg of my heartless patron the paltry favor
of the minor orders!" Tears were running down the
abate's cheeks, and he paused to wipe them with a
corner of his tattered bands.

Though Odo had been bred in an abhorrence of
the theatre the strange creature's aspect so pricked
his compassion that he asked him what he was now
engaged in; at which Cantapresto piteously cried,
"Alas, what am I not engaged in, if the occasion offers? For whatever a man's habit, he will not wear
it long if it cover an empty belly; and he that re-
spects his calling must find food enough to continue
in it. But as for me, sir, I have put a hand to every
trade, from composing scenarios for the ducal company of Pianura to writing satirical sonnets for noblemen that desire to pass for wits. I've a pretty taste,
too, in compiling almanacks, and when nothing else
served I have played the public scrivener at the street

corner; nay, sir, necessity has even driven me to hold the candle in one or two transactions I would not more actively have mixed in; and it was to efface the remembrance of one of these—for my conscience is still over-nice for my condition—that I set out on this laborious pilgrimage."

Much of this was unintelligible to Odo; but he was moved by any mention of Pianura, and in the abate's first pause he risked the question—"Do you know the humpbacked boy Brutus?"

His companion stared and pursed his soft lips. "Brutus—?" says he. "Brutus? Is he about the Duke's person?"

"He lives in the palace," said Odo doubtfully.

The fat ecclesiastic clapped a hand to his thigh. "Can it be your excellency has in mind the foundling boy Carlo Gamba? Does the jackanapes call himself Brutus now? He was always full of his classical allusions! Why, sir, I think I know him very well; he is even rumored to be a brother of Don Lelio Trescorre's, and I believe the Duke has lately given him to the Marquess of Cerveno, for I saw him not long since in the Marquess's livery at Pontesordo."

"Pontesordo?" cried Odo. "It was there I lived."

"Did you indeed, cavaliere? But I think you will have been at the Duke's manor of that name; and it was the hunting-lodge on the edge of the chase that

I had in mind. The Marquess uses it, I believe, as a kind of casino; though not without risk of a distemper. Indeed, there is much wonder at his frequenting it, and 't is said he does so against the Duke's wishes."

The name of Pontesordo had set Odo's memories humming like a hive of bees, and without heeding his companion's allusions he asked—"And did you see the Momola?"

The other looked his perplexity.

"She's an Innocent too," Odo hastened to explain. "She is Filomena's servant at the farm."

The abate at this, standing still in the road, screwed up his eyelids and protruded a relishing lip. "Eh, eh," said he, "the girl from the farm, you say?" And he gave a chuckle. "You've an eye, cavaliere, you've an eye," he cried, his soft body shaking with enjoyment; but before Odo could make a guess at his meaning their conversation was interrupted by a sharp call from the litter. The abate at once disappeared in the crowd, and a moment later the litter had debouched on the grassy quadrangle before the outer gates of the monastery. This space was set in beech-woods, amid which gleamed the white-pillared chapels of the Way of the Cross; and the devouter pilgrims, dispersed beneath the trees, were ascending from one chapel to another, preparatory to entering the church. The quadrangle itself was crowded with people, and the sellers of votive offerings, in their booths roofed with acacia-boughs, were driving a noisy trade in scapulars and Agnus Deis, images of the Black Virgin of Oropa, silver hearts and crosses, and phials of Jordan water warranted to effect the immediate conversion of Jews and heretics. In one corner a Carmelite missionary had set up his portable pulpit and, crucifix in hand, was exhorting the crowd; in another, an improvisatore intoned canticles to the miraculous Virgin; a barefoot friar sat selling indulgences at the monastery gate, and pedlars with trays of rosaries and religious prints pushed their way among the pilgrims. Young women of less pious aspect solicited the attention of the better-dressed travellers, and jugglers, mountebanks and quacks of every description hung on the outskirts of the square. The sight speedily turned Odo's thoughts from his late companion, and the litter coming to a halt he was leaning forward to observe the antics of a tumbler who had spread his carpet beneath the trees, when the abate's face suddenly rose to the surface of the throng and his hand thrust a crumpled paper between the curtains of the litter. Odo was quick-witted enough to capture this missive without attracting the notice of his grand-aunts, and stealing a glance at it he read—"Cavaliere, I starve. When the illustrious ladies descend, for Christ's sake beg a scudo of them for the unhappy Cantapresto."

By this the litter had disengaged itself and was moving toward the outer gates. Odo, aware of the disfavor with which the theatre was viewed at Donnaz, and unable to guess how far the soprano's present habit would be held to palliate the scandal of his former connection, was perplexed how to communicate his petition to the canonesses. A moment later, however, the question solved itself; for as the aunts descended at the door of the Rector's lodging the porter, running to meet them, stumbled on a black mass under the arcade, and raised the cry that here was a man dropped dead. A crowd gathering, some one called out that it was an ecclesiastic had fallen; whereat the great-aunts were hurrying forward when Odo whispered the eldest, Donna Livia, that the sick man was indeed an abate from Pianura. Donna Livia immediately bid her servants lift him into the porter's lodge, where, with the administering of spirits, the poor soprano presently revived and cast a drowning glance about the chamber.

"Eight years ago, illustrious ladies," he gurgled, "I had nearly died one night of a surfeit of ortolans; and now it is of a surfeit of emptiness that I am perishing."

The ladies at this, with exclamations of pity, called on the lay-brothers for broth and cordials, and bidding the porter inquire more particularly into the history of the unhappy ecclesiastic, hastened away with Odo to the Rector's parlor.

Next morning betimes all were afoot for the procession, which the canonesses were to witness from the monastery windows. The apothecary had brought word that the abate, whose seizure was indeed the result of hunger, was still too weak to rise; and Donna Livia, eager to open her devotions with an act of pity, pressed a sequin in the man's hand and bid him spare no care for the sufferer's comfort.

This sent Odo in a cheerful mood to the red-hung windows, whence, peering between the folds of his aunts' gala habits, he admired the great court enclosed in nobly-ordered cloisters and strewn with fresh herbs and flowers. Thence one of the Rector's chaplains conducted them to the church, placing them, in company with the monastery's other noble guests, in a tribune constructed above the choir. It was Odo's first sight of a great religious ceremony, and as he looked down on the church glimmering with votive offerings and gold-fringed draperies, and seen through rolling incense in which the altar-candles swam like stars reflected in a river, he felt an almost sensual thrill of pleasure at the thought that his life was to be passed amid scenes of such mystic beauty. The sweet singing of the choir raised his spirit to a higher view of the scene; and the sight of the huddled misery on the floor of the church revived in him the old longing for the Franciscan cowl.

From these raptures he was speedily diverted by the

sight awaiting him at the conclusion of the mass. Hardly had the spectators returned to the Rector's windows when, the doors of the church swinging open, a procession headed by the Rector himself descended the steps and began to make the circuit of the court. Odo's eyes swam with the splendor of this burst of banners, images and jewelled reliquaries, surmounting the long train of tonsured heads and bathed in a light almost blinding after the mild penumbra of the church. As the monks advanced, the pilgrims, pouring after them, filled the court with a dark undulating mass through which the procession wound like a ray of sunlight down the brown bosom of a torrent. Branches of oleander swung in air, devout cries hailed the approach of the Black Madonna's canopy, and hoarse voices swelled to a roar the measured litanies of the friars.

The ceremonies over, Odo, with the canonesses, set out to visit the chapels studding the beech-knoll above the monastic buildings. Passing out of Juvara's great portico they stood a moment above the grassy common, which presented a scene in curious contrast to that they had just quitted. Here refreshment-booths had been set up, musicians were fiddling, jugglers unrolling their carpets, dentists shouting out the merits of their panaceas, and light women drinking with the liveried servants of the nobility. The very cripples who had groaned the loudest in church now rollicked with the mountebanks and dancers; and no trace remained of the celebration just concluded but the medals and relics strung about the necks of those engaged in these gross diversions.

It was strange to pass from this scene to the solitude of the grove where, in a twilight rustling with streams, the chapels lifted their white porches. Peering through the grated door of each little edifice, Odo beheld within a group of terra-cotta figures representing some scene of the Passion—here a Last Supper, with a tigerish Judas and a Saint John resting his yellow curls on his Master's bosom, there an Entombment or a group of stricken Maries. These figures, though rudely modelled and daubed with bright colors, yet, by a vivacity of attitude and gesture which the mystery of their setting enhanced, conveyed a thrilling impression of the sacred scenes set forth; and Odo was yet at an age when the distinction between flesh-and-blood and its plastic counterfeits is not clearly defined, or when at least the sculptured image is still a mysterious half-sentient thing, denizen of some strange borderland between art and life. It seemed to him, as he gazed through the chapel-gratings, that those long-distant episodes of the divine tragedy had been here preserved in some miraculous state of suspended animation, and as he climbed from one shrine to another he had the sense of treading the actual stones of Gethsemane and Calvary.

As was usual with him the impressions of the moment had effaced those preceding it, and it was almost with surprise that, at the Rector's door, he beheld the primo soprano of Pianura totter forth to the litter and offer his knee as a step for the canonesses. The charitable ladies cried out on him for this imprudence, and his pallor still giving evidence of distress, he was bidden to wait on them after supper with his story. He presented himself promptly in the parlor, and being questioned as to his condition at once rashly proclaimed his former connection with the ducal theatre of Pianura. No avowal could have been more disastrous to his cause. The canonesses crossed themselves with horror, and the abate, seeing his mistake, hastened to repair it by exclaiming—"What! ladies, would you punish me for following a vocation to which my frivolous parents condemned me when I was too young to resist their purpose? And have not my subsequent sufferings, my penances and pilgrimages, and the state to which they have reduced me, sufficiently effaced the record of an involuntary error?"

Seeing the effect of this appeal the abate made haste to follow up his advantage. "Ah, illustrious ladies," he cried, "am I not a living example of the fate of those who leave all to follow righteousness? For while I remained on the stage, among the most dissolute surroundings, fortune showered me with every benefit she heaps on her favorites. I had my seat at every table in Pianura; the Duke's chair to carry me to the theatre; and more money than I could devise how to spend; while now that I have resigned my calling to embrace the religious life, you see me reduced to begging a crust from the very mendicants I formerly nourished. For," said he, moved to tears by his own recital, "my super-fluity was always spent in buying the prayers of the unfortunate; and to judge how I was esteemed by those acquainted with my private behavior, you need only learn that, on my renouncing the stage, 't was the Bishop of Pianura who himself accorded me the tonsure."

This discourse, which Odo admired for its adroit-ness, visibly excited the commiseration of the ladies; but at mention of the Bishop Donna Livia exchanged a glance with her sister, who inquired, with a quaint air of astuteness, "But how comes it, abate, that with so powerful a protector you have been exposed to such incredible reverses?"

Cantapresto rolled a meaning eye. "Alas, Madam, it was through my protector that misfortune attacked me; for his lordship having appointed me secretary to his favorite nephew, Don Serafino, that imprudent nobleman required of me services so incompatible with my cloth that disobedience became a duty; whereupon, not satisfied with dismissing me in disgrace, he punished me by blackening my character to his uncle. To defend myself was to traduce Don Serafino; and rather than reveal his courses to the Bishop I sank to the state in which you see me; a state," he added with emotion, "that I have travelled this long way to commend to the adorable pity of Her whose Son had not where to lay his head."

This stroke visibly touched the canonesses, still soft from the macerations of the morning; and Donna Livia compassionately asked how he had subsisted since his rupture with the Bishop.

"Madam, by the sale of my talents in any service not at odds with my calling: as the compiling of pious almanacks, the inditing of rhymed litanies and canticles, and even the construction of theatrical pieces—" the ladies lifted hands of reprobation—"of theatrical pieces," Cantapresto impressively repeated, "for the use of the Carmelite nuns of Pianura. But," said he with a deprecating smile, "the wages of virtue are less liberal than those of sin, and spite of a versatility I think I may honestly claim, I have often had to subsist on the gifts of the pious, and sometimes, Madam, to starve on their compassion."

This ready discourse, and the soprano's evident distress, so worked on the canonesses that, having little money at their disposal, it was fixed, after some private consultation, that he should attend them to Donnaz,

where Don Gervaso, in consideration of his edifying
conduct in renouncing the stage, might be interested in
helping him to a situation; and when the little party
set forth from Oropa the abate Cantapresto closed the
procession on one of the baggage-mules, with Odo riding pillion at his back. Good fortune loosened the poor
soprano's tongue, and as soon as the canonesses' litter
was a safe distance ahead he began to beguile the way
with fragments of reminiscence and adventure. Though
few of his allusions were clear to Odo, the glimpse they
gave of the motley theatrical life of the north Italian
cities—the quarrels between Goldoni and the supporters
of the expiring *commedia dell' arte*, the rivalries of the
prime donne and the arrogance of the popular comedians—all these peeps into a tinsel world of mirth,
cabal and folly, enlivened by the recurring names of
the Four Masks, those lingering gods of the older dis-
pensation, so lured the boy's fancy and set free his vagrant wonder, that he was almost sorry to see the keep
of Donnaz reddening in the second evening's sunset.
Such regrets, however, their arrival at the castle soon
effaced; for in the doorway stood the old Marquess, a
letter in hand, who springing forward caught his grandson by the shoulders, and cried with his great boar-
hunting shout, "Cavaliere, you are heir-presumptive of
Pianura!"

THE OLD ORDER

VII

THE Marquess of Cerveno had succumbed to the tertian ague contracted at the hunting-lodge of Pontesordo; and this unforeseen calamity left but one life, that of the sickly ducal infant, between Odo and the succession to the throne of Pianura. Such was the news conveyed post-haste from Turin by Donna Laura; who added the Duke's express wish that his young kinsman should be fitted for the secular career, and the information that Count Valdù had already entered his stepson's name at the Royal Academy of Turin.

The Duke of Pianura being young and in good health, and his wife having already given him an heir, the most sanguine imagination could hardly view Odo as being brought much nearer the succession; yet the change in his condition was striking enough to excuse the fancy of those about him for shaping the future to their liking. The priestling was to turn courtier and perhaps soldier; Asti was to be exchanged for Turin, the seminary for the academy; and even the old chief of Donnaz betrayed, in his grumbling counsels to the boy, a sense of the exalted future in which they might some day serve him.

The preparations of departure and the wonder of his new state left Odo little space wherein to store his thought with impressions of what he was leaving; and

it was only in after years, when the accretion of super-
ficial incident had dropped from his past, that those
last days at Donnaz gained their full distinctness. He
saw them then, heavy with the warmth of the long
summer, from the topmost pine-belt to the bronzed
vineyards turning their metallic clusters to the sun;
and in the midst his small bewildered figure, netted in
a web of association, and seeming, as he broke away, to
leave a shred of himself in every corner of the castle.

Sharpest of all, there remained with him the vision
of his last hour with Don Gervaso. The news of Odo's
changed condition had been received in silence by the
chaplain. He was not the man to waste words and he
knew the futility of asserting the Church's claim to the
heir-presumptive of a reigning house. Therefore if he
showed no enthusiasm he betrayed no resentment; but,
the evening before the boy's departure, led him, still in
silence, to the chapel. Here the priest knelt with Odo;
then, raising him, sat on one of the benches facing the
high altar, and spoke a few grave words.

"You are setting out," said he, "on a way far different from that in which it has been my care to guide
you; yet the high-road and the mountain-path may, by
diverse windings, lead to the same point; and whatever
walk a man chooses, it will surely carry him to the end
that God has appointed. If you are called to serve Him
in the world, the journey on which you are now starting

[74]

may lead you to the throne of Pianura; but even so,"
he went on, "there is this I would have you remember:
that should this dignity come to you it may come as
a calamity rather than a joy; for when God confers
earthly honors on a child of His predilection, He sometimes deigns to render them as innocuous as misfortune;
and my chief prayer for you is that should you be
raised to this eminence, it may be at a moment when
such advancement seems to thrust you in the dust."

The words burned themselves into Odo's heart like
some mystic writing on the walls of memory, long afterward to start into fiery meaning. At the time he felt
only that the priest spoke with a power and dignity no
human authority could give; and for a moment all the
stored influences of his faith reached out to him from
the dimly-gleaming altar.

The next sun rose on a new world. He was to set out
at daylight, and dawn found him at the casement, footing it in thought down the road as yet undistinguish-
able in a dying glimmer of stars. Bruno was to attend
him to Turin; but one of the women presently brought
word that the old huntsman's rheumatism had caught
him in the knee, and that the Marquess, resolved not
to delay his grandson's departure, had chosen Cantapresto as the boy's companion. The courtyard, when
Odo descended, fairly bubbled with the voluble joy of

the fat soprano, who was giving directions to the servants, receiving commissions and instructions from the aunts, assuring everybody of his undying devotion to the heir-presumptive of Pianura, and citing impressive instances of the responsibilities with which the great of the earth had formerly entrusted him.

As a companion for Odo the abate was clearly not to Don Gervaso's taste; but he stood silent, turning the comment of a cool eye on the soprano's protestations, and saying only, as Cantapresto swept the company into the circle of an obsequious farewell:—"Remember, signor abate, it is to your cloth this business is entrusted." The abate's answer was a rush of purple to the forehead; but Don Gervaso imperturbably added, "And you lie but one night on the road."

Meanwhile the old Marquess, visibly moved, was charging Odo to respect his elders and superiors, while in the same breath warning him not to take up with the frenchified notions of the court, but to remember that for a lad of his condition the chief virtues were a tight seat in the saddle, a quick hand on the sword and a slow tongue in counsel. "Mind your own business," he concluded, "and see that others mind theirs."

The Marchioness thereupon, with many tears, hung a scapular about Odo's neck, bidding him shun the theatre and be regular at confession; one of the can-

onesses reminded him not to omit a visit to the chapel
of the Holy Winding-sheet, while the other begged
him to burn a candle for her at the Consolata; and the
servants pressed forward to embrace and bless their
little master.

Day was high by this and as the Marquess's travel-
ling-chariot rumbled down the valley the shadows
seemed to fly before it. Odo at first lay numb; but
presently his senses woke to the call of the brightening
landscape. The scene was such as Salvator might have
painted: wild blocks of stone heaped under walnut-
shade; here the white plunge of water down a wall of
granite, and there, in bluer depths, a charcoal burner's
hut sending up its spiral of smoke to the dark raftering
of branches. Though it was but a few hours since Odo
had travelled from Oropa, years seemed to have passed
over him, and he saw the world with a new eye. Each
sound and scent plucked at him in passing: the roadside started into detail like the foreground of some
minute Dutch painter; every pendent mass of fern,
dark dripping rock, late tuft of harebell called out to
him: "Look well, for this is your last sight of us!" His
first sight too, it seemed: since he had lived through
twelve Italian summers without sense of the sun-steeped
quality of atmosphere that, even in shade, gives each
object a golden salience. He was conscious of it now

only as it suggested fingering a missal stiff with gold-leaf and edged with a swarming diversity of buds and insects. The carriage moved so slowly that he was in no haste to turn the pages; and each spike of yellow foxglove, each clouding of butterflies about a patch of speedwell, each quiver of grass over a hidden thread of moisture, became a marvel to be thumbed and treasured.

From this mood he was detached by the next bend of the road. The way, hitherto winding through narrow glens, now swung to a ledge overhanging the last escarpment of the mountains; and far below, the Piedmontese plain unrolled to the southward its interminable blue-green distances mottled with forest. A sight to lift the heart; for on those sunny reaches Ivrea, Novara, Vercelli lay like sea-birds on a summer sea. It was the future unfolding itself to the boy; dark forests, wide rivers, strange cities and a new horizon: all the mystery of the coming years figured to him in that great plain stretching away to the greater mystery of heaven.

To all this Cantapresto turned a snoring countenance. The lively air of the hills, the good fare of Donnaz, and the satisfaction, above all, of rolling on cushions over a road he had thought to trudge on foot, had lapped the abate in Capuan slumber. The midday halt aroused him. The travellers rested at an inn on the edge of the hills, and here Cantapresto proved to his charge that, as he phrased it, his belly had as short a memory for food as his heart for injuries. A flask of Asti put him in the talking mood, and as they drove on he regaled Odó with a lively picture of the life on which he was about to enter.

"You are going," said he, "to one of the first cities of Europe; one that has all the beauty and elegance of the French capital without its follies and excesses. Turin is blessed with a court where good manners and a fine tone are more highly prized than the extravagances of genius; and I have heard it said of his Majesty, that he was delighted to see his courtiers wearing the French fashions outside their heads, provided they did n't carry the French ideas within. You are too young, doubtless, cavaliere, to have heard of the philosophers, who are raising such a pother north of the Alps: a set of madmen that, because their birth does n't give them the entrée of Versailles, are preaching that men should return to a state of nature, great ladies suckle their young like animals, and the peasantry own their land like nobles. Luckily you 'll hear little of this infectious talk in Turin: the King stamps out the philosophers like vermin or packs them off to splutter their heresies in Milan or Venice. But to a nobleman mindful of the privileges of his condition there is no more agreeable sojourn in Europe. The wines are delicious, the women—er—accomplished—and though the *sbirri* may hug one a trifle close now and then, why, with money and discretion, a friend or two in the right quarters, and the wit to stand well with the Church, there's no city in Europe where a man may have pleasanter sins to confess."

The carriage, by this, was descending the last curves above the valley, and before them, in a hollow of the hills, blinked the warm shimmer of maize and vine, like some bright vintage brimming its cup. The soprano waved a convivial hand.

"Look," he cried, "what Nature has done for this happy region! Where herself has spread the table so bountifully, should her children hang back from the feast? I vow, cavaliere, if the mountains were built for hermits and ascetics, then the plain was made level for dancing, banqueting, and the pleasures of the villeggiatura. If God had meant us to break our teeth on nuts and roots, why did He hang the vine with fruit and draw three crops of wheat from this indulgent soil? I protest, when I look on such a scene as this it is sufficient incentive to lowliness to remember that the meek shall inherit the earth!"

This mood held Cantapresto till his after-dinner sleep overtook him; and when he woke again the chariot was clattering across the bridge of Chivasso. The Po rolled its sunset crimson between flats that

seemed dull and featureless after the broken scenery of
the hills; but beyond the bridge rose the towers and
roofs of the town, with its cathedral-front catching the
last slant of light. In the streets dusk had fallen and a
lamp flared under the arch of the inn before which the
travellers halted. Odo's head was heavy and he hardly
noticed the figures thronging the *caffè* into which they
were led; but presently there rose a shout of "Cantapresto!" and a ring of waving arms and flashing teeth
encircled his companion.

These appendages belonged to a troop of men and
women, some masked and in motley, others in discolored travel-stained garments, who pressed about the
soprano with cries of joyous recognition. He was evidently an old favorite of the band, for a duenna in
tattered velvet fell on his neck with genial unreserve,
a pert soubrette caught him by the arm the duenna
left free, and a terrific Matamor with a nose like a
scimitar slapped him on the back with a tin sword.

Odo's glimpse of the square at Oropa told him that
here was a band of strolling players such as Cantapresto had talked of on the ride back to Donnaz. Don
Gervaso's instructions and the old Marchioness's warning against the theatre were present enough in the
boy's mind to add a touch of awe to the curiosity with
which he observed these strange objects of the Church's
reprobation. They struck him, it must be owned, as

more pitiable than alarming, for the duenna's toes were coming through her shoes and one or two of the children who hung on the outskirts of the group looked as lean and hungry under their spangles as the foundling-girl of Pontesordo. Spite of this they seemed a jolly crew, and ready (at Cantapresto's expense) to celebrate their encounter with the ex-soprano in unlimited libations of Asti and Val Pulicello. The singer, however, hung back with protesting gestures.

"Gently, then, gently, dear friends—dear companions! When was it we parted? In the spring of the year—and we meet now in the late summer. As the seasons change, so do our conditions: if spring is a season of folly, then is harvest-time the period for reflection. When we last met I was a strolling poet, glad to serve your gifted company within the scope of my talents —now, ladies and gentlemen, now—" he drew himself up with pride—"now you behold in me the governor and friend of the heir-presumptive of Pianura."

Cries of incredulity and derision greeted this announcement, and one of the girls called out laughingly, "Yet you have the same old cassock to your back!"

"And the same old passage from your mouth to your belly," added an elastic Harlequin, reaching an arm across the women's shoulders. "Come, Cantapresto, we'll help you line it with good wine, to the health of his most superlatively Serene Highness, the Heir-presumptive of Pianura; and where is that fabulous personage, by the way?"

Odo at this retreated hastily behind the soprano; but a pretty girl catching sight of him, he found himself dragged into the centre of the company, who hailed him with fantastic obeisances. Supper meanwhile was being laid on the greasy table down the middle of the room. The Matamor, who seemed the director of the troupe, thundered out his orders for macaroni, fried eels and sausages; the inn-servants flanked the plates with wine-flasks and lumps of black bread, and in a moment the hungry comedians, thrusting Odo into a high seat at the head of the table, were falling on the repast with a prodigious clatter of cutlery.

Of the subsequent incidents of the feast—the banter of the younger women, the duenna's lachrymose confidences, the incessant interchange of theatrical jargon and coarse pleasantry—there remained to Odo but a confused image, obscured by the smoke of guttering candles, the fumes of wine and the stifling air of the low-ceilinged tavern. Even the face of the pretty girl who had dragged him from his concealment, and who now sat at his side, plying him with sweets from her own plate, began to fade into the general blur; and his last impression was of Cantapresto's figure dilating to immense proportions at the other end of the table, as the soprano rose with shaking wine-glass to favor the company with a song. The chorus, bursting forth in response, surged over Odo's drowning senses, and he was barely aware, in the tumult of noise and lights, of an arm slipped about him, a softly-heaving pillow beneath his head, and the gradual subsidence into dark delicious peace.

So, on the first night of his new life, the heir-presumptive of Pianura fell asleep with his head in a dancing-girl's breast.

VIII

THE travellers were to journey by vettura from Chivasso to Turin; and when Odo woke next morning the carriage stood ready in the courtyard.

Cantapresto, mottled and shame-faced, with his bands awry and an air of tottering dignity, was gathering their possessions together, and the pretty girl who had pillowed Odo's slumbers now knelt by his bed and laughingly drew on his stockings. She was a slim brown morsel, not much above his age, with a glance that flitted like a bird, and round shoulders slipping out of her kerchief. A wave of shyness bathed Odo to the forehead as their eyes met: he hung his head stupidly and turned away when she fetched the comb to dress his hair.

His toilet completed, she called out to the abate to

go below and see that the cavaliere's chocolate was ready; and as the door closed she turned and kissed Odo on the lips.

"Oh, how red you are!" she cried laughingly. "Is that the first kiss you've ever had? Then you'll remember me when you're Duke of Pianura—Mirandolina of Chioggia, the first girl you ever kissed!" She was pulling his collar straight while she talked, so that he could not get away from her. "You will remember me, won't you?" she persisted. "I shall be a great actress by that time, and you'll appoint me *prima amorosa* to the ducal theatre of Pianura, and throw me a diamond bracelet from your Highness's box, and make all the court ladies ready to poison me for rage!" She released his collar and drooped away from him. "Ah, no, I shall be a poor strolling player and you a great prince," she sighed, "and you'll never, never think of me again; but I shall always remember that I was the first girl you ever kissed!"

She hung back in a dazzle of tears, looking so bright and tender that Odo's bashfulness melted like a spring frost.

"I shall never be Duke," he cried, "and I shall never forget you!" and with that he turned and kissed her boldly and then bolted down the stairs like a hare. And all that day he scorched and froze with the thought that perhaps she had been laughing at him.

Cantapresto was torpid after the feast, and Odo detected in him an air of guilty constraint. The boy was glad enough to keep silence, and they rolled on without speaking through the wide glowing landscape. Already the nearness of a great city began to make itself felt. The bright champaign was scattered over with farm-houses, their red-tiled pigeon-cots and their granges latticed with openwork terra-cotta pleasantly breaking the expanse of maize and mulberry; villages lay along the banks of the canals intersecting the plain; and the hills beyond the Po were planted with villas and monasteries.

All the afternoon they drove between umbrageous parks and under the walls of terraced vineyards. It was a region of delectable shade, with glimpses here and there of gardens flashing with fountains and villa-roofs decked with statues and vases; and at length, toward sunset, a bend of the road brought them out on a fair-spreading city, so flourishing in buildings, so beset with smiling hills, that Odo, springing from his seat, cried out in sheer joy of the spectacle.

They had still the suburbs to traverse; and darkness was falling when they entered the gates of Turin. This brought the fresh amazement of wide lamp-lit streets, clean and bright as a ball-room, lined with palaces and filled with well-dressed loungers: officers in the brilliant Sardinian uniforms, fine gentlemen in French tie-wigs

and narrow-sleeved coats, merchants hurrying home
from business, ecclesiastics in high-swung carriages, and
young bloods dashing by in their curricles. The tables
before the coffee-houses were thronged with idlers taking their chocolate and reading the gazettes; and here
and there the arched doorway of a palace showed some
gay party supping *al fresco* in a garden hung with
lamps.

The flashing of lights and the noise of the streets
roused Cantapresto, who sat up with a sudden assumption of dignity.

"Ah, cavaliere," said he, "you now see a great city,
a famous city, a city aptly called 'the Paris of Italy.'
Nowhere else shall you find such well-lit streets, such
fair pavements, shops so full of Parisian wares, prome-
nades so crowded with fine carriages and horses. What
a life a young gentleman may lead here! The court is
hospitable, society amiable, the theatres are the best-
appointed in Italy." Here Cantapresto paused with a
deprecating cough. "Only one thing is necessary," he
went on, "to complete enjoyment of the fruits of this
garden of Eden; and that is—" he coughed again—
"discretion. His Majesty, cavaliere, is a father to his
subjects; the Church is their zealous mother; and between two such parents, and the innumerable delegates
of their authority, why you may fancy, sir, that a man
has to wear his eyes on all sides of his head. Discretion

is a virtue the Church herself commends; it is natural, then, that she should afford her children full opportunity to practise it. And look you, cavaliere, it is like gymnastics: the younger you acquire it, the less effort it costs. Our Maker Himself has taught us the value of silence by putting us speechless into the world: if we learn to talk later we do it at our own risk! But for your own part, cavaliere—since the habit cannot too early be exercised—I would humbly counsel you to say nothing to your illustrious parents of our little diversion of last evening."

The Countess Valdù lived on the upper floor of a rococo palace near the Piazza San Carlo; and here Odo, led by Cantapresto, presently found himself shown into an apartment where several ladies and gentlemen sat at cards. His mother, detaching herself from the group, embraced him with unusual warmth, and the old Count, more painted and perfumed than ever, hurried up with an obsequious greeting. Odo for the first time found himself of consequence in the world; and as he was passed from guest to guest, questioned about his journey, praised for his good color and stout looks, complimented on his high prospects, and laughingly entreated not to forget his old friends when fortune should advance him to the duchy, he began to feel himself a reigning potentate already.

His mother, as he soon learned, had sunk into a life almost as dull and restricted as that she had left Donnaz to escape. Count Valdù's position at court was more ornamental than remunerative, the income from his estates was growing annually smaller, and he was involved in costly litigation over the sale of some entailed property. Such conditions were little to the Countess's humor, and the society to which her narrow means confined her offered few distractions to her vanity. The frequenters of the house were chiefly poor relations and hangers-on of the Count's, the parasites who in those days were glad to subsist on the crumbs of the slenderest larder. Half-a-dozen hungry Countesses, their lean admirers, a superannuated abate or two, and a flock of threadbare ecclesiastics, made up Donna Laura's circle; and even her cicisbeo, selected in family council under the direction of her confessor, was an austere gentleman of middle age, who collected ancient coins and was engaged in composing an essay on the Martellian verse. This company, which devoted hours to the new French diversion of the *parfilage*, and spent the evenings in drinking lemonade and playing basset for small stakes, found its chief topic of conversation in the only two subjects safely discussed in Turin at that day—the doings of the aristocracy and of the clergy. The fashion of the Queen's head-dress at the last circle, the marked manner in which his Majesty had lately distinguished the brilliant young cavalry officer, Count Roberto di Tournanches, the third marriage of the Countess Alfieri of Asti, the incredibility of the rumor that the court ladies of Versailles had taken to white muslin and Leghorn hats, the probable significance of the Vicar-general's visit to Rome, the subject of the next sacred representation to be given by the nuns of Santa Croce—such were the questions that engaged the noble frequenters of Casa Valdù.

This was the only society that Donna Laura saw; for she was too poor to dress to her taste and too proud to show herself in public without the appointments becoming her station. Her sole distraction consisted in visits to the various shrines—the Sudario, the Consolata, the Corpus Domini—at which the feminine aristocracy offered up its devotions and implored absolution for sins it had often no opportunity to commit: for though fashion accorded cicisbei to the fine ladies of Turin, the Church usually restricted their intercourse to the exchange of the most harmless amenities.

Meanwhile the antechamber was as full of duns as the approach to Donna Laura's apartment at Pianura; and Odo guessed that the warmth of the maternal welcome sprang less from natural affection than from the hope of using his expectations as a sop to her creditors. The pittance which the ducal treasury allowed for his education was scarce large enough to be worth diverting to other ends; but a potential prince is a shield to the most vulnerable fortunes. In this character Odo for the first time found himself flattered, indulged, and made the centre of the company. The contrast to his life of subjection at Donnaz; the precocious initiation into motives that tainted the very fount of filial piety; the taste of this mingled draught of adulation and disillusionment might have perverted a nature more self-centred than his. From this perversion, and from many subsequent perils, he was saved by a kind of imaginative sympathy, a wondering joy in the mere spectacle of life, that tinged his most personal impressions with a streak of the philosophic temper. If this trait did not save him from sorrow, it at least lifted him above pettiness; if it could not solve the difficulties of life it could arm him to endure them. It was the best gift of the past from which he sprang; but it was blent with another quality, a deep moral curiosity that ennobled his sensuous enjoyment of the outward show of life; and these elements were already tending in him, as in countless youths of his generation, to the formation of a new spirit, the spirit that was to destroy one world without surviving to create another.

Of all this none could have been less conscious than the lad just preparing to enter on his studies at the Royal Academy of Turin. That institution, adjoining the royal palace, was a kind of nursery or forcing-house

for the budding nobility of Savoy. In one division
of the sumptuous building were housed his Majesty's
pages, a corps of luxurious indolent young fops; another wing accommodated the regular students of the
Academy, sons of noblemen and gentlemen destined
for the secular life, while a third was set aside for the
forestieri or students from foreign countries and from
the other Italian states. To this quarter Odo Valsecca
was allotted; though it was understood that on leaving
the Academy he was to enter the Sardinian service.

It was customary for a young gentleman of Odo's
rank to be attended at the Academy not only by a
body-servant but by a private governor or pedant,
whose business it was to overlook his studies, attend
him abroad, and have an eye to the society he frequented. The old Marquess of Donnaz had sent his
daughter, by Odo's hand, a letter recommending her
to select her son's governor with particular care, choos-
ing rather a person of grave behavior and assured morality than one of your glib ink-spatterers who may
know the inside of all the folios in the King's library
without being the better qualified for the direction of
a young gentleman's conduct; and to this letter Don
Gervaso appended the terse postscript: "Your excellency is especially warned against according this or
any other position of trust to the merry-andrew who
calls himself the abate Cantapresto."

Donna Laura, with a shrug, handed the letter to her husband; Count Valdù, adjusting his glasses, observed it was notorious that people living in the depths of the country thought themselves qualified to instruct their city relatives on all points connected with the social usages; and the cicisbeo suggested that he could recommend an abate who was proficient in the construction of the Martellian verse, and who would make no extra charge for that accomplishment.

"Charges!" the Countess cried. "There's a matter my father does n't deign to consider. It's not enough, nowadays, to give the lads a governor, but they must maintain their servants too, an idle gluttonous crew that prey on their pockets and get a commission off every tradesman's bill."

Count Valdù lifted a deprecating hand.

"My dear, nothing could be more offensive to his Majesty than any attempt to reduce the way of living of the pupils of the Academy."

"Of course," she shrugged—"But who's to pay? The Duke's beggarly pittance hardly clothes him."

The cicisbeo suggested that the cavaliere Odo had expectations; at which Donna Laura flushed and turned uneasy; while the Count, part of whose marital duty it was to intervene discreetly between his lady and her knight, now put forth the remark that the abate Cantapresto seemed a shrewd serviceable fellow.

"Nor do I like to turn him adrift," cried the Countess instantly, "after he has obliged us by attending my son on his journey."

"And I understand," added the Count, "that he would be glad to serve the cavaliere in any capacity you might designate."

"Why not in all?" said the cicisbeo thoughtfully. "There would be undoubted advantages to the cavaliere in possessing a servant who would explain the globes while powdering his hair and not be above calling his chair when he attended him to a lecture."

And the upshot of it was that when Odo, a few days later, entered on his first term at the Academy, he was accompanied by the abate Cantapresto, who had agreed, for a minimum of pay, to serve him faithfully in the double capacity of pedagogue and lacquey.

The considerable liberty accorded the foreign students made Odo's first year at the Academy at once pleasanter and less profitable than had he been one of the regular pupils. The companions among whom he found himself were a set of lively undisciplined young gentlemen, chiefly from England, Russia and the German principalities; all in possession of more or less pocket-money and attended by governors either pedantic and self-engrossed or vulgarly subservient. These young sprigs, whose ambition it was to ape the dress and manners of the royal pages, led a life of dissipation

barely interrupted by a few hours of attendance at the
academic classes. From the ill-effects of such surroundings Odo was preserved by an intellectual curiosity
that flung him ravening on his studies. It was not that
he was of a bookish habit, or that the drudgery of the
classes was less irksome to him than to the other pupils; but not even the pedantic methods then prevail-
ing, or the distractions of his new life, could dull the
flush of his first encounter with the past. His imagination took fire over the dry pages of Cornelius Nepos,
glowed with the mild pastoral warmth of the Georgics
and burst into flame at the first hexameters of the
Æneid. He caught but a fragment of meaning here
and there, but the sumptuous imagery, the stirring
names, the glimpses into a past where Roman sena-
tors were mingled with the gods of a gold-pillared
Olympus, filled his mind with a misty pageant of im-
mortals. These moments of high emotion were interspersed with hours of plodding over the Latin gram-
mar and the text-books of philosophy and logic. Books
were unknown ground to Cantapresto, and among
masters and pupils there was not one who could help
Odo to the meaning of his task, or who seemed aware
that it might have a meaning. To most of the lads
about him the purpose of the Academy was to fit
young gentlemen for the army or the court; to give
them the chance of sweating a shirt every morning

with the fencing-master, and of learning to thread the intricacies of the court minuet. They modelled themselves on the dress and bearing of the pages, who were always ruffling it about the quadrangle in court dress and sword, or booted and spurred for a day's hunting at the King's chase of Stupinigi. To receive a nod or a word from one of these young demigods on his way to the King's opera-box or just back from a pleasure-party at her Majesty's villa above the Po—to hear of their tremendous exploits and thrilling escapades— seemed to put the whole school in touch with the fine gentleman's world of intrigue, cards and duelling: the world in which ladies were subjugated, fortunes lost, adversaries run through and tradesmen ruined with that imperturbable grace which distinguished the man of quality from the plebeian.

Among the privileges of the foreign pupils were frequent visits to the royal theatre; and here was to Odo a source of unimagined joys. His superstitious dread of the stage (a sentiment, he soon discovered, that not even his mother's director shared) made his heart beat oppressively as he first set foot in the theatre. It was a gala night, boxes and stalls were thronged, and the audience-hall unfolded its glittering curves like some poisonous flower enveloping him in rich malignant fragrance. This impression was dispelled by the rising of the curtain on a scene of such Claude-like loveliness as it would have been impossible to associate with the bugbear tales of Donnaz or with the coarse antics of the comedians at Chivasso. A temple girt with mysterious shade, lifting its colonnades above a sunlit harbor; and before the temple, vine-wreathed nymphs waving their thyrsi through the turns of a melodious dance— such was the vision that caught up Odo and swept him leagues away from the rouged and starred assemblage gathered in the boxes to gossip, flirt, eat ices and chocolates, and incidentally, in the pauses of their talk, to listen for a moment to the ravishing airs of Metastasio's Achilles in Scyros.

The distance between such performances—magic evocations of light and color and melody—and the gross buffoonery of the popular stage, still tainted with the obscenities of the old *commedia dell' arte*, in a measure explains the different points from which at that period the stage was viewed in Italy: a period when in such cities as Milan, Venice, Turin, actors and singers were praised to the skies and loaded with wealth and favors, while the tatterdemalion players who set up their boards in the small towns at market-time or on feast-days were despised by the people and flung like carrion into unconsecrated graves. The impression Odo had gathered from Don Gervaso's talk was of the provincial stage in all its pothouse license; but here was a spectacle as lofty and harmonious as some great reli-

gious pageant. As the action developed and the beauty
of the verse was borne to Odo on the light hurrying
ripples of Caldara's music he turned instinctively to
share his pleasure with those about him. Cantapresto,
in a new black coat and ruffles, was conspicuously taking snuff from a tortoiseshell box which the Countess's
cicisbeo had given him; but Odo saw that he took less
pleasure in the spectacle than in the fact of accompany-
ing the heir-presumptive of Pianura to a gala performance at the royal theatre; and the lads about them
were for the most engaged either with their own dress
and appearance, or in exchanging greetings with the
royal pages and the older students. A few of these sat
near Odo, disdainfully superior in their fob-chains and
queues; and as the boy glanced about him he met the
fixed stare of one of the number, a tall youth seated at
his elbow, and conspicuous, even in that modish company, for the exaggerated elegance of his dress. This
young man, whose awkward bearing and long lava-hued
face crowned with flamboyant hair contrasted oddly
with his finical apparel, returned Odo's look with a gaze
of eager comprehension. He too, it was clear, felt the
thrill and wonder, or at least re-lived them in the
younger lad's emotion; and from that moment Odo felt
himself in mute communion with his neighbor.

The quick movement of the story—the succession of
devices by which the wily Ulysses lures Achilles to

throw off his disguise, while Deidamia strives to conceal his identity; the scenic beauties of the background, shifting from sculpture-gallery to pleasance, from pleasance to banquet-hall; the pomp and glitter of the royal train, the melting graces of Deidamia and her maidens; seemed, in their multiple appeal, to develop in Odo new faculties of perception. It was his first initiation into Italian poetry, and the numbers, now broken, harsh and passionate, now flowing into liquid sweetness, were so blent with sound and color that he scarce knew through which sense they reached him. Deidamia's strophes thrilled him like the singing-girl's kiss, and at the young hero's cry—

Ma lo so ch'io sono Achille,
E mi sento Achille in sen—

his fists tightened and the blood hummed in his ears.

In the scene of the banquet-hall, where the followers of Ulysses lay before Lycomedes the offerings of the Greek chieftains, and, while the King and Deidamia are marvelling at the jewels and the Tyrian robes, Achilles, unmindful of his disguise, bursts out

Ah, chi vide finora armi più belle?—

at this supreme point Odo again turned to his neighbor. They exchanged another look, and at the close of the act the youth leaned forward to ask with an air

[99]

of condescension: "Is this your first acquaintance with the divine Metastasio?"

"I have never been in a play-house before," said Odo reddening.

The other smiled. "You are fortunate in having so worthy an introduction to the stage. Many of our operas are merely vulgar and ridiculous; but Metastasio is a great poet." Odo nodded a breathless assent. "A great poet," his new acquaintance resumed, "and handling a great theme. But do you not suffer from the silly songs that perpetually interrupt the flow of the verse? To me they are intolerable. Metastasio might have been a great tragic dramatist if Italy would have let him. But Italy does not want tragedies—she wishes to be sung to, danced to, made eyes at, flattered and amused! Give her anything, anything that shall help her to forget her own abasement. *Pancm et circenses!* that is always her cry. And who can wonder that her sovereigns and statesmen are willing to humor her, when even her poets stoop to play the mountebank for her diversion?" The speaker, ruffling his locks with a hand that scattered the powder, turned on the brilliant audience his strange corrugated frown. "Fools! simpletons!" he cried, "not to see that in applauding the Achilles of Metastasio they are smiling at the allegory of their own abasement! What are the Italians of to-day but men tricked out in women's finery, when they should be waiting full-armed to rally at the first signal of revolt? Oh, for the day when a poet shall arise who dares tell them the truth, not disguised in sentimental frippery, not ending in a maudlin reconciliation of love and glory—but the whole truth, naked, cold and fatal as a patriot's blade; a poet who dares show these bedizened courtiers they are no freer than the peasants they oppress, and tell the peasants they are entitled to the same privileges as their masters!" He paused and drew back with a supercilious smile. "But doubtless, sir," said he, "I offend you in thus arraigning your sacred caste; for unless I mistake you belong to the race of demi-gods—the Titans whose downfall is at hand?" He swept the boxes with a contemptuous eye.

Little of this tirade was clear to Odo; but something in the speaker's tone moved him to answer, with a quick lifting of his head: "My name is Odo Valsecca, of the Dukes of Pianura;" when, fearing he had seemed to parade his birth before one evidently of inferior station, he at once added with a touch of shyness: "And you, sir, are perhaps a poet, since you speak so beautifully?"

At which, with a stare and a straightening of his long awkward body, the other haughtily returned: "A poet, sir? I am the Count Vittorio Alfieri of Asti."

IX

THE singular being with whom chance had thus brought him acquainted was to have a lasting influence on the formation of Odo's character.

Vittorio Alfieri, then just concluding, at the age of sixteen, his desultory years of academic schooling, was probably the most extraordinary youth in Charles Emmanuel's dominion. Of the future student, of the tragic poet who was to prepare the liberation of Italy by raising the political ideals of his generation, this moody boy with his craze for dress and horses, his pride of birth and contempt for his own class, his liberal theories and insolently aristocratic practice, must have given small promise to the most discerning observer. It seems indeed probable that none thought him worth observing and that he passed among his townsmen merely as one of the most idle and extravagant young noblemen in a society where idleness and extravagance were held to be the natural attributes of the great. But in the growth of character the light on the road to Damascus is apt to be preceded by faint premonitory gleams; and even in his frivolous days at the Academy Alfieri carried a Virgil in his pocket and wept and trembled over Ariosto's verse.

It was the instant response of Odo's imagination that drew the two together. Odo, as one of the foreign

pupils, was quartered in the same wing of the Academy
with the students of Alfieri's class, and enjoyed an almost equal freedom. Thus, despite the difference of age,
the lads found themselves allied by taste and circumstances. Among the youth of their class they were perhaps the only two who already felt, however obscurely,
the stirring of unborn ideals, the pressure of that tide
of renovation that was to sweep them, on widely-sun-
dered currents, to the same uncharted deep. Alfieri,
at any rate, represented to the younger lad the seer
who held in his hands the keys of knowledge and
beauty. Odo could never forget the youth who first
lent him Annibale Caro's Æneid and Metastasio's opera
libretti, Voltaire's Zaïre and the comedies of Goldoni;
while Alfieri perhaps found in his companion's sympathy with his own half-dormant tastes the first incentive to a nobler activity. Certain it is that, in the
interchange of their daily comradeship, the elder gave
his friend much that he was himself unconscious of possessing, and perhaps first saw reflected in Odo's more
vivid sensibility an outline of the formless ideals coiled
in the depths of his own sluggish nature.

The difference in age, and the possession of an independent fortune, which the laws of Savoy had left
Alfieri free to enjoy since his fifteenth year, gave
him an obvious superiority over Odo; but if Alfieri's
amusements separated him from his young friend, his

tastes were always drawing them together; and Odo was happily of those who are more engaged in profiting by what comes their way than in pining for what escapes them. Much as he admired Alfieri, it was somehow impossible for the latter to condescend to him; and the equality of intercourse between the two was perhaps its chief attraction to a youth surfeited with adulation.

Of the opportunities his new friendship brought him, none became in after years a pleasanter memory to Odo than his visits with Vittorio to the latter's uncle, the illustrious architect Count Benedetto Alfieri. This accomplished and amiable man, who had for many years devoted his talents to the King's service, was lodged in a palace adjoining the Academy; and thither, one holiday afternoon, Vittorio conducted his young friend.

Ignorant as Odo was of all the arts, he felt on the very threshold the new quality of his surroundings. These tall bare rooms, where busts and sarcophagi were ranged as in the twilight of a temple, diffused an influence that lowered the voice and hushed the step. In the semi-Parisian capital where French architects designed the King's pleasure-houses and the nobility imported their boudoir-panellings from Paris and their damask hangings from Lyons, Benedetto Alfieri represented the old classic tradition, the tradition of the "grand manner," which had held its own through all later variations of taste, running parallel with the *baroc-*

chismo of the seventeenth century and the effeminate caprices of the rococo period. He had lived much in Rome, in the company of men like Winckelmann and Maffei, in that society where the revival of classical research was being forwarded by the liberality of Princes and Cardinals and by the indefatigable zeal of the scholars in their pay. From this centre of æsthetic reaction Alfieri had returned to the Gallicized Turin, with its preference for the graceful and ingenious rather than for the large, the noble, the restrained; bringing to bear on the taste of his native city the influence of a view raised but perhaps narrowed by close study of the past: the view of a generation of architects in whom archæological curiosity had stifled the artistic instinct, and who, instead of assimilating the spirit of the past like their great predecessors, were engrossed in a sterile restoration of the letter. It may be said of this school of architects that they were of more service to posterity than to their contemporaries; for while they opened the way to modern antiquarian research, their pedantry checked the natural development of a style which, if left to itself, might in time have found new and more vigorous forms of expression.

To Odo, happily, Count Benedetto's surroundings spoke more forcibly than his theories. Every object in the calm severe rooms appealed to the boy with the pure eloquence of form. Casts of the Vatican busts

stood against the walls and a niche at one end of the
library contained a marble copy of the Apollo Belve-
dere. The sarcophagi with their winged genii, their
garlands and bucranes, the porphyry tazzas, the fragments of Roman mosaic and Pompeian fresco-painting,
roused Odo's curiosity as if they had been the scattered
letters of a new alphabet; and he saw with astonish-
ment his friend Vittorio's indifference to these wonders.
Count Benedetto, it was clear, was resigned to his
nephew's lack of interest. The old man doubtless knew
that he represented to the youth only the rich uncle
whose crotchets must be humored for the sake of what
his pocket may procure; and such kindly tolerance
made Odo regret that Vittorio should not at least
affect an interest in his uncle's pursuits.

Odo's eagerness to see and learn filled Count Benedetto with a simple joy. He brought forth all his
treasures for the boy's instruction and the two spent
many an afternoon poring over Piranesi's Roman etch-
ings, Maffei's Verona Illustrata, and Count Benedetto's
own elegant pencil-drawings of classical remains. Like
all students of his day, he had also his cabinet of antique gems and coins, from which Odo obtained more
intimate glimpses of that buried life so marvellously
exhumed before him: hints of traffic in far-off market-
places and familiar gestures of hands on which those
very jewels might have sparkled. Nor did the Count

restrict the boy's inquiries to that distant past; and for the first time Odo heard of the masters who had maintained the great classical tradition on Latin soil: Sanmichele, Vignola, Sansovino, and the divine Michel Angelo, whom the old architect never named without baring his head. From the works of these architects Odo formed his first conception of the earlier, more virile manner which the first contact with Græco-Roman antiquity had produced. The Count told him, too, of the great painters whose popularity had been lessened, if their fame had not been dimmed, by the more recent achievements of Correggio, Guido, Guercino, and the Bolognese school. The splendor of the stanze of the Vatican, the dreadful majesty of the Sistine ceiling, revealed to Odo the beauty of that unmatched moment before grandeur broke into bombast. His early association with the expressive homely art of the chapel at Pontesordo and with the half-pagan beauty of Luini's compositions had formed his taste on soberer lines than the fashion of the day affected; and his imagination breathed freely on the heights of the Latin Parnassus. Thus, while his friend Vittorio stormed up and down the quiet rooms, chattering about his horses, boasting of his escapades, or ranting against the tyranny of the Sardinian government, Odo, at the old Count's side, was entering on the great inheritance of the past.

[107]

Such an initiation was the more precious to him from the indifference of those about him to all forms of liberal culture. Among the greater Italian cities, Turin was at that period the least open to new influences, the most rigidly bound up in the formulas of the past. While Milan, under the Austrian rule, was becoming a centre of philosophic thought; while Naples was producing a group of economists such as Galiani, Gravina and Filangieri; while ecclesiastical Rome was dedicating herself to the investigation of ancient art and polity, and even flighty Venice had her little set of "liberals," who read Voltaire and Hume and wept over the rights of man, the old Piedmontese capital lay in the grasp of a bigoted clergy and of a reigning house which was already preparing to superimpose Prussian militarism on the old feudal discipline of the border. Generations of hard fighting and rigorous living had developed in the nobles the qualities which were preparing them for the great part their country was to play; and contact with the Waldensian and Calvinist heresies had stiffened Piedmontese piety into a sombre hatred of schism and a minute observance of the mechanical rules of the faith. Such qualities could be produced only at the expense of intellectual freedom; and if Piedmont could show a few nobles like Massimo d'Azeglio's father, who "made the education of his children his first and gravest thought" and supplemented the deficiencies of his wife's conventual training by "consecrating to her daily four hours of reading, translating and other suitable exercises," the commoner view was that of Alfieri's own parents, who frequently repeated in their son's hearing "the old maxim of the Piedmontese nobility" that there is no need for a gentleman to be a scholar. Such at any rate was the opinion of the old Marquess of Donnaz, and of all the frequenters of Casa Valdù. Odo's step-father was engrossed in the fulfilment of his duties about the court, and Donna Laura, under the influence of poverty and ennui, had sunk into a state of rigid pietism; so that the lad, on his visits to his mother, found himself in a world where art was represented by the latest pastel-portrait of a court beauty, literature by Liguori's Glories of Mary or the Blessed Battista's Mental Sorrows of Christ, and history by the conviction that Piedmont's efforts to stamp out the enemies of the Church had distinguished her above every other country of Europe. Donna Laura's cicisbeo was indeed a member of the local Arcadia, and given to celebrating in verse every incident in the noble household of Valdù, from its lady's name-day to the death of a pet canary; but his own tastes inclined to the elegant Bettinelli, whose Lettere Virgiliane had so conclusively shown Dante to be a writer of barbarous doggerel; and among the dilettanti of the day one heard less of

Raphael than of Carlo Maratta, less of Ariosto and Petrarch than of the Jesuit poet Padre Cevo, author of the sublime "heroico-comic" poem on the infancy of Jesus.

It was in fact mainly to the Jesuits that Italy, in the early part of the eighteenth century, owed her literature and her art as well as the direction of her religious life. Though the reaction against the order was everywhere making itself felt, though one Italian sovereign after another had been constrained to purchase popularity or even security by banishing the Society from his dominions, the Jesuits maintained their hold on the aristocracy, whose pretensions they flattered, whose tastes they affected, and to whom they represented the spirit of religious and political conservatism against which invisible forces were already felt to be moving. For the use of their noble supporters, the Jesuits had devised a religion as elaborate and ceremonious as the social usages of the aristocracy: a religion which decked its chapels in imitation of great ladies' boudoirs and prescribed observances in keeping with the vapid and gossiping existence of their inmates.

To Odo, fresh from the pure air of Donnaz, where the faith of his kinsfolk expressed itself in charity, self-denial and a noble decency of life, there was something stifling in the atmosphere of languishing pietism

in which his mother's friends veiled the emptiness of
their days. Under the instruction of the Countess's director the boy's conscience was enervated by the casuis-
tries of Liguorianism and his devotion dulled by the
imposition of interminable "pious practices." It was in
his nature to grudge no sacrifice to his ideals, and he
might have accomplished without question the monoto-
nous observances his confessor exacted, but for the
changed aspect of the Deity in whose name they were
imposed. As with most thoughtful natures, Odo's first
disillusionment was to come from discovering not what
his God condemned, but what He condoned. Between
Cantapresto's coarse philosophy of pleasure and the re-
fined complaisances of his new confessor he felt the distinction to be one rather of taste than of principle;
and it seemed to him that the religion of the aristocracy might not unfairly be summed up in the ex-
soprano's cynical aphorism: "As respectful children of
our Heavenly Father it behoves us not to speak till
we are spoken to." Even the religious ceremonies he
witnessed did not console him for that chill hour of
dawn, when, in the chapel at Donnaz, he had served
the mass for Don Gervaso, with a heart trembling at
its own unworthiness yet uplifted by the sense of the
Divine Presence. In the churches adorned like aristocratic drawing-rooms, of which some Madonna wreathed
in artificial flowers seemed the amiable and indulgent

hostess, and where the florid passionate music of the mass was rendered by the King's opera singers before a throng of chattering cavaliers and ladies, Odo prayed in vain for a reawakening of the old emotion. The sense of sonship was gone. He felt himself an alien in the temple of this affable divinity, and his heart echoed no more the cry which had once lifted him on wings of praise to the very threshold of the hidden glory—

Domine, dilexi decorem domus tuæ et locum habitationis gloriæ tuæ!

It was in the first reaction from this dimly-felt loss that he lit one day on a volume which Alfieri had smuggled into the Academy—the Lettres Philosophiques of François Arouet de Voltaire.

BOOK II

THE NEW LIGHT

Zu neuen Ufern lockt ein neuer Tag.

BOOK II

THE NEW LIGHT

I

ONE afternoon of April in the year 1774 Odo Valsecca, riding down the hillside below the church of the Superga, had reined in his horse at a point where a group of Spanish chestnuts overhung the way. The air was light and pure, the shady turf invited him, and dismounting he bid his servant lead the horses to the wayside inn half-way down the slope.

The spot he had chosen, though secluded as some nook above the gorge of Donnaz, commanded a view of the Po rolling at his feet like a flood of yellowish metal, and beyond, outspread in clear spring sunshine, the great city in the bosom of the plain. The spectacle was fair enough to touch any fancy: brown domes and façades set in new-leaved gardens and surrounded by vineyards extending to the nearest acclivities; country-houses glancing through the fresh green of planes and willows; monastery-walls cresting the higher ridges; and westward the Po winding in sunlit curves toward the Alps.

Odo had lost none of his sensitiveness to such impressions; but the sway of another mood turned his eye from the outstretched beauty of the city to the

vernal solitude about him. It was the season when old
memories of Donnaz worked in his blood; when the
banks and hedges of the fresh hill-country about Turin
cheated him with a breath of budding beech-groves
and the fragrance of crushed fern in the glens of the
high Pennine valleys. It was a mere waft, perhaps, from
some clod of loosened earth, or the touch of cool elastic moss as he flung himself face downward under the
trees; but the savor, the contact filled his nostrils with
mountain air and his eyes with dim-branched distances.
At Donnaz the slow motions of the northern spring
had endeared to him all those sweet incipiencies preceding the full choral burst of leaf and flower: the
mauve mist over bare woodlands, the wet black gleams
in frost-bound hollows, the thrust of fronds through
withered bracken, the primrose-patches spreading like
pale sunshine along wintry lanes. He had always felt
a sympathy for these delicate unnoted changes; but
the feeling which had formerly been like the blind stir
of sap in a plant was now a conscious sensation that
groped for speech and understanding.

He had grown up among people to whom such emotions were unknown. The old Marquess's passion for
his fields and woods was the love of the agriculturist
and the hunter, not that of the naturalist or the poet;
and the aristocracy of the cities regarded the country
merely as so much soil from which to draw their main-

tenance. The gentlefolk never absented themselves from
town but for a few weeks of autumn, when they went
to their villas for the vintage, transporting thither all
the diversions of city life and venturing no farther
afield than the pleasure-grounds that were but so many
open-air card-rooms, concert-halls and theatres. Odo's
tenderness for every sylvan function of renewal and de-
cay, every shifting of light and color on the flying surface of the year, would have been met with the same
stare with which a certain enchanting Countess had
received the handful of wind-flowers that, fresh from a
sunrise on the hills, he had laid one morning among
her toilet-boxes. The Countess Clarice had stared and
laughed, and every one of his acquaintance, Alfieri
even, would have echoed her laugh; but one man at
least had felt the divine commotion of nature's touch,
had felt and interpreted it, in words as fresh as spring
verdure, in the pages of a volume that Odo now drew
from his pocket.

"I longed to dream, but some unexpected spectacle
continually distracted me from my musings. Here immense rocks hung their ruinous masses above my head;
there the thick mist of roaring waterfalls enveloped
me; or some unceasing torrent tore open at my very
feet an abyss into which the gaze feared to plunge.
Sometimes I was lost in the twilight of a thick wood;
sometimes, on emerging from a dark ravine, my eyes

were charmed by the sight of an open meadow. . .
Nature seemed to revel in unwonted contrasts; such
varieties of aspect had she united in one spot. Here
was an eastern prospect bright with spring flowers,
while autumn fruits ripened to the south, and the
northern face of the scene was still locked in wintry
frosts. . . Add to this the different angles at which
the peaks took the light, the chiar'oscuro of sun and
shade, and the variations of light resulting from it at
morning and evening . . . sum up the impressions I
have tried to describe and you will be able to form an
idea of the enchanting situation in which I found myself. . . The scene has indeed a magical, a supernatural quality, which so ravishes the spirit and senses
that one seems to lose all exact notion of one's surroundings and identity."

This was a new language to eighteenth-century readers. Already it had swept through the length and
breadth of France, like a spring storm-wind bursting
open doors and windows, and filling close candle-lit
rooms with wet gusts and the scent of beaten blossoms;
but south of the Alps the new ideas travelled slowly,
and the Piedmontese were as yet scarce aware of the
man who had written thus of their own mountains. It
was true that, some thirty years earlier, in one of the
very monasteries on which Odo now looked down, a
Swiss vagrant called Rousseau had embraced the true

faith with the most moving signs of edification; but
the rescue of Helvetian heretics was a favorite occupa-
tion of the Turinese nobility and it is doubtful if any
recalled the name of the strange proselyte who had
hastened to signalize his conversion by robbing his em-
ployers and slandering an innocent maid-servant.

Odo in fact owed his first acquaintance with the
French writers to Alfieri, who, in the intervals of his
wandering over Europe, now and then reappeared in
Turin laden with the latest novelties in Transalpine
literature and haberdashery. What his eccentric friend
failed to provide, Odo had little difficulty in obtaining
for himself; for though most of the new writers were
on the Index, and the Sardinian censorship was notoriously severe, there was never yet a barrier that could
keep out books, and Cantapresto was a skilled purveyor
of contraband dainties. Odo had thus acquainted himself with the lighter literature of England and France;
and though he had read but few philosophical treatises,
was yet dimly aware of the new standpoint from which,
north of the Alps, men were beginning to test the accepted forms of thought. The first disturbance of his
childish faith, and the coincident reading of the Lettres
Philosophiques, had been followed by a period of moral
perturbation, during which he suffered from that sense
of bewilderment, of inability to classify the phenomena
of life, that is one of the keenest trials of inexperience.

Youth and nature had their way with him, however, and a wholesome reaction of indifference set in. The invisible world of thought and conduct had been the frequent subject of his musings; but the other, tangible world was close to him too, spreading like a rich populous plain between himself and the distant heights of speculation. The old doubts, the old dissatisfactions, hung on the edge of consciousness; but he was too profoundly Italian not to linger awhile in that atmosphere of careless acquiescence that is so pleasant a medium for the unhampered enjoyment of life. Some day, no doubt, the intellectual curiosity and the moral disquietude would revive; but what he wanted now were books which appealed not to his reason but to his emotions, which reflected as in a mirror the rich and varied life of the senses: books that were warm to the touch, like the little volume in his hand.

For it was not only of nature that the book spoke. Amid scenes of such rustic freshness were set human passions as fresh and natural: a great romantic love, subdued to duty, yet breaking forth again and again as young shoots spring from the root of a felled tree. To eighteenth-century readers such a picture of life was as new as its setting. Duty, in that day, to people of quality, meant the observance of certain fixed conventions: the correct stepping of a moral minuet; as an inner obligation, as a voluntary tribute to Diderot's "divinity on earth", it had hardly yet drawn breath. To depict a personal relation so much purer and more profound than any form of sentiment then in fashion, and then to subordinate it, unflinchingly, to the ideal of those larger relations that link the individual to the group—this was a stroke of originality for which it would be hard to find a parallel in modern fiction. Here at last was an answer to the blind impulses agrope in Odo's breast—the loosening of those springs of emotion that gushed forth in such fresh contrast to the stagnant rills of the sentimental pleasure-garden. To renounce a Julie would be more thrilling than—

Odo, with a sigh, thrust the book in his pocket and rose to his feet. It was the hour of the promenade at the Valentino and he had promised the Countess Clarice to attend her. The old high-roofed palace of the French princess lay below him, in its gardens along the river: he could figure, as he looked down on it, the throng of carriages and chairs, the modishly dressed riders, the pedestrians crowding the foot-path to watch the quality go by. The vision of all that noise and glitter deepened the sweetness of the woodland hush. He sighed again. Suddenly voices sounded in the road below—a man's speech flecked with girlish laughter. Odo hung back listening: the girl's voice rang like a bird-call through his rustling fancies. Presently she came in sight: a slender black-mantled figure hung on the arm of an elderly man in the sober dress of one of the learned professions—a physician or a lawyer, Odo guessed. Their being afoot, and the style of the man's dress, showed that they were of the middle class; their demeanor, that they were father and daughter. The girl moved with a light forward flowing of her whole body that seemed the pledge of grace in every limb: of her face Odo had but a bright glimpse in the eclipse of her flapping hat-brim. He stood under his tree unheeded; but as they rose abreast of him the girl paused and dropped her companion's arm.

"Look! The cherry flowers!" she cried, and stretched her arms to a white gush of blossoms above the wall across the road. The movement tilted back her hat, and Odo caught her small fine profile, wide-browed as the head on some Sicilian coin, with a little harp-shaped ear bedded in dark ripples.

"Oh," she wailed, straining on tiptoe, "I can't reach them!"

Her father smiled. "May temptation," said he philosophically, "always hang as far out of your reach."

"Temptation?" she echoed.

"Is it not theft you 're bent on?"

"Theft? This is a monks' orchard, not a peasant's plot."

"Confiscation, then," he humorously conceded.

"Since they pay no taxes on their cherries they

might at least," she argued, "spare a few to us poor tax-payers."

"Ah," said her father, "I want to tax their cherries, not to gather them." He slipped a hand through her arm. "Come, child," said he, "does not the philosopher tell us that he who enjoys a thing possesses it? The flowers are yours already!"

"Oh, are they?" she retorted. "Then why does n't the loaf in the baker's window feed the beggar that looks in at it?"

"Casuist!" he cried and drew her up the bend of the road.

Odo stood gazing after them. Their words, their aspect, seemed an echo of his reading. The father in his plain broadcloth and square-buckled shoes, the daughter with her unpowdered hair and spreading hat, might have stepped from the pages of the romance. What a breath of freshness they brought with them! The girl's cheek was clear as the cherry-blossoms, and with what lovely freedom did she move! Thus Julie might have led Saint Preux through her "Elysium". Odo crossed the road and, breaking one of the blossoming twigs, thrust it in the breast of his uniform. Then he walked down the hill to the inn where the horses waited. Half an hour later he rode up to the house where he lodged in the Piazza San Carlo.

In the archway Cantapresto, heavy with a nine

years' accretion of fat, laid an admonishing hand on his bridle.

"Cavaliere, the Countess's black boy—"

"Well?"

"Three several times has battered the door down with a missive."

"Well?"

"The last time, I shook him off with the message that you would be there before him."

"Be where?"

"At the Valentino; but that was an hour ago!"

Odo slipped from the saddle.

"I must dress first. Call a chair; or no—write a letter for me first. Let Antonio carry it."

The ex-soprano, wheezing under the double burden of flesh and consequence, had painfully labored after Odo up the high stone flights to that young gentleman's modest lodgings, and they stood together in a study lined with books and hung with prints and casts from the antique. Odo threw off his dusty coat and called the servant to remove his boots.

"Will you read the lady's letters, cavaliere?" Cantapresto asked, obsequiously offering them on a lacquered tray.

"No—no: write first. Begin 'My angelic lady'—"

"You began the last letter in those terms, cavaliere," his scribe reminded him with suspended pen.

"The devil! Well, then—wait. 'Throned goddess'—"

"You ended the last letter with 'throned goddess.'"

"Curse the last letter! Why did you send it?" Odo sprang up and slipped his arms into the dress-tunic his servant had brought him. "Write anything. Say that I am suddenly summoned by—"

"By the Count Alfieri?" Cantapresto suggested.

"Count Alfieri? Is he here? He has returned?"

"He arrived an hour ago, cavaliere. He sent you this Moorish scimitar with his compliments. I understand he comes recently from Spain."

"Imbecile, not to have told me before! Quick, Antonio—my gloves, my sword." Odo, flushed and animated, buckled his sword-belt with impatient hands. "Write anything—anything to free my evening. To-morrow morning—to-morrow morning I shall wait on the lady. Let Antonio carry her a nosegay with my compliments. Did you see him, Cantapresto? Was he in good health? Does he sup at home? He left no message? Quick, Antonio, a chair!" he cried with his hand on the door.

Odo had acquired, at twenty-two, a nobility of carriage not incompatible with the boyish candor of his gaze, and becomingly set off by the brilliant dress-uniform of a lieutenant in one of the provincial regiments. He was tall and fair, and a certain languor of complexion, inherited from his father's house, was corrected in him by the vivacity of the Donnaz blood. This now sparkled in his grey eye and gave a glow to his cheek, as he stepped across the threshold, treading on a sprig of cherry-blossom that had dropped unnoticed to the floor.

Cantapresto, looking after him, caught sight of the flowers and kicked them aside with a contemptuous toe.

"I sometimes think he botanizes," he murmured with a shrug. "The Lord knows what queer notions he gets out of all those books!"

II

AS an infusion of fresh blood to Odo were Alfieri's meteoric returns to Turin. Life moved languidly in the strait-laced city, even to a young gentleman a-tiptoe for adventure and framed to elicit it as the hazel-wand draws water. Not that vulgar distractions were lacking. The town, as Cantapresto had long since advised him, had its secret leniencies, its posterns opening on clandestine pleasure; but there was that in Odo which early turned him from such cheap counterfeits of living. He accepted the diversions of his age, but with a clear sense of their worth; and the youth who calls his pleasures by their true name has learned the secret of resisting them.

Alfieri's coming set deeper springs in motion. His follies and extravagances were on a less provincial scale than those of Odo's daily associates. The breath of a freer life clung to him and his allusions were so many glimpses into a larger world. His political theories were but the enlargement of his private grievances, but the mere play of criticism on accepted institutions was an exercise more novel and exhilarating than the wildest ride on one of his half-tamed thoroughbreds. Still chiefly a man of pleasure, and the slave, as always, of some rash infatuation, Alfieri was already shaking off the intellectual torpor of his youth; and the first stirrings of his curiosity roused an answering passion in Odo. Their tastes were indeed divergent, for to that external beauty which was to Odo the very bloom of life, Alfieri remained insensible; while of its imaginative counterpart, its prolongation in the realm of thought and emotion, he had but the most limited conception. But his love of ringing deeds woke the chivalrous strain in Odo, and his vague celebration of Liberty, that unknown goddess to whom altars were everywhere building, chimed with the other's scorn of oppression and injustice. So far, it is true, their companionship had been mainly one of pleasure; but the temper of both gave their follies that provisional character which saves them from vulgarity.

Odo, who had slept late on the morning after his

friend's return, was waked by the pompous mouthing of certain lines just then on every lip in Italy:—

> *Meet was it that, its ancient seats forsaking,*
> *An Empire should set forth with dauntless sail,*
> *And braving tempests and the deep's betrayal,*
> *Break down the barriers of inviolate worlds—*
> *That Cortez and Pizarro should esteem*
> *The blood of man a trivial sacrifice*
> *When, flinging down from their ancestral thrones*
> *Incas and Mexicans of royal line,*
> *They wrecked two Kingdoms to refresh thy palate—*

They were the verses in which the Abate Parini, in his satire of "The Morning," apostrophizes the cup of chocolate which the lacquey presents to his master. Cantapresto had in fact just entered with a cup of this beverage, and Alfieri, who stood at his friend's bedside with unpowdered locks and a fashionable undress of Parisian cut, snatching the tray from the soprano's hands presented it to Odo in an attitude of mock servility.

The young man sprang up laughing. It was the fashion to applaud Parini's verse in the circles at which his satire was aimed, and none recited his mock heroics with greater zest than the young gentlemen whose fopperies he ridiculed. Odo's toilet was indeed a rite almost as elaborate as that of Parini's hero; and this accomplished, he was on his way to fulfil the very duty the

poet most unsparingly derides: the morning visit of the
cicisbeo to his lady; but meanwhile he liked to show
himself above the follies of his class by joining in the
laugh against them. When he issued from the powder-
room in his gold-laced uniform, with scented gloves and
carefully-adjusted queue, he presented the image of a
young gentleman so clearly equal to the most flattering
emergencies that Alfieri broke into a smile of half-ironi-
cal approval. "I see, my dear cavaliere, that it were idle
to invite you to try one of the new Arabs I have brought
with me from Spain, since it is plain other duties engage you; but I come to lay claim to your evening."

Odo hesitated. "The Queen holds a circle this evening," he said.

"And her lady-in-waiting is in attendance?" returned
Alfieri. "And the lady-in-waiting's gentleman-in-wait-
ing also?"

Odo made an impatient movement. "What induce
ments do you offer?" said he carelessly.

Alfieri stepped close and tapped him on the sleeve.
"Meet me at ten o'clock at the turn of the lane behind
the Corpus Domini. Wear a cloak and a mask, and
leave this gentleman at home with a flask of Asti." He
glanced at Cantapresto.

Odo hesitated a moment. He knew well enough where
such midnight turnings led, and across the vision evoked
by his friend's words a girl's face flitted suddenly.

"Is that all?" he said with a shrug. "You find me, I fear, in no humor for such exploits."

Alfieri smiled. "And if I say that I have promised to bring you?"

"Promised—?"

"To one as chary of exacting such pledges as I of giving them. If I say that you stake your life on the adventure, and that the stake is not too great for the reward—?"

His sallow face had reddened with excitement, and Odo's forehead reflected the flush. Was it possible—? but the thought set him tingling with disgust.

"Why, you say little," he cried lightly, "at the rate at which I value my life."

Alfieri turned on him. "If your life is worthless make it worth something!" he exclaimed. "I offer you the opportunity to-night."

"What opportunity?"

"The sight of a face that men have laid down their lives to see."

Odo laughed and buckled on his sword. "If you answer for the risk, I agree to take it," said he. "At ten o'clock then, behind the Corpus Domini."

If the ladies whom gallant gentlemen delight to serve could guess what secret touchstones of worth these same gentlemen sometimes carry into the adored presence, many a handsome head would be carried with less assurance and many a fond exaction less confidently imposed. If, for instance, the Countess Clarice di Tournanches, whose high-colored image reflected itself so complacently in her Venetian toilet-glass, could have known that the Cavaliere Odo Valsecca's devoted glance saw her through the medium of a countenance compared to which her own revealed the most unexpected shortcomings, she might have received him with less airy petulance of manner. But how could so accomplished a mistress doubt the permanence of her rule? The Countess Clarice, in singling out young Odo Valsecca (to the despair of a score of more experienced cavaliers), had done him an honor that she could no more imagine his resigning than an adventurer a throne to which he is unexpectedly raised. She was a finished example of the pretty woman who views the universe as planned for her convenience. What could go wrong in a world where noble ladies lived in palaces hung with tapestry and damask, with powdered lacqueys to wait on them, a turbaned blackamoor to tend their parrots and monkeys, a coronet-coach at the door to carry them to mass or the ridotto, and a handsome cicisbeo to display on the promenade? Everything had combined to strengthen the Countess Clarice's faith in the existing order of things. Her husband, Count Roberto di Tournanches, was one of the King's

equerries and distinguished for his brilliant career as
an officer of the Piedmontese army—a man marked for
the highest favors in a society where military influences
were paramount. Passing at sixteen from an aristocratic
convent to the dreary magnificence of the palazzo Tournanches, Clarice had found herself a lady-in-waiting at
the dullest court in Europe and the wife of an army
officer engrossed in his profession, and pledged by eti-
quette to the service of another lady. Odo Valsecca represented her escape from this bondage—the dash of
romance and folly in a life of elegant formalities; and
the Countess, who would not have sacrificed to him one
of her rights as a court-lady or a *nobil donna* of the
Golden Book, regarded him as the reward which Providence accords to a well-regulated conduct.

Her room, when Odo entered it on taking leave of
Alfieri, was crowded, as usual at that hour, with the
hangers-on of the noble lady's *lever:* the *abatino* in
lace ruffles, handing about his latest rhymed acrostic,
the jeweller displaying a set of enamelled buckles
newly imported from Paris, and the black-breeched
doctor with white bands, who concocted remedies for
the Countess's vapors and megrims. These personages,
grouped about the toilet-table where the Countess sat
under the hands of a Parisian hair-dresser, were pic-
turesquely relieved against the stucco panelling and
narrow mirrors of the apartment, with its windows

[132]

looking on a garden set with mossy statues. To Odo,
however, the scene suggested the most tedious part of
his day's routine. The compliments to be exchanged,
the silly verses to be praised, the gew-gaws from Paris
to be admired, were all contrasted in his mind with
the vision of that other life which had come to him
on the hillside of the Superga. On this mood the
Countess Clarice's sarcasms fell without effect. To be
pouted at because he had failed to attend the promenade of the Valentino was to Odo but a convenient
pretext for excusing himself from the Queen's circle
that evening. He had engaged with little ardor to
join Alfieri in what he guessed to be a sufficiently
commonplace adventure; but as he listened to the
Countess's chatter about the last minuet-step, and the
relative merits of Sanspareil water and oil-of-lilies, of
gloves from Blois and Vendôme, his impatience hailed
any alternative as a release. Meanwhile, however, long
hours of servitude intervened. The lady's toilet completed, to the adjusting of the last patch, he must
attend her to dinner, where, placed at her side, he
was awarded the honor of carving the roast; must sit
through two hours of biribì in company with the *abatino*, the doctor, and half-a-dozen parasites of the noble
table; and for two hours more must ride in her gilt
coach up and down the promenade of the Valentino.

Escaping from this ceremonial, with the conscious-

[133]

ness that it must be repeated on the morrow, Odo
was seized with that longing for freedom that makes
the first street-corner an invitation to flight. How he
envied Alfieri, whose travelling-carriage stood at the
beck of such moods! Odo's scant means forbade evasion, even had his military duties not kept him in
Turin. He felt himself no more than a puppet dancing to the tune of Parini's satire, a puny doll con-
demmed, as the strings of custom pulled, to feign
the gestures of immortal passions.

III

THE night was moonless, with cold dashes of rain,
and though the streets of Turin were well-lit no
lantern-ray reached the windings of the lane behind the
Corpus Domini.

As Odo, alone under the wall of the church, awaited
his friend's arrival, he wondered what risk had constrained the reckless Alfieri to such unwonted caution.
Italy was at that time a vast network of espionage, and
the Piedmontese capital passed for one of the best-
policed cities in Europe; but even on a moonless night
the law distinguished between the noble pleasure-seeker
and the obscure delinquent whose fate it was to pay
the other's shot. Odo knew that he would probably be
followed and his movements reported to the authori-

ties; but he was almost equally certain that there would
be no active interference in his affairs. What chiefly
puzzled him was Alfieri's insistence that Cantapresto
should not be privy to the adventure. The soprano had
long been the confidant of his pupil's escapades, and
his adroitness had often been of service in intrigues
such as that on which Odo now fancied himself engaged. The place, again, perplexed him: a sober quarter of convents and private dwellings, in the very
eye of the royal palace, scarce seeming the theatre
for a light adventure. These incongruities revived his
former wonder; nor was this dispelled by Alfieri's approach.

The poet, masked and unattended, rejoined his friend
without a word; and Odo guessed in him an eye and
ear alert for pursuit. Guided by the pressure of his
arm, Odo was hurried round the bend of the lane, up
a transverse alley and across a little square lost between high shuttered buildings. Alfieri, at his first word,
gripped his arm with a backward glance; then urged
him on under the denser blackness of an arched passage-way, at the end of which an oil-light glimmered.
Here a gate in a wall confronted them. It opened at
Alfieri's tap, and Odo scented wet box-borders and felt
the gravel of a path underfoot. The gate was at once
locked behind them and they entered the ground-floor
of a house as dark as the garden. Here a maid-servant

of close aspect met them with a lamp and preceded them upstairs to a bare landing hung with charts and *portulani*. On Odo's flushed anticipations this ante-chamber, which seemed the approach to some pedant's cabinet, had an effect undeniably chilling; but Alfieri, heedless of his surprise, had cast off cloak and mask, and now led the way into a long conventual-looking room lined with book-shelves. A knot of middle-aged gentlemen of sober dress and manner, gathered about a cabinet of fossils in the centre of this apartment, looked up at the entrance of the two friends; then the group divided, and Odo with a start recognized the girl he had seen on the road to the Superga.

She bowed gravely to the young men. "My father," said she, in a clear voice without trace of diffidence, "has gone to his study for a book, but will be with you in a moment."

She wore a dress in keeping with her manner, its black stuff folds and the lawn kerchief crossed on her bosom giving height and authority to her slight figure. The dark unpowdered hair drawn back over a cushion made a severer setting for her face than the fluctuating brim of her shade-hat; and this perhaps added to the sense of estrangement with which Odo gazed at her; but she met his look with a smile, and instantly the rosy girl flashed through her grave exterior.

"Here is my father," said she; and her companion of

the previous day stepped into the room with several folios under his arm.

Alfieri turned to Odo. "This, my dear Odo," said he, "is my distinguished friend, Professor Vivaldi, who has done us the honor of inviting us to his house." He took the Professor's hand. "I have brought you," he continued, "the friend you were kind enough to include in your invitation—the Cavaliere Odo Valsecca."

Vivaldi bowed. "Count Alfieri's friends," said he, "are always welcome to my house; though I fear there is here little to interest a young gentleman of the Cavaliere Valsecca's years." And Odo detected a shade of doubt in his glance.

"The Cavaliere Valsecca," Alfieri smilingly rejoined, "is above his years in wit and learning, and I answer for his interest as I do for his discretion."

The Professor bowed again. "Count Alfieri, sir," he said, "has doubtless explained to you the necessity that obliges me to be so private in receiving my friends; and now perhaps you will join these gentlemen in examining some rare fossil fish newly sent me from the Monte Bolca."

Odo murmured a civil rejoinder; but the wonder into which the sight of the young girl had thrown him was fast verging on stupefaction. What mystery was here? What necessity compelled an elderly professor to receive his scientific friends like a band of political conspirators? How, above all, in the light of the girl's presence, was Odo to interpret Alfieri's extravagant allusions to the nature of their visit?

The company having returned to the cabinet of fossils, none seemed to observe his disorder but the young lady who was its cause; and seeing him stand apart she advanced with a smile, saying, "Perhaps you would rather look at some of my father's other curiosities."

Simple as the words were, they failed to restore Odo's self-possession, and for a moment he made no answer. Perhaps she partly guessed the cause of his commotion; yet it was not so much her beauty that silenced him, as the spirit that seemed to inhabit it. Nature, in general so chary of her gifts, so prone to use one good feature as the palliation of a dozen deficiencies, to wed the eloquent lip with the ineffectual eye, had indeed compounded her of all fine meanings, making each grace the complement of another and every outward charm expressive of some inward quality. Here was as little of the convent-bred miss as of the flippant and vaporish fine lady; and any suggestion of a less fair alternative vanished before such candid graces. Odo's confusion had in truth sprung from Alfieri's ambiguous hints; and these shrivelling to nought in the gaze that encountered his, constraint gave way to a sense of wondering pleasure.

"I should like to see whatever you will show me," said he, as simply as one child speaking to another; and she answered in the same tone, "Then we'll glance at my father's collections before the serious business of the evening begins."

With these words she began to lead him about the room, pointing out and explaining the curiosities it contained. It was clear that, like many scholars of his day, Professor Vivaldi was something of an eclectic in his studies, for while one table held a fine orrery, a cabinet of coins stood near, and the book-shelves were surmounted by specimens of coral and petrified wood. Of all these rarities his daughter had a word to say, and though her explanations were brief and without affectation of pedantry, they put her companion's ignorance to the blush. It must be owned, however, that had his learning been a match for hers it would have stood him in poor stead at the moment; his faculties being lost in the wonder of hearing such discourse from such lips. To his compliments on her erudition she returned with a smile that what learning she had was no merit, since she had been bred in a library; to which she suddenly added:—"You are not unknown to me, cavaliere; but I never thought to see you here."

The words renewed her hearer's surprise; but giving him no time to reply, she went on in a lower tone: —"You are young and the world is fair before you.

Have you considered that before risking yourself among us?"

She colored under Odo's wondering gaze, and at his random rejoinder that it was a risk any man would gladly take without considering, she turned from him with a gesture in which he fancied a shade of disappointment.

By this they had reached the cabinet of fossils, about which the interest of the other guests still seemed to centre. Alfieri, indeed, paced the farther end of the room with the air of awaiting the despatch of some tedious business; but the others were engaged in an animated discussion necessitating frequent reference to the folios Vivaldi had brought from his study.

The latter turned to Odo as though to include him in the group. "I do not know, sir," said he, "whether you have found leisure to study these enigmas of that mysterious Sphinx, the earth; for though Count Alfieri has spoken to me of your unusual acquirements, I understand your tastes have hitherto lain rather in the direction of philosophy and letters;" and on Odo's prompt admission of ignorance, he courteously continued: "The physical sciences seem, indeed, less likely to appeal to the imaginative and poetical faculty in man, and, on the other hand, religion has appeared to prohibit their too close investigation; yet I question if any thoughtful mind can enter on the study of these curious phenomena without feeling, as it were, an affinity between such investigations and the most abstract forms of thought. For whether we regard these figured stones as of terrigenous origin, either mere *lusus naturæ*, or mineral formations produced by a plastic virtue latent in the earth, or whether as in fact organic substances lapidified by the action of water; in either case, what speculations must their origin excite, leading us back into that dark and unexplored period of time when the breath of Creation was yet moving on the face of the waters!"

Odo had listened but confusedly to the first words of this discourse; but his intellectual curiosity was too great not to respond to such an appeal, and all his perplexities slipped from him in the pursuit of the Professor's thought.

One of the other guests seemed struck by his look of attention. "My dear Vivaldi," said this gentleman, laying down a fossil, and fixing his gaze on Odo while he addressed the Professor, "why use such superannuated formulas in introducing a neophyte to a study designed to subvert the very foundations of the Mosaic cosmogony? I take it the Cavaliere is one of us, since he is here this evening: why, then, permit him to stray even for a moment in the labyrinth of theological error?"

The Professor's deprecating murmur was cut short

by an outburst from another of the learned group, a red-faced spectacled personage in a doctor's gown.

"Pardon me for suggesting," he exclaimed, "that the conditional terms in which our host was careful to present his hypotheses are better suited to the instruction of the neophyte than our learned friend's positive assertions. But if the Vulcanists are to claim the cavaliere Valsecca, may not the Diluvials also have a hearing? How often must it be repeated that theology as well as physical science is satisfied by the Diluvial explanation of the origin of petrified organisms, whereas inexorable logic compels the Vulcanists to own that their thesis is subversive of all dogmatic belief?"

The first speaker answered with a gesture of disdain. "My dear doctor, you occupy a chair in our venerated University. From that exalted *cathedrā* the Mosaic theory of creation must still be expounded; but in the security of these surroundings—the catacombs of the new faith—why keep up the forms of an obsolete creed? As long ago as Pythagoras, man was taught that all things were in a state of flux, without end as without beginning; and must we still, after more than two thousand years, pretend to regard the universe as some gigantic toy manufactured in six days by a Superhuman Artisan, who is presently to destroy it at his pleasure?"

"Sir," cried the other, flushing from red to purple

at this assault, "I know not on what ground you insinuate that my private convictions differ from my public doctrine—"

But here, with a firmness tempered by the most scrupulous courtesy, Professor Vivaldi intervened.

"Gentlemen," said he, "the discussion in which you are engaged, interesting as it is, must, I fear, distract us from the true purpose of our meeting. I am happy to offer my house as the asylum of all free research; but you must remember that the first object of these reunions is not the special study of any one branch of modern science, but the application of physical investigation to the origin and destiny of man. In other words, we ask the study of nature to lead us to the knowledge of ourselves; and it is because we approach this great problem from a point as yet unsanctioned by dogmatic authority, that I am reluctantly obliged—" and here he turned to Odo with a smile—"to throw a veil of privacy over these inoffensive meetings."

Here at last was the key to the enigma. The gentlemen assembled in Professor Vivaldi's rooms were met there to discuss questions not safely aired in public. They were conspirators indeed, but the liberation they planned was intellectual rather than political; though the acuter among them doubtless saw whither such innovations tended. Meanwhile they were content to linger in that wide field of speculation which the development of the physical sciences had recently opened to philosophic thought. As, at the Revival of Learning, the thinker imprisoned in mediæval dialectics suddenly felt under his feet the firm ground of classic argument, so, in the eighteenth century, philosophy, long suspended in the void of metaphysic, touched earth again and, Antæus-like, drew fresh life from the contact. It was clear that Professor Vivaldi, whose very name had been unknown to Odo, was an important figure in the learned world, and one uniting the tact and firmness necessary to control those dissensions from which philosophy itself does not preserve its disciples. His words calmed the two disputants who were preparing to do battle over Odo's unborn scientific creed, and the talk growing more general, the Professor turned to his daughter, saying, "My Fulvia, is the study prepared?"

She signed her assent, and her father led the way to an inner cabinet, where seats were drawn about a table scattered with pamphlets, gazettes and dictionaries, and set out with modest refreshments. Here began a conversation ranging from chemistry to taxation, and from the perfectibility of man to the secondary origin of the earth's surface. It was evident to Odo that, though the Professor's guests represented all shades of opinion, some being clearly loth to leave the safe anchorage of orthodoxy, while others already braved the seas of free

[144]

enquiry, yet all were at one as to the need of unhampered action and discussion. Odo's dormant curiosity
woke with a start at the summons of fresh knowledge. Here were worlds to explore, or rather the actual
world about him, a region then stranger and more
unfamiliar than the lost Atlantis of fable. Liberty was
the word on every lip, and if to some it represented
the right to doubt the Diluvial origin of fossils, to
others that of reforming the penal code, to a third (as
to Alfieri) merely personal independence and relief
from civil restrictions; yet these fragmentary conceptions seemed, to Odo's excited fancy, to blend in the
vision of a New Light encircling the whole horizon of
thought. He understood at last Alfieri's allusion to a
face for the sight of which men were ready to lay down
their lives; and if, as he walked home before dawn,
those heavenly lineaments were blent in memory with
features of a mortal cast, yet these were pure and grave
enough to stand for the image of the goddess.

IV

PROFESSOR ORAZIO VIVALDI, after filling with distinction the chair of Philosophy at the University
of Turin, had lately resigned his office that he might
have leisure to complete a long-contemplated work on
the Origin of Civilization. His house was the meeting-

place of a Society calling itself of the Honey-Bees and ostensibly devoted to the study of the classical poets, from whose pages the members were supposed to cull mellifluous nourishment; but under this guise the so-called *literati* had for some time indulged in free discussion of religious and scientific questions. The Academy of the Honey-Bees comprised among its members all the independent thinkers of Turin: doctors of law, of philosophy and medicine, chemists, philologists and naturalists, with one or two members of the nobility, who, like Alfieri, felt, or affected, an interest in the graver problems of life, and could be trusted not to betray the true character of the association.

These details Odo learned the next day from Alfieri; who went on to say that, owing to the increased vigilance of the government, and to the banishment of several distinguished men accused by the Church of heretical or seditious opinions, the Honey-Bees had of late been obliged to hold their meetings secretly, it being even rumored that Vivaldi, who was their president, had resigned his professorship and withdrawn behind the shelter of literary employment in order to elude the observation of the authorities. Men had not yet forgotten the fate of the Neapolitan historian, Pietro Giannone, who for daring to attack the censorship and the growth of the temporal power had been driven from Naples to Vienna, from Vienna back to Venice, and at length, at the prompting of the Holy See, lured across the Piedmontese frontier by Charles Emmanuel of Savoy, and imprisoned for life in the citadel of Turin. The memory of his tragic history—most of all, perhaps, of his recantation and the "devout ending" to which solitude and persecution had forced the freest spirit of his day—hovered like a warning on the horizon of thought and constrained political speculation to hide itself behind the study of fashionable trifles. Alfieri had lately joined the association of the Honey-Bees, and the Professor, at his suggestion, had invited Odo, for whose discretion his friend declared himself ready to answer. The Honey-Bees were in fact desirous of attracting young men of rank who felt an interest in scientific or economic problems; for it was hoped that in this manner the new ideas might imperceptibly permeate the class whose privileges and traditions presented the chief obstacle to reform. In France, it was whispered, free-thinkers and political agitators were the honored guests of the nobility, who eagerly embraced their theories and applied them to the remedy of social abuses. Only by similar means could the ideals of the Piedmontese reformers be realized; and in those early days of universal illusion none appeared to suspect the danger of arming inexperienced hands with untried weapons. Utopia was already in sight; and all the world was setting out for it as for some heavenly picnic ground.

[147]

Of Vivaldi himself, Alfieri spoke with extravagant admiration. His affable exterior was said to conceal the moral courage of one of Plutarch's heroes. He was a man after the antique pattern, ready to lay down fortune, credit and freedom in defence of his convictions. "An Agamemnon," Alfieri exclaimed, "who would not hesitate to sacrifice his daughter to obtain a favorable wind for his enterprise!"

The metaphor was perhaps scarcely to Odo's taste; but at least it gave him the chance for which he had waited. "And the daughter?" he asked.

"The lovely doctoress?" said Alfieri carelessly. "Oh, she's one of your prodigies of female learning, such as our topsy-turvy land produces: an incipient Laura Bassi or Gaetana Agnesi, to name the most distinguished of their tribe; though I believe that hitherto her father's good sense or her own has kept her from aspiring to academic honors. The beautiful Fulvia is a good daughter, and devotes herself, I'm told, to helping Vivaldi in his work; a far more becoming employment for one of her age and sex than defending Latin theses before a crew of ribald students."

In this Odo was of one mind with him; for though Italy was used to the spectacle of the *Improvisatrice* and the female doctor of philosophy, it is doubtful if the character was one in which any admirer cared to see his divinity figure. Odo, at any rate, felt a distinct

satisfaction in learning that Fulvia Vivaldi had thus far
made no public display of her learning. How much
pleasanter to picture her as her father's aid, perhaps
a sharer in his dreams: a vestal cherishing the flame of
Liberty in the secret sanctuary of the goddess! He
scarce knew as yet of what his feeling for the girl was
compounded. The sentiment she had roused was one for
which his experience had no name: an emotion in which
awe mingled with an almost boyish sense of fellowship,
sex as yet lurking out of sight as in some hidden am-
bush. It was perhaps her association with a world so
unfamiliar and alluring that lent her for the moment
her greatest charm. Odo's imagination had been profoundly stirred by what he had heard and seen at the
meeting of the Honey-Bees. That impatience with the
vanity of his own pursuits and with the injustice of
existing conditions, which hovered like a phantom at
the feast of life, had at last found form and utterance.
Parini's satires and the bitter mockery of the *Frusta
Letteraria* were but instruments of demolition; but the
arguments of the Professor's friends had that constructive quality so appealing to the urgent temper of youth.
Was the world in ruins? Then here was a plan to re-
build it. Was humanity in chains? Behold the angel
on the threshold of the prison!

Odo, too impatient to await the next reunion of the
Honey-Bees, sought out and frequented those among

the members whose conversation had chiefly attracted
him. They were grave men, of studious and retiring
habit, leading the frugal life of the Italian middle-
class, a life in dignified contrast to the wasteful and
aimless existence of the nobility. Odo's sensitiveness to
outward impressions made him peculiarly alive to this
contrast. None was more open than he to the seduce-
ments of luxurious living, the polish of manners, the
tacit exclusion of all that is ugly or distressing; but it
seemed to him that fine living should be but the flower
of fine feeling, and that such external graces, when
they adorned a dull and vapid society, were as incon-
gruous as the royal purple on a clown. Among certain
of his new friends he found a clumsiness of manner
somewhat absurdly allied with an attempt at Roman
austerity; but he was fair-minded enough to see that
the middle-class doctor or lawyer who tries to play the
Cicero is, after all, a more respectable figure than the
Marquess who apes Caligula or Commodus. Still, his
lurking dilettantism made him doubly alive to the
elegance of the Palazzo Tournanches when he went
thither from a coarse meal in the stuffy dining-parlor
of one of his new acquaintances; as he never relished
the discourse of the latter more than after an afternoon
in the society of the Countess's parasites.

Alfieri's allusions to the learned ladies for whom
Italy was noted made Odo curious to meet the wives

and daughters of his new friends; for he knew it was only in their class that women received something more than the ordinary conventual education; and he felt a secret desire to compare Fulvia Vivaldi with other young girls of her kind. Learned ladies he met, indeed; for though the women-folk of some of the philosophers were content to cook and darn for them (and perhaps secretly burn a candle in their behalf to Saint Thomas Aquinas or Saint Dominick, refuters of heresy), there were others who aspired to all the honors of scholarship, and would order about their servant-girls in Tuscan, and scold their babies in Ciceronian Latin. Among these fair grammarians, however, he met none that wore her learning lightly. They were forever tripping in the folds of their doctors' gowns, and delivering their most trivial views ex cathedrâ; and too often the poor philosophers, their lords and fathers, cowered under their harangues like frightened boys under the tongue of a schoolmaster.

It was in fact only in the household of Orazio Vivaldi that Odo found the simplicity and grace of living for which he longed. Alfieri had warned him not to visit the Professor too often, since the latter, being under observation, might be compromised by the assiduity of his friends. Odo therefore waited for some days before presenting himself, and when he did so it was at the angelus, when the streets were crowded and a man's

comings and goings the less likely to be marked. He
found Vivaldi reading with his daughter in the long
library where the Honey-Bees held their meetings; but
Fulvia at once withdrew, nor did she show herself again
during Odo's visit. It was clear that, proud of her as
Vivaldi was, he had no wish to parade her attainments,
and that in her daily life she maintained the Italian
habit of seclusion; but to Odo she was everywhere present in the quiet room with its well-ordered books and
curiosities, and the scent of flowers rising through the
shuttered windows. He was sensible of an influence per-
meating even the inanimate objects about him, so that
they seemed to reflect the spirit of those who dwelt
there. No room had given him this sense of companionship since he had spent his boyish holidays in the old
Count Benedetto's apartments; but it was of another,
intangible world that his present surroundings spoke.
Vivaldi received him kindly and asked him to repeat
his visit; and Odo returned as often as he thought
prudent.

The Professor's conversation engaged him deeply.
Vivaldi's familiarity with French speculative literature,
and with its sources in the experiential philosophy of
the English school, gave Odo his first clear conception
of the origin and tendency of the new movement. This
coördination of scattered ideas was aided by his read-
ings in the Encyclopædia, which, though placed on the

Index in Piedmont, was to be found behind the concealed panels of more than one private library. From
his talks with Alfieri, and from the pages of Plutarch,
he had gained a certain insight into the Stoical view of
reason as the measure of conduct, and of the inherent
sufficiency of virtue as its own end. He now learned
that all about him men were endeavoring to restore
the human spirit to that lost conception of its dignity;
and he longed to join the band of new crusaders who
had set out to recover the tomb of truth from the forces
of superstition. The distinguishing mark of eighteenth-
century philosophy was its eagerness to convert its
acquisitions in every branch of knowledge into instruments of practical beneficence; and this quality appealed peculiarly to Odo, who had ever been moved by
abstract theories only as they explained or modified the
destiny of man. Vivaldi, pleased by his new pupil's
eagerness to learn, took pains to set before him this
aspect of the struggle.

"You will now see," he said, after one of their long
talks about the Encyclopædists, "why we who have at
heart the mental and social regeneration of our countrymen are so desirous of making a concerted effort against
the established system. It is only by united action that
we can prevail. The bravest mob of independent fighters
has little chance against a handful of disciplined sol-
diers, and the Church is perfectly logical in seeing her

chief danger in the Encyclopædia's systematized mar-
shalling of scattered truths. As long as the attacks on
her authority were isolated, and as it were sporadic, she
had little to fear even from the assaults of genius; but
the most ordinary intellect may find a use and become
a power in the ranks of an organized opposition. Seneca
tells us the slaves in ancient Rome were at one time so
numerous that the government prohibited their wearing
a distinctive dress lest they should learn their strength
and discover that the city was in their power; and the
Church knows that when the countless spirits she has
enslaved without subduing have once learned their
number and efficiency they will hold her doctrines at
their mercy.—The Church again," he continued, "has
proved her astuteness in making faith the gift of grace
and not the result of reason. By so doing she placed
herself in a position which was well-nigh impregnable
till the school of Newton substituted observation for
intuition and his followers showed with increasing clear-
ness the inability of the human mind to apprehend anything outside the range of experience. The ultimate
claim of the Church rests on the hypothesis of an in-
tuitive faculty in man. Disprove the existence of this
faculty, and reason must remain the supreme test of
truth. Against reason the fabric of theological doctrine
cannot long hold out, and the Church's doctrinal authority once shaken, men will no longer fear to test by

ordinary rules the practical results of her teaching. We have not joined the great army of truth to waste our time in vain disputations over metaphysical subtleties. Our aim is, by freeing the mind of man from superstition to relieve him from the practical abuses it entails. As it is impossible to examine any fiscal or industrial problem without discovering that the chief obstacle to improvement lies in the Church's countless privileges and exemptions, so in every department of human activity we find some inveterate wrong taking shelter under the claim of a divinely-revealed authority. This claim demolished, the stagnant current of human progress will soon burst its barriers and set with a mighty rush toward the wide ocean of truth and freedom. . ."

That general belief in the perfectibility of man which cheered the eighteenth-century thinkers in their struggle for intellectual liberty colored with a delightful brightness this vision of a renewed humanity. It threw its beams on every branch of research, and shone like an aureole round those who laid down fortune and advancement to purchase the new redemption of mankind. Foremost among these, as Odo now learned, were many of his own countrymen. In his talks with Vivaldi he first explored the course of Italian thought and heard the names of the great jurists, Vico and Gravina, and of his own contemporaries, Filangieri, Verri and Beccaria. Vivaldi lent him Beccaria's famous volume and several numbers of the *Caffè*, the brilliant gazette which Verri and his associates were then publishing in Milan, and in which all the questions of the day, theological, economic and literary, were discussed with a freedom possible only under the lenient Austrian rule.

"Ah," Vivaldi cried, "Milan is indeed the home of the free spirit, and were I not persuaded that a man's first duty is to improve the condition of his own city and state, I should long ago have left this unhappy kingdom; indeed I sometimes fancy I may yet serve my own people better by proclaiming the truth openly at a distance than by whispering it in their midst."

It was a surprise to Odo to learn that the new ideas had already taken such hold in Italy, and that some of the foremost thinkers on scientific and economic subjects were among his own countrymen. Like all eighteenth-century Italians of his class he had been taught to look to France as the source of all culture, intellectual and social; and he was amazed to find that in jurisprudence, and in some of the natural sciences, Italy led the learning of Europe.

Once or twice Fulvia showed herself for a moment; but her manner was retiring and almost constrained, and her father always contrived an excuse for dismissing her. This was the more noticeable as she continued to appear at the meetings of the Honey-Bees, where she joined freely in the conversation, and sometimes diverted the guests by playing on the harpsichord or by recitations from the poets; all with such art and grace, and withal so much simplicity, that it was clear she was accustomed to the part. Odo was thus driven to the not unflattering conclusion that she had been instructed to avoid his company; and after the first disappointment he was too honest to regret it. He was deeply drawn to the girl; but what part could she play in the life of a man of his rank? The cadet of an empoverished house, it was unlikely that he would marry; and should he do so, custom forbade even the thought of taking a wife outside of his class. Had he been admitted to free intercourse with Fulvia, love might have routed such prudent counsels; but in the society of her father's associates, where she moved, as in a halo of learning, amid the respectful admiration of middle-aged philosophers and jurists, she seemed as inaccessible as a young Minerva.

Odo, at first, had been careful not to visit Vivaldi too often; but the Professor's conversation was so instructive, and his library so inviting, that inclination got the better of prudence, and the young man fell into the habit of turning almost daily down the lane behind the Corpus Domini. Vivaldi, too proud to betray any concern for his personal safety, showed no sign of resenting the frequency of these visits; indeed, he received Odo with an increasing cordiality that, to an older observer, might have betokened an effort to hide his apprehension.

One afternoon, escaping later than usual from the Valentino, Odo had again bent toward the quiet quarter behind the palace. He was afoot, with a cloak over his laced coat, and the day being Easter Monday the streets were filled with a throng of pleasure-seekers amid whom it seemed easy enough for a man to pass unnoticed. Odo, as he crossed the Piazza Castello, thought it had never presented a gayer scene. Booths with brightly-striped awnings had been set up under the arcades, which were thronged with idlers of all classes; court-coaches dashed across the square or rolled in and out of the palace-gates; and the Palazzo Madama, lifting against the sunset its ivory-tinted columns and statues, seemed rather some pictured fabric of Claude's or Bibbiena's than an actual building of brick and marble. The turn of a corner carried him from this spectacle into the solitude of a by-street where his own tread was the only sound. He walked on carelessly; but suddenly he heard what seemed an echo of his step. He stopped and faced about. No one was in sight but a blind beggar crouching at the side-door of the Corpus Christi. Odo walked on, listening, and again he heard the step, and again turned to find himself alone. He tried to fancy that his ear had tricked him; but he knew too much of the subtle methods of Italian espionage not to feel a secret uneasiness. His better judgment warned him back; but the desire to spend a pleasant hour prevailed. He took a turn through the neighboring streets, in the hope of diverting suspicion, and ten minutes later was at the Professor's gate.

It opened at once, and to his amazement Fulvia stood before him. She had thrown a black mantle over her head, and her face looked pale and vivid in the fading light. Surprise for a moment silenced Odo and before he could speak the girl, without pausing to close the gate, had drawn him toward her and flung her arms about his neck. In the first disorder of his senses he was conscious only of seeking her lips; but an instant later he knew it was no kiss of love that met his own, and he felt her tremble violently in his arms. He saw in a flash that he was on unknown ground; but his one thought was that Fulvia was in trouble and looked to him for aid. He gently freed himself from her hold and tried to shape a soothing question; but she caught his arm and, laying a hand over his mouth, drew him across the garden and into the house. The lower floor stood dark and empty. He followed Fulvia up the stairs and into the library, which was also empty. The shutters stood wide, admitting the evening freshness, and a drowsy scent of jasmine from the garden.

Odo could not control a thrill of strange anticipation as he found himself alone in this silent room with the girl whose heart had so lately beat against his own. She had sunk into a chair, with her face hidden, and for a moment or two he stood before her without speaking. Then he knelt at her side and took her hands with a murmur of endearment.

At his touch she started up. "And it was I," she cried, "who persuaded my father that he might trust you!" And she sank back sobbing.

Odo rose and moved away, waiting for her over-wrought emotion to subside. At length he gently asked, "Do you wish me to leave you?"

She raised her head. "No," she said firmly, though her lip still trembled; "you must first hear an expla-nation of my conduct; though it is scarce possible," she added, flushing to the brow, "that you have not already guessed the purpose of this lamentable comedy."

"I guess nothing," he replied, "save that perhaps I may in some way serve you."

"Serve me?" she cried, with a flash of anger through her tears. "It is a late hour to speak of service, after what you have brought on this house!"

Odo turned pale. "Here indeed, Madam," said he, "are words that need an explanation."

"Oh," she broke forth, "and you shall have it; though I think to any other it must be writ large upon my countenance." She rose and paced the floor impetuously. "Is it possible," she began again, "you do not yet perceive the sense of that execrable scene? Or do you think, by feigning ignorance, to prolong my humiliation? Oh," she said, pausing before him, her breast in a tumult, her eyes alight, "it was I who persuaded my father of your discretion and prudence, it was through my influence that he opened himself to you so freely; and is this the return you make? Alas, why did you leave your fashionable friends and a world in which you are so fitted to shine, to bring unhappiness on an obscure household that never dreamed of courting your notice?"

As she stood before him in her radiant anger, it went hard with Odo not to silence with a kiss a resentment that he guessed to be mainly directed against herself; but he controlled himself and said quietly: "Madam, I were a dolt not to perceive that I have had the misfortune to offend; but when or how, I swear to heaven I know not; and till you enlighten me I can neither excuse nor defend myself."

She turned pale, but instantly recovered her composure. "You are right," she said; "I rave like a foolish girl; but indeed I scarce know if I am in my waking senses—" She paused, as if to check a fresh rush of emotion. "Oh, sir," she cried, "can you not guess what has happened? You were warned, I believe, not to frequent this house too openly; but of late you have been an almost daily visitor, and you never come here but you are followed. My father's doctrines have long been under suspicion, and to be accused of perverting a man of your rank must be his ruin. He was too proud to tell you this, and profiting to-day by his absence, and knowing that if you came the spies would be at your heels, I resolved to meet you at the gate, and welcome you in such a way that our enemies should be deceived as to the true cause of your visits."

Her voice wavered on the last words but she faced him proudly, and it was Odo whose gaze fell. Never perhaps had he been conscious of cutting a meaner figure; yet shame was so blent in him with admiration for the girl's nobility and courage, that compunction was swept away in the impulse that flung him at her feet.

"Ah," he cried, "I have been blind indeed, and what you say abases me to earth. Yes, I was warned that my visits might compromise your father; nor had I any pretext for returning so often but my own selfish pleasure in his discourse; or so at least," he added in a lower voice, "I chose to fancy—but when we met just now at the gate, if you acted a comedy, believe me, I did not; and if I have come day after day to this house, it is because, unknowingly, I came for you."

The words had escaped him unawares, and he was too sensible of their untimeliness not to be prepared for the gesture with which she cut him short.

"Oh," said she, in a tone of the liveliest reproach,

"spare me this last affront if you wish me to think the harm you have already done was done unknowingly!"

Odo rose to his feet, tingling under the rebuke. "If respect and admiration be an affront, Madam," he said, "I cannot remain in your presence without offending, and nothing is left me but to withdraw; but before going I would at least ask if there is no way of repairing the harm that my over-assiduity has caused."

She flushed high at the question. "Why, that," she said, "is in part, I trust, already accomplished; indeed," she went on with an effort, "it was when I learned the authorities suspected you of coming here on a gallant adventure that I devised the idea of meeting you at the gate; and for the rest, sir, the best reparation you can make is one that will naturally suggest itself to a gentleman whose time must already be so fully engaged." And with that she made him a deep reverence, and withdrew to the inner room.

V

WHEN the Professor's gate closed on Odo night was already falling and the oil-lamp at the end of the arched passage-way shed its weak circle of light on the pavement. This light, as Odo emerged, fell on a retreating figure which resembled that of the blind beggar he had seen crouching on the steps of the Corpus

Domini. He ran forward, but the man hurried across
the little square and disappeared in the darkness. Odo
had not seen his face; but though his dress was tattered, and he leaned on a beggar's staff, something
about his broad rolling back recalled the well-filled
outline of Cantapresto's cassock.

Sick at heart, Odo rambled on from one street to another, avoiding the more crowded quarters, and losing
himself more than once in the districts near the river,
where young gentlemen of his figure seldom showed
themselves unattended. The populace, however, was all
abroad, and he passed as unregarded as though his
sombre thoughts had enveloped him in actual darkness.

It was late when at length he turned again into the
Piazza Castello, which was brightly lit and still thronged
with pleasure-seekers. As he approached, the crowd
divided to make way for three or four handsome travel-
ling-carriages, preceded by linkmen and liveried out-
riders and followed by a dozen mounted equerries. The
people, evidently in the humor to greet every incident
of the streets as part of a show prepared for their diversion, cheered lustily as the carriages dashed across the
square; and Odo, turning to a man at his elbow, asked
who the distinguished visitors might be.

"Why, sir," said the other laughing, "I understand
it is only an Embassage from some neighboring state;

but when our good people are in their Easter mood they are ready to take a mail-coach for Elijah's chariot and their wives' scolding for the Gift of Tongues."

Odo spent a restless night face to face with his first humiliation. Though the girl's rebuff had cut him to the quick, it was the vision of the havoc his folly had wrought that stood between him and sleep. To have endangered the liberty, the very life, perhaps, of a man he loved and venerated, and who had welcomed him without heed of personal risk, this indeed was bitter to his youthful self-sufficiency. The thought of Giannone's fate was like a cold clutch at his heart; nor was there any balm in knowing that it was at Fulvia's request he had been so freely welcomed; for he was persuaded that, whatever her previous feeling might have been, the scene just enacted must render him forever odious to her. Turn whither it would, his tossing vanity found no repose; and dawn rose for him on a thorny waste of disillusionment.

Cantapresto broke in early on this vigil, flushed with the importance of a letter from the Countess Valdù. The lady summoned her son to dinner, "to meet an old friend and distinguished visitor"; and a verbal message bade Odo come early and wear his new uniform. He was too well acquainted with his mother's exaggerations to attach much importance to the summons; but being glad of an excuse to escape his daily visit at the

[165]

Palazzo Tournanches, he sent Donna Laura word that he would wait on her at two.

On the very threshold of Casa Valdù, Odo perceived that unwonted preparations were afoot. The shabby liveries of the servants had been refurbished and the marble floor newly scoured; and he found his mother seated in the drawing-room, an apartment never un-shrouded save on the most ceremonious occasions. As to Donna Laura, she had undergone the same process of renovation, and with more striking results. It seemed to Odo, when she met him sparkling under her rouge and powder, as though some withered flower had been dipped in water, regaining for the moment a languid semblance of freshness. Her eyes shone, her hand trembled under his lips, and the diamonds rose and fell on her eager bosom.

"You are late!" she tenderly reproached him; and before he had time to reply, the double doors were thrown open, and the major-domo announced in an awed voice: "His excellency Count Lelio Trescorre."

Odo turned with a start. To his mind, already crowded with a confusion of thoughts, the name summoned a throng of memories. He saw again his mother's apartments at Pianura, and the handsome youth with lace ruffles and a clouded amber cane, who came and went among her other visitors with an air of such superiority, and who rode beside the travelling-carriage on the first stage of their journey to Donnaz. To that handsome youth the gentleman just announced bore the likeness of the finished portrait to the sketch. He was a man of about two-and-thirty, of the middle height, with a delicate dark face and an air of arrogance not unbecomingly allied to an insinuating courtesy of address. His dress of sombre velvet, with a star on the breast, and a profusion of the finest lace, suggested the desire to add dignity and weight to his appearance without renouncing the softer ambitions of his age.

He received with a smile Donna Laura's agitated phrases of welcome. "I come," said he kissing her hand, "in my private character, not as the Envoy of Pianura, but as the friend and servant of the Countess Valdù; and I trust," he added turning to Odo, "of the Cavaliere Valsecca also."

Odo bowed in silence.

"You may have heard," Trescorre continued, addressing him in the same engaging tone, "that I am come to Turin on a mission from his Highness to the court of Savoy: a trifling matter of boundary-lines and customs, which I undertook at the Duke's desire, the more readily, it must be owned, since it gave me the opportunity to renew my acquaintance with friends whom absence has not taught me to forget." He smiled again at Donna Laura, who blushed like a girl.

The curiosity which Trescorre's words excited was

lost to Odo in the painful impression produced by his mother's agitation. To see her, a woman already past her youth, and aged by her very efforts to preserve it, trembling and bridling under the cool eye of masculine indifference, was a spectacle the more humiliating that he was too young to be moved by its human and pathetic side. He recalled once seeing a *memento mori* of delicately-tinted ivory, which represented a girl's head, one side all dewy freshness, the other touched with death; and it seemed to him that his mother's face resembled this tragic toy, the side her mirror reflected being still rosy with youth, while that which others saw was already a ruin. His heart burned with disgust as he followed Donna Laura and Trescorre into the dining-room, which had been set out with all the family plate, and decked with rare fruits and flowers. The Countess had excused her husband on the plea of his official duties, and the three sat down alone to a meal composed of the costliest delicacies.

Their guest, who ate little and drank less, entertained them with the latest news of Pianura, touching discreetly on the growing estrangement between the Duke and Duchess, and speaking with becoming gravity of the heir's weak health. It was clear that the speaker, without filling an official position at the court, was already deep in the Duke's counsels, and perhaps also in the Duchess's; and Odo guessed under his smiling indiscretions the cool aim of the man who never wastes a shot.

Toward the close of the meal, when the servants had withdrawn, he turned to Odo with a graver manner. "You have perhaps guessed, cavaliere," he said, "that in venturing to claim the Countess's hospitality in so private a manner, I had in mind the wish to open myself to you more freely than would be possible at court." He paused a moment, as though to emphasize his words; and Odo fancied he cultivated the trick of deliberate speaking to counteract his natural arrogance of manner. "The time has come," he went on, "when it seems desirable that you should be more familiar with the state of affairs at Pianura. For some years it seemed likely that the Duchess would give his Highness another son; but circumstances now appear to preclude that hope; and it is the general opinion of the court physicians that the young prince has not many years to live." He paused again, fixing his eyes on Odo's flushed face. "The Duke," he continued, "has shown a natural reluctance to face a situation so painful both to his heart and his ambitions; but his feelings as a parent have yielded to his duty as a sovereign, and he recognizes the fact that you should have an early opportunity of acquainting yourself more nearly with the affairs of the Duchy, and also of seeing something of the other courts of Italy. I am persuaded," he added, "that, young as you are, I need not point out to you on what slight contingencies all human fortunes hang, and how completely the heir's recovery or the birth of another prince must change the aspect of your future. You have, I am sure, the heart to face such chances with becoming equanimity, and to carry the weight of conditional honors without any undue faith in their permanence."

The admonition was so lightly uttered that it seemed rather a tribute to Odo's good sense than a warning to his inexperience; and indeed it was difficult for him, in spite of an instinctive aversion to the man, to quarrel with anything in his address or language. Trescorre in fact possessed the art of putting younger men at their ease, while appearing as an equal among his elders: a gift doubtless developed by the circumstances of court life, and the need of at once commanding respect and disarming diffidence.

He took leave upon his last words, declaring, in reply to the Countess's protests, that he had promised to accompany the court that afternoon to Stupinigi. "But I hope," he added, turning to Odo, "to continue our talk at greater length, if you will favor me with a visit to-morrow at my lodgings."

No sooner was the door closed on her illustrious visitor than Donna Laura flung herself on Odo's bosom.

"I always knew it," she cried, "my dearest; but, oh,

that I should live to see the day!" and she wept and clung to him with a thousand endearments, from the nature of which he gathered that she already beheld him on the throne of Pianura. To his laughing reminder of the distance that still separated him from that dizzy eminence, she made answer that there was far more than he knew, that the Duke had fallen into all manner of excesses which had already gravely impaired his health, and that for her part she only hoped her son, when raised to a station so far above her own, would not forget the tenderness with which she had ever cherished him, or the fact that Count Valdù's financial situation was one quite unworthy the stepfather of a reigning Prince.

Escaping at length from this parody of his own sensations, Odo found himself in a tumult of mind that solitude served only to increase. Events had so pressed upon him within the last few days that at times he was reduced to a passive sense of spectatorship, an inability to regard himself as the centre of so many converging purposes. It was clear that Trescorre's mission was mainly a pretext for seeing the Duke's young kinsman; and that some special motive must have impelled the Duke to show such sudden concern for his cousin's welfare. Trescorre need hardly have cautioned Odo against fixing his hopes on the succession. The Duke himself was a man not above five-and-thirty, and more than one chance stood between Odo and the Duchy; nor was it this contingency that set his pulses beating, but rather the promise of an immediate change in his condition. The Duke wished him to travel, to visit the different courts of Italy: what was the prospect of ruling over a stagnant principality to this near vision of the world and the glories thereof, suddenly discovered from the golden height of opportunity? Save for a few weeks of autumn *villeggiatura* at some neighboring chase or vineyard, Odo had not left Turin for nine years. He had come there a child and had grown to manhood among the same narrow influences and surroundings. To be turned loose on the world at two-and-twenty, with such an arrears of experience to his credit, was to enter on a richer inheritance than any duchy; and in Odo's case the joy of the adventure was doubled by its timeliness. That fate should thus break at a stroke the meshes of habit, should stoop to play the advocate of his secret inclinations, seemed to promise him the complicity of the gods. Once in a lifetime, chance will thus snap the toils of a man's making; and it is instructive to see the poor puppet adore the power that connives at his evasion. . .

Trescorre remained a week in Turin; and Odo saw him daily at court, at his lodgings, or in company. The little sovereignty of Pianura being an important factor in the game of political equilibrium, her envoy was sure of a flattering reception from the neighboring powers; and Trescorre's person and address must have commended him to the most fastidious company. He continued to pay particular attention to Odo, and the rumor was soon abroad that the Cavaliere Valsecca had been sent for to visit his cousin, the reigning Duke; a rumor which, combined with Donna Laura's confidential hints, made Odo the centre of much feminine solicitude, and roused the Countess Clarice to a vivid sense of her rights. These circumstances, and his own tendency to drift on the current of sensation, had carried Odo more easily than he could have hoped past the painful episode of the Professor's garden. He was still tormented by the sense of his inability to right so grave a wrong; but he found solace in the thought that his absence was after all the best reparation he could make.

Trescorre, though distinguishing Odo by his favors, had not again referred to the subject of their former conversation; but on the last day of his visit he sent for Odo to his lodgings and at once entered upon the subject.

"His Highness," said he, "does not for the present recommend your resigning your commission in the Sardinian army; but as he desires you to visit him at Pianura, and to see something of the neighboring courts,

he has charged me to obtain for you a two years' leave
of absence from his Majesty's service: a favor the King
has already been pleased to accord. The Duke has moreover resolved to double your present allowance and has
entrusted me with the sum of two hundred ducats,
which he desires you to spend in the purchase of a
travelling-carriage, and such other appointments as are
suitable to a young gentleman of your rank and expectations." As he spoke, he unlocked his despatch-box
and handed a purse to Odo. "His Highness," he continued, "is impatient to see you; and once your preparations are completed, I should advise you to set out
without delay; that is," he added, after one of his char-
acteristic pauses, "if I am right in supposing that there
is no obstacle to your departure."

Odo, inferring an allusion to the Countess Clarice,
smiled and colored slightly. "I know of none," he said.

Trescorre bowed. "I am glad to hear it," he said, "for
I know that a man of your age and appearance may
have other inclinations than his own to consider. Indeed, I have had reports of a connection that I should
not take the liberty of mentioning, were it not that
your interest demands it." He waited a moment, but
Odo remained silent. "I am sure," he went on, "you
will do me the justice of believing that I mean no re-
flexion on the lady, when I warn you against being
seen too often in the quarter behind the Corpus

[174]

Domini. Such attachments, though engaging at the
outset to a fastidious taste, are often more troublesome than a young man of your age can foresee; and
in this case the situation is complicated by the fact
that the girl's father is in ill odor with the authorities, so that, should the motive of your visits be mistaken, you might find yourself inconveniently involved
in the proceedings of the Holy Office."

Odo, who had turned pale, controlled himself sufficiently to listen in silence, and with as much pretence
of indifference as he could assume. It was the peculiar
misery of his situation that he could not defend Fulvia
without betraying her father, and that of the two al-
ternatives prudence bade him reject the one that chiv-
alry would have chosen. It flashed across him, however,
that he might in some degree repair the harm he had
done by finding out what measures were to be taken
against Vivaldi; and to this end he carelessly asked:—

"Is it possible that the Professor has done anything
to give offence in such quarters?"

His assumption of carelessness was perhaps overdone;
for Trescorre's face grew as blank as a shuttered house-
front.

"I have heard rumors of the kind," he rejoined;
"but they would scarcely have attracted my notice had
I not learned of your honoring the young lady with
your favors." He glanced at Odo with a smile. "Were

I a father," he added, "with a son of your age, my first advice to him would be to form no sentimental ties but in his own society or in the world of pleasure—the only two classes where the rules of the game are understood."

VI

ODO had appointed to leave Turin some two weeks after Trescorre's departure; but the preparations for a young gentleman's travels were in those days a momentous business, and one not to be discharged without vexatious postponements. The travelling-carriage must be purchased and fitted out, the gold-mounted dressing-case selected and engraved with the owner's arms, servants engaged and provided with liveries, and the noble tourist's own wardrobe stocked with an assortment of costumes suited to the vicissitudes of travel and the requirements of court life.

Odo's impatience to be gone increased with every delay, and at length he determined to go forward at all adventure, leaving Cantapresto to conclude the preparations and overtake him later. It had been agreed with Trescorre that Odo, on his way to Pianura, should visit his grandfather, the old Marquess, whose increasing infirmities had for some years past imprisoned him on his estates, and accordingly about the Ascension he set out in the saddle for Donnaz, attended only by one servant, and having appointed that Cantapresto should meet him with the carriage at Ivrea.

The morning broke cloudy as he rode out of the gates. Beyond the suburbs a few drops fell, and as he pressed forward the country lay before him in the emerald freshness of a spring rain, vivid strips of vine-yard alternating with silvery bands of oats, the domes of the walnut-trees dripping above the roadside, and the poplars along the water-courses all slanting one way in the soft continuous downpour. He had left Turin in that mood of clinging melancholy which waits on the most hopeful departures, and the land-scape seemed an image of anticipations clouded with regret. He had had a stormy but tender parting with Clarice, whose efforts to act the forsaken Ariadne were somewhat marred by her irrepressible pride in her lover's prospects, and whose last word had charged him to bring her back one of the rare lap-dogs bred by the monks of Bologna. Seen down the lengthening vista of separation even Clarice seemed regrettable; and Odo would have been glad to let his mind linger on their farewells. But another thought importuned him. He had left Turin without news of Vivaldi or Fulvia, and without having done anything to conjure the peril to which his rashness had exposed them. More than once he had been about to reveal his trouble to Alfieri; but shame restrained him when he remembered that it was Alfieri who had vouched for his discretion. After his conversation with Trescorre he had tried to find some way of sending a word of warning to Vivaldi; but he had no messenger whom he could trust; and would not Vivaldi justly resent a warning from such a source? He felt himself the prisoner of his own folly, and as he rode along the wet country roads an invisible jailer seemed to spur beside him.

The clouds lifted at noon; and leaving the plain he mounted into a world sparkling with sunshine and quivering with new-fed streams. The first breath of mountain-air lifted the mist from his spirit, and he began to feel himself a boy again as he entered the high gorges in the cold light after sunset. It was about the full of the moon, and in his impatience to reach Donnaz he resolved to push on after night-fall. The forest was still thinly-leaved, and the rustle of wind in the branches and the noise of the torrents recalled his first approach to the castle, in the wild winter twilight. The way lay in darkness till the moon rose, and once or twice he took a wrong turn and found himself engaged in some overgrown woodland track; but he soon regained the high-road, and his servant, a young fellow of indomitable cheerfulness, took the edge off their solitude by frequent snatches of song. At length the moon rose, and toward midnight Odo, spurring out of a dark glen, found himself at the opening of the valley of Donnaz. A cold radiance bathed the familiar pastures, the houses of the village along the stream, and the turrets and crenellations of the castle at the head of the gorge. The air was bitter, and the horses' hoofs struck sharply on the road as they trotted past the slumbering houses and halted at the gateway through which Odo had first been carried as a sleepy child. It was long before the travellers' knock was answered, but a bewildered porter at length admitted them, and Odo cried out when he recognized in the man's face the features of one of the lads who had taught him to play pallone in the castle court.

Within doors all were abed; but the cavaliere was expected, and supper was laid for him in the very chamber where he had slept as a lad. The sight of so much that was strange and yet familiar—of the old stone walls, the banners, the flaring lamps and worn slippery stairs—all so much barer, smaller, more dilapidated than he had remembered—stirred the deep springs of his piety for inanimate things, and he was seized with a fancy to snatch up a light and explore the recesses of the castle. But he had been in the saddle since dawn, and the keen air and the long hours of riding were in his blood. They weighted his lids, relaxed his limbs, and gently divesting him of his hopes and fears, pressed him down in the deep sepulchre of a dreamless sleep. . .

[179]

Odo remained a month at Donnaz. His grandfather's happiness in his presence would in itself have sufficed to detain him, apart from his natural tenderness for old scenes and associations. It was one of the compensations of his rapidly travelling imagination that the past, from each new vantage-ground of sensation, acquired a fascination which to the more sober-footed fancy only the perspective of years can give. Life, in childhood, is a picture-book of which the text is undecipherable; and the youth now revisiting the unchanged setting of his boyhood was spelling out for the first time the legend beneath the picture.

The old Marquess, though broken in body, still ruled his household from his seat beside the hearth. The failure of bodily activity seemed to have doubled his moral vigor, and the walls shook with the vehemence of his commands. The Marchioness was sunk in a state of placid apathy from which only her husband's outbursts roused her; one of the canonesses was dead, and the other, drier and more shrivelled than ever, pined in her corner like a statue whose mate is broken. Bruno was dead too; his old dog's bones had long since enriched a corner of the vineyard; and some of the younger lads that Odo had known about the place were grown to sober-faced men with wives and children.

Don Gervaso was still chaplain of Donnaz; and Odo saw with surprise that the grave ecclesiastic who had formerly seemed an old man to him was in fact scarce past the middle age. In general aspect he was unchanged; but his countenance had darkened, and what Odo had once taken for harshness of manner he now perceived to be a natural melancholy. The young man had not been long at Donnaz without discovering that in that little world of crystallized traditions the chaplain was the only person conscious of the new forces abroad. It had never occurred to the Marquess that anything short of a cataclysm such as it would be blasphemy to predict could change the divinely established order whereby the territorial lord took tithes from his peasantry and pastured his game on their crops. The hierarchy which rested on the bowed back of the toiling serf and culminated in the figure of the heaven-sent King seemed to him as immutable as the everlasting hills. The men of his generation had not learned that it was built on a human foundation and that a sudden movement of the underlying mass might shake the structure to its pinnacle. The Marquess, who, like Donna Laura, already beheld Odo on the throne of Pianura, was prodigal of counsels which showed a touching inability to discern the new aspect under which old difficulties were likely to present themselves. That a ruler should be brave, prudent, personally abstemious, and nobly lavish in his official display; that he should repress any attempts on the privileges of the Church, while at the same time protecting his authority from the encroachments of the Holy See; these axioms seemed to the old man to sum up the sovereign's duty to the state. The relation, to his mind, remained a distinctly personal and paternal one; and Odo's attempts to put before him the new theory of government, as a service performed by the ruler in the interest of the ruled, resulted only in stirring up the old sediment of absolutism which generations of feudal power had deposited in the Donnaz blood.

Only the chaplain perceived what new agencies were at work; but even he looked on as a watcher from a distant tower, who sees opposing armies far below him in the night, without being able to follow their movements or guess which way the battle goes.

"The days," he said to Odo, "are evil. The Church's enemies, the basilisks and dragons of unbelief and license, are stirring in their old lairs, the dark places of the human spirit. It is time that a fresh purification by blood should cleanse the earth of its sins. That hour has already come in France, where the blood of heretics has lately fertilized the soil of faith; it will come here, as surely as I now stand before you; and till it comes the faithful can only weary heaven with their entreaties, if haply thereby they may mitigate the evil. I shall remain here," he continued, "while the Marquess needs me; but that task discharged, I intend to retire to one

of the contemplative orders, and with my soul perpetually uplifted like the arms of Moses, wear out my
life in prayer for those whom the latter days shall
overtake."

Odo had listened in silence; but after a moment he
said: "My father, among those who have called into
question the old order of things there are many animated by no mere desire for change, no idle inclination
to pry into the divine mysteries, but who earnestly long
to ease the burden of mankind and let light into what
you have called the dark places of the spirit. How is it,
they ask, that though Christ came to save the poor and
the humble, it is on them that life presses most heavily
after eighteen hundred years of His rule? All cannot
be well in a world where such contradictions exist, and
what if some of the worst abuses of the age have found
lodgment in the very ramparts that faith has built
against them?"

Don Gervaso's face grew stern and his eyes rested
sadly on Odo. "You speak," said he, "of bringing light
into dark places; but what light is there on earth save
that which is shed by the Cross, and where shall they
find guidance who close their eyes to that divine illumination?"

"But is there not," Odo rejoined, "a divine illumination within each of us, the light of truth which we must
follow at any cost—or have the worst evils and abuses

only to take refuge in the Church to find sanctuary there, as malefactors find it?"

The chaplain shook his head. "It is as I feared," he said, "and Satan has spread his subtlest snare for you; for if he tempts some in the guise of sensual pleasure, or of dark fears and spiritual abandonment, it is said that to those he most thirsts to destroy he appears in the likeness of their Saviour. You tell me it is to right the wrongs of the poor and the humble that your new friends, the philosophers, have assailed the authority of Christ. I have only one answer to make: Christ, as you said just now, died for the poor—how many of your philosophers would do as much? Because men hunger and thirst, is that a sign that He has forsaken them? And since when have earthly privileges been the token of His favor? May He not rather have designed that, by continual sufferings and privations, they shall lay up for themselves treasures in Heaven such as your eyes and mine shall never see or our ears hear? And how dare you assume that any temporal advantages could atone for that of which your teachings must deprive them— the heavenly consolations of the love of Christ?"

Odo listened with a sense of deepening discouragement. "But is it necessary," he urged, "to confound Christ with His ministers, the law with its exponents? May not men preserve their hope of heaven and yet lead more endurable lives on earth?"

"Ah, my child, beware, for this is the heresy of private judgment, which has already drawn down thousands into the pit. It is one of the most insidious errors in which the Spirit of evil has ever masqueraded; for it is based on the fallacy that we, blind creatures of a day, and ourselves in the meshes of sin, can penetrate the counsels of the Eternal, and test the balances of the heavenly Justice. I tremble to think into what an abyss your noblest impulses may fling you, if you abandon yourself to such illusions; and more especially if it pleases God to place in your hands a small measure of that authority of which He is the supreme repository. —When I took leave of you here nine years since," Don Gervaso continued in a gentler tone, "we prayed together in the chapel; and I ask you, before setting out on your new life, to return there with me and lay your doubts and difficulties before Him who alone is able to still the stormy waves of the soul."

Odo, touched by the appeal, accompanied him to the chapel, and knelt on the steps whence his young spirit had once soared upward on the heavenly pleadings of the Mass. The chapel was as carefully tended as ever; and amid the comely appointments of the altar shone forth that Presence which speaks to men of an act of love perpetually renewed. But to Odo the voice was mute, the divinity wrapped in darkness; and he remembered reading in some Latin author that the ancient oracles had ceased to speak when their questioners lost faith in them. He knew not whether his own faith was lost; he felt only that it had put forth on a sea of difficulties across which he saw the light of no divine command.

In this mood there was no more help to be obtained from Don Gervaso than from the Marquess. Odo's last days at Donnaz were clouded by a sense of the deep estrangement between himself and that life of which the outward aspect was so curiously unchanged. His past seemed to look at him with unrecognizing eyes, to bar the door against his knock; and he rode away saddened by that sense of isolation which follows the first encounter with a forgotten self.

At Ivrea the sight of Cantapresto and the travelling-carriage roused him as from a waking dream. Here, at his beck, were the genial realities of life, embodied, humorously enough, in the bustling figure which for so many years had played a kind of comic accompaniment to his experiences. Cantapresto was in a fever of expectation. To set forth on the road again, after nine years of well-fed monotony, and under conditions so favorable to his physical well-being, was to drink the wine of romance from a golden cup. Odo was at the age when the spirit lies as naturally open to variations of mood as a lake to the shifting of the breeze; and Cantapresto's exuberant humor, and the novel details of his travelling

equipment, had soon effaced the graver influences of
Donnaz. Life stretched before him alluring and various
as the open road; and his pulses danced to the tune of
the postilion's whip as the carriage rattled out of the
gates.

It was a bright morning and the plain lay beneath
them like a planted garden, in all the flourish and verdure of June; but the roads being deep in mire, and un-
repaired after the ravages of the winter, it was past noon
before they reached the foot of the hills. Here matters
were little better, for the highway was ploughed deep by
the wheels of the numberless vans and coaches journey-
ing from one town to another during the Whitsun holidays, so that even a young gentleman travelling post
must resign himself to a plebeian rate of progression.
Odo at first was too much pleased with the novelty of
the scene to quarrel with any incidental annoyances; but
as the afternoon wore on the way began to seem long,
and he was just giving utterance to his impatience when
Cantapresto, putting his head out of the window, announced in a tone of pious satisfaction that just ahead
of them were a party of travellers in far worse case than
themselves. Odo, leaning out, saw that, a dozen yards
ahead, a modest chaise of antique pattern had in fact
come to grief by the roadside. He called to his postilion
to hurry forward, and they were soon abreast of the
wreck, about which several people were grouped in anx-

ious colloquy. Odo sprang out to offer his services; but as he alit he felt Cantapresto's hand on his sleeve.

"Cavaliere," the soprano whispered, "these are plainly people of no condition, and we have yet a good seven miles to Vercelli, where all the inns will be crowded for the Whitsun fair. Believe me, it were better to go forward."

Odo advanced without heeding this admonition; but a moment later he had almost regretted his action; for in the centre of the group about the chaise stood the two persons whom, of all the world, he was at that moment least wishful of meeting.

VII

IT was in fact Vivaldi who, putting aside the knot of idlers about the chaise, stepped forward at Odo's approach. The philosopher's countenance was perturbed, his travelling-coat spattered with mud, and his daughter, hooded and veiled, clung to him with an air of apprehension that smote Odo to the heart. He caught a blush of recognition beneath her veil; and as he drew near she raised a finger to her lip and faintly shook her head.

The mute signal reassured him. "I see, sir," said he, turning courteously to Vivaldi, "that you are in a bad plight, and I hope that I or my carriage may be of service to you." He ventured a second glance at Fulvia, but she had turned aside and was inspecting the wheel of the chaise with an air of the most disheartening detachment.

Vivaldi, who had returned Odo's greeting without any sign of ill-will, bowed slightly and seemed to hesitate a moment. "Our plight, as you see," he said, "is indeed a grave one; for the wheel has come off our carriage and my driver here tells me there is no smithy this side Vercelli, where it is imperative we should lie to-night. I hope, however," he added, glancing down the road, "that with all the traffic now coming and going we may soon be overtaken by some vehicle that will carry us to our destination."

He spoke calmly, but it was plain some pressing fear underlay his composure, and the nature of the emergency was but too clear to Odo.

"Will not my carriage serve you?" he hastily rejoined. "I am for Vercelli, and if you will honor me with your company we can go forward at once."

Fulvia, during this exchange of words, had affected to be engaged with the luggage, which lay in a heap beside the chaise; but at this point she lifted her head and shot a glance at her father from under her black travelling-hood.

Vivaldi's constraint increased. "This, sir," said he, "is a handsome offer, and one for which I thank you; but

I fear our presence may incommode you and the additional weight of our luggage perhaps delay your progress. I have little fear but some van or wagon will overtake us before nightfall; and should it chance otherwise," he added with a touch of irresistible pedantry, "why, it behoves us to remember that we shall be none the worse off, since the sage is independent of circumstances."

Odo could hardly repress a smile. "Such philosophy, sir, is admirable in principle, but in practice hardly applicable to a lady unused to passing her nights in a rice-field. The region about here is notoriously unhealthy and you will surely not expose your daughter to the risk of remaining by the roadside or of finding a lodging in some peasant's hut."

Vivaldi drew himself up. "My daughter," said he, "has been trained to face graver emergencies with an equanimity I have no fear of putting to the touch— 'the calm of a mind blest in the consciousness of its virtue'; and were it not that circumstances are somewhat pressing—" he broke off and glanced at Cantapresto, who was fidgeting about Odo's carriage or talking in undertones with the driver of the chaise.

"Come, sir," said Odo urgently, "let my servants put your luggage up and we'll continue this argument on the road."

Vivaldi again paused. "Sir," he said at length, "will you first step aside with me a moment?" He led Odo a few paces down the road. "I make no pretence," he went on when they were out of Cantapresto's hearing, "of concealing from you that this offer comes very opportune to our needs, for it is urgent we should be out of Piedmont by to-morrow. But before accepting a seat in your carriage, I must tell you that you offer it to a proscribed man; since I have little reason to doubt that by this time the *sbirri* are on my track."

It was impossible to guess from Vivaldi's manner whether he suspected Odo of being the cause of his misadventure; and the young man, though flushing to the forehead, took refuge in the thought of Fulvia's signal and maintained a self-possessed silence.

"The motive of my persecution," Vivaldi continued, "I need hardly explain to one acquainted with my house and with the aims and opinions of those who frequent it. We live, alas, in an age when it is a moral offence to seek enlightenment, a political crime to share it with others. I have long foreseen that any attempt to raise the condition of my countrymen must end in imprisonment or flight; and though perhaps to have suffered the former had been a more impressive vindication of my views, why, sir, the father at the last moment overruled the philosopher, and thinking of my poor girl there, who but for me stands alone in the world, I resolved to take refuge in a state where a man may work for the liberty of others without endangering his own."

[191]

Odo had listened with rising eagerness. Was not here an opportunity, if not to atone, at least to give practical evidence of his contrition?

"What you tell me, sir," he exclaimed, "cannot but increase my zeal to serve you. Here is no time to palter. I am on my way to Lombardy, which, from what you say, I take to be your destination also; and if you and your daughter will give me your company across the border I think you need fear no farther annoyance from the police, since my passports, as the Duke of Pianura's cousin, cover any friends I choose to take in my company."

"Why, sir," said Vivaldi, visibly moved by the readiness of the response, "here is a generosity so far in excess of our present needs that it encourages me to accept the smaller favor of travelling with you to Vercelli. There we have friends with whom we shall be safe for the night, and soon after sunrise I hope we may be across the border."

Odo at once followed up his advantage by pointing out that it was on the border that difficulties were most likely to arise; but after a few moments of debate Vivaldi declared he must first take counsel with his daughter, who still hung like a mute interrogation on the outskirts of their talk.

After a few words with her, he returned to Odo. "My daughter," said he, "whose good sense puts my wisdom to the blush, wishes me first to enquire if you purpose returning to Turin; since in that case, as she points out, your kindness might result in annoyances to which we have no right to expose you."

Odo colored. "Such considerations, I beg your daughter to believe, would not weigh with me an instant; but as I am leaving Piedmont for two years I am not so happy as to risk anything by serving you."

Vivaldi on this assurance at once consented to accept a seat in his carriage as far as Boffalora, the first village beyond the Sardinian frontier. It was agreed that at Vercelli Odo was to set down his companions at an inn whence, alone and privately, they might gain their friend's house; that on the morrow at daybreak he was to take them up at a point near the convent of the Umiliati, and that thence they were to push forward without a halt for Boffalora.

This agreement reached, Odo was about to offer Fulvia a hand to the carriage when an unwelcome thought arrested him.

"I hope, sir," said he, again turning to Vivaldi, and blushing furiously as he spoke, "that you feel assured of my discretion; but I ought perhaps to warn you that my companion yonder, though the good-naturedest fellow alive, is not one to live long on good terms with a secret, whether his own or another's."

"I am obliged to you," said Vivaldi, "for the hint;

[193]

but my daughter and I are like those messengers who, in time of war, learn to carry their despatches beneath their tongues. You may trust us not to betray ourselves; and your friend may, if he chooses, suppose me to be travelling to Milan to act as governor to a young gentleman of quality."

The Professor's luggage had by this been put on Odo's carriage, and the latter advanced to Fulvia. He had drawn a favorable inference from the concern she had shown for his welfare; but to his mortification she merely laid two reluctant finger-tips in his hand and took her seat without a word of thanks or so much as a glance at her rescuer. This unmerited repulse, and the constraint occasioned by Cantapresto's presence, made the remainder of the drive interminable. Even the Professor's apposite reflections on rice-growing and the culture of the mulberry did little to shorten the way; and when at length the bell-towers of Vercelli rose in sight Odo felt the relief of a man who has acquitted himself of a tedious duty. He had looked forward with the most romantic anticipations to the outcome of this chance encounter with Fulvia; but the unforgiving humor which had lent her a transitory charm now became as disfiguring as some physical defect; and his heart swelled with the defiance of youthful disappointment.

It was near the angelus when they entered the city.

Just within the gates Odo set down his companions,
who took leave of him, the one with the heartiest ex-
pressions of gratitude, the other with a hurried inclination of her veiled head. Thence he drove on to the
Three Crowns, where he designed to lie. The streets
were still crowded with holiday-makers and decked out
with festal hangings. Tapestries and silken draperies
adorned the balconies of the houses, innumerable tiny
lamps framed the doors and windows, and the street-
shrines were dressed with a profusion of flowers; while
every square and open space in the city was crowded
with booths, with the tents of ambulant comedians
and dentists, and with the outspread carpets of snake-
charmers, posture-makers and jugglers. Among this
mob of quacks and pedlars circulated other fantastic
figures, the camp-followers of the army of hucksters:
dwarfs and cripples, mendicant friars, gypsy fortune-
tellers, and the itinerant reciters of Ariosto and Tasso.
With these mingled the townspeople in holiday dress,
the well-to-do farmers and their wives, and a throng of
nondescript idlers, ranging from the servants of the nobility pushing their way insolently through the crowd,
to those sinister vagabonds who lurk, as it were, in the
interstices of every concourse of people.

It was not long before the noise and animation about
him had dispelled Odo's ill-humor. The world was too
fair to be darkened by a girl's disdain, and a reaction

of feeling putting him in tune with the humors of the
market-place, he at once set forth on foot to view the
city. It was now near sunset and the day's decline irra-
diated the stately front of the Cathedral, the walls of
the ancient Hospital that faced it, and the groups
gathered about the stalls and platforms obstructing
the square. Even in his travelling-dress Odo was not a
figure to pass unnoticed, and he was soon assailed by
laughing compliments on his looks and invitations to
visit the various shows concealed behind the flapping
curtains of the tents. There were enough pretty faces
in the crowd to justify such familiarities, and even so
modest a success was not without solace to his vanity.
He lingered for some time in the square, answering the
banter of the blooming market-women, inspecting the
filigree-ornaments from Genoa, and watching a little
yellow bitch in a hooped petticoat and lappets dance
the *furlana* to the music of an armless fiddler who held
the bow in his teeth. As he turned from this show Odo's
eye was caught by a handsome girl who, on the arm
of a dashing cavalier in somewhat shabby velvet, was
cheapening a pair of gloves at a neighboring stall. The
girl, who was masked, shot a dark glance at Odo from
under her three-cornered Venetian hat; then, tossing
down a coin, she gathered up the gloves and drew her
companion away. The manœuvre was almost a chal-
lenge, and Odo was about to take it up when a pretty

boy in a Scaramouch habit, waylaying him with various
graceful antics, thrust a play-bill in his hand; and on
looking round he found the girl and her gallant had
disappeared. The play-bill, with a wealth of theatrical
rhetoric, invited Odo to attend the Performance to be
given that evening at the Philodramatic Academy by
the celebrated Capo Comico Tartaglia of Rimini and
his world-renowned company of Comedians, who, in the
presence of the aristocracy of Vercelli, were to present
a new comedy entitled *Le Gelosie di Milord Zambò*, with
an Intermezzo of singing and dancing by the best Per-
formers of their kind.

Dusk was already falling, and Odo, who had brought
no letters to the gentry of Vercelli, where he intended
to stay but a night, began to wonder how he should
employ his evening. He had hoped to spend it in Vivaldi's company, but the Professor not having invited
him, he saw no prospect but to return to the inn and
sup alone with Cantapresto. In the doorway of the
Three Crowns he found the soprano awaiting him. Cantapresto, who had been as mute as a fish during the
afternoon's drive, now bustled forward with a great
show of eagerness.

"What poet was it," he cried, "that paragoned youth
to the Easter sunshine, which, wherever it touches,
causes a flower to spring up? Here we are scarce alit
in a strange city, and already a messenger finds the

way to our inn with a most particular word from his lady to the Cavaliere Odo Valsecca." And he held out a perfumed billet sealed with a flaming dart.

Odo's heart gave a leap at the thought that the letter might be from Fulvia; but on breaking the seal he read these words, scrawled in an unformed hand:—

"Will the Cavaliere Valsecca accept from an old friend, who desires to renew her acquaintance with him, the trifling gift of a side-box at Don Tartaglia's entertainment this evening?"

Vexed at his credulity, Odo tossed the invitation to Cantapresto; but a moment later, recalling the glance of the pretty girl in the market-place, he began to wonder if the billet might not be the prelude to a sufficiently diverting adventure. It at least offered a way of passing the evening; and after a hurried supper he set out with Cantapresto for the Philodramatic Academy. It was late when they entered their box, and several masks were already capering before the footlights, exchanging *lazzi* with the townsfolk in the pit, and addressing burlesque compliments to the quality in the boxes. The theatre seemed small and shabby after those of Turin, and there was little in the old-fashioned fopperies of a provincial audience to interest a young gentleman fresh from the capital. Odo looked about for any one resembling the masked beauty of the market-place; but he beheld only ill-dressed dowagers and matrons, or ladies of the town more conspicuous for their effrontery than for their charms.

The main diversion of the evening was by this begun. It was a comedy in the style of Goldoni's earlier pieces, representing the actual life of the day, but interspersed with the antics of the masks, to whose improvised drolleries the people still clung. A terrific Don Spavento in cloak and sword played the jealous English nobleman, Milord Zambò, and the part of Tartaglia was taken by the manager, one of the best-known interpreters of the character in Italy. Tartaglia was the guardian of the *prima amorosa*, whom the enamoured Briton pursued; and in the Columbine, when she sprang upon the stage with a pirouette that showed her slender ankles and embroidered clocks, Odo instantly recognized the graceful figure and killing glance of his masked beauty. Her face, which was now uncovered, more than fulfilled the promise of her eyes, being indeed as arch and engaging a countenance as ever flashed distraction across the footlights. She was greeted with an outburst of delight that cost her a sour glance from the *prima amorosa*, and presently the theatre was ringing with her improvised sallies, uttered in the gay staccato of the Venetian dialect. There was to Odo something perplexingly familiar in this accent and in the light darting movements of her little head framed in a Columbine's ruff, with a red rose thrust behind one ear; but after a rapid glance about

the house she appeared to take no notice of him and he
began to think it must be to some one else he owed his
invitation.

From this question he was soon diverted by his increasing enjoyment of the play. It was not indeed a remarkable example of its kind, being crudely enough put
together, and turning on a series of ridiculous and dis-
connected incidents; but to a taste formed on the frigid
elegancies of Metastasio and the French stage there
was something refreshing in this plunge into the coarse
homely atmosphere of the old popular theatre. Extem-
poraneous comedies were no longer played in the great
cities, and Odo listened with surprise to the swift thrust
and parry, the inexhaustible flow of jest and repartee,
the readiness with which the comedians caught up each
other's leads, like dancers whirling without a false step
through the mazes of some rapid contra-dance.

So engaged was he that he no longer observed the
Columbine save as a figure in this flying reel; but presently a burst of laughter fixed his attention and he saw
that she was darting across the stage pursued by Milord Zambò, who, furious at the coquetries of his be-
trothed, was avenging himself by his attentions to the
Columbine. Half-way across, her foot caught and she fell
on one knee. Zambò rushed to the rescue; but springing
up instantly, and feigning to treat his advance as a part
of the play, she cried out with a delicious assumption of

[200]

outraged dignity: "Not a step farther, villain! Know that it is sacrilege for a common mortal to embrace one who has been kissed by his most illustrious Highness the Heir-presumptive of Pianura!"

Mirandolina of Chioggia! sprang to Odo's lips. At the same instant the Columbine turned about and swept him a deep curtsey, to the delight of the audience, who had no notion of what was going forward, but were in the humor to clap any whim of their favorite's; then she turned and darted off the stage, and the curtain fell on a tumult of applause.

Odo had hardly recovered from his confusion when the door of the box opened and the young Scaramouch he had seen in the market-place peeped in and beckoned to Cantapresto. The soprano rose with alacrity, leaving Odo alone in the dimly-lit box, his mind agrope in a labyrinth of memories. A moment later Cantapresto returned with that air of furtive relish that always proclaimed him the bearer of a tender message. The one he now brought was to the effect that the Signorina Miranda Malmocco, justly renowned as one of the first Columbines of Italy, had charged him to lay at the Cavaliere Valsecca's feet her excuses for the liberty she had taken with his illustrious name, and to entreat that he would show his magnanimity by supping with her after the play in her room at the Three Crowns—a request she was emboldened to make by the fact that she

was lately from Pianura, and could give him the last
news of the court.

The message chimed with Odo's mood, and the play
over he hastened back to the inn with Cantapresto and
bid the landlord send to the Signorina Miranda's room
whatever delicacies the town could provide. Odo on ar-
riving that afternoon had himself given orders that his
carriage should be at the door the next morning an
hour before sunrise; and he now repeated these instructions to Cantapresto, charging him on his life to see
that nothing interfered with their fulfilment. The soprano objected that the hour was already late, and that
they could easily perform the day's journey without
curtailing their rest; but on Odo's reiteration of the
order he resigned himself, with the remark that it was
a pity old age had no savings-bank for the sleep that
youth squandered.

VIII

IT was something of a disappointment to Odo, on
entering the Signorina Miranda's room, to find that
she was not alone. Engaged in feeding her pet monkey
with sugar-plums was the young man who had given
her his arm in the Piazza. This gentleman, whom she
introduced to Odo as her cousin and travelling-com-
panion, the Count of Castelrovinato, had the same air of

tarnished elegance as his richly-laced coat and discolored ruffles. He seemed, however, of a lively and obliging humor, and Mirandolina observed with a smile that she could give no better notion of his amiability than by mentioning that he was known among her friends as the *Cavaliere Frattanto*. This praise, Odo thought, seemed scarcely to the cousin's liking; but he carried it off with the philosophic remark that it is the mortar between the bricks that holds the building together.

"At present," said Mirandolina laughing, "he is engaged in propping up a ruin; for he has fallen desperately in love with our *prima amorosa*, a lady who lost her virtue under the Pharaohs, but whom, for his sake, I have been obliged to include in our little supper."

This, it was clear, was merely a way of palliating the Count's infatuation for herself; but he took the second thrust as good naturedly as the first, remarking that he had been bred for an archæologist and had never lost his taste for the antique.

Odo's servants now appearing with a pasty of *beccafichi*, some bottles of old Malaga, and a tray of ices and fruits, the three seated themselves at the table, which Mirandolina had decorated with a number of wax candles stuck in the cut-glass bottles of the Count's dressing-case. Here they were speedily joined by the actress's monkey and parrot, who had soon spread devastation among the dishes. While Miranda was restoring order

by boxing the monkey's ears and feeding the shrieking
bird from her lips, the door opened to admit the *prima
amorosa*, a lady whose mature charms and mellifluous
manner suggested a fine fruit preserved in syrup. The
new-comer was clearly engrossed in captivating the
Count, and the latter amply justified his nickname by
the cynical complaisance with which he cleared the way
for Odo by responding to her advances.

The tête-à-tête thus established, Miranda at once began to excuse herself for the means she had taken to
attract Odo's attention at the theatre. She had heard
from the innkeeper that the Duke of Pianura's cousin,
the cavaliere Valsecca, was expected that day in Vercelli;
and seeing in the Piazza a young gentleman in travelling-dress and French *toupet*, had at once guessed him
to be the distinguished stranger from Turin. At the
theatre she had been much amused by the air of apprehension with which Odo had appeared to seek, among
the dowdy or vulgar inmates of the boxes, the sender
of the mysterious billet; and the contrast between the
elegant gentleman in embroidered coat and gold-hilted
sword, and the sleepy bewildered little boy of the midnight feast at Chivasso, had seized her with such comic
effect that she could not resist a playful allusion to
their former meeting. All this was set forth with so
sprightly an air of mock-contrition that, had Odo felt
the least resentment, it must instantly have vanished.

He was, however, in the humor to be pleased by whatever took his mind off his own affairs, and none could be more skilled than Mirandolina in profiting by such a mood.

He pressed her to tell him something of what had befallen her since they had met, but she replied by questioning him about his own experiences, and on learning that he had been called to Pianura on account of the heir's ill-health she declared it was notorious that the little prince had not long to live, and that the Duke could not hope for another son.

"The Duke's life, however," said Odo, "is as good as mine, and in truth I am far less moved by my remote hopes of the succession than by the near prospect of visiting so many famous cities and seeing so much that is novel and entertaining."

Miranda shrugged her pretty shoulders. "Why, as to the Duke's life," said she, "there are some that would not give a counterfeit penny for it; but indeed his Highness lives so secluded from the world, and is surrounded by persons so jealous to conceal his true condition even from the court, that the reports of his health are no more to be trusted than the other strange rumors about him. I was told in Pianura that but four persons are admitted to his familiarity: his confessor, his mistress, Count Trescorre, who is already comptroller of finance and will soon be prime-minister, and a strange German doctor or astrologer that is lately come to the court. As to the Duchess, she never sees him; and were it not for Trescorre, who has had the wit to stand well with both sides, I doubt if she would know more of what goes on about her husband than any scullion in the ducal kitchens."

She spoke with the air of one well-acquainted with the subject, and Odo, curious to learn more, asked her how she came to have such an insight into the intrigues of the court.

"Why," said she, "in the oddest way imaginable—by being the guest of his lordship the Bishop of Pianura; and since you asked me just now to tell you something of my adventures, I will, if you please, begin by relating the occurrences that procured me this extraordinary honor. But first," she added with a smile, "would it not be well to open another bottle of Malaga?"

MIRANDOLINA'S STORY.

YOU must know, she continued, when Odo had complied with her request, that soon after our parting at Chivasso, the company with which I was travelling came to grief through the dishonesty of the Harlequin, who ran away with the Capo Comico's wife, carrying with him, besides the lady, the far more irretrievable treasure of our modest earnings. This brought us to destitution, and the troop was disbanded. I had nothing but the spangled frock on my back, and thinking to make some use of my sole possession I set out as a dancer with the flute-player of the company, a good-natured fellow that had a performing marmozet from the Indies. We three wandered from one town to another, spreading our carpet wherever there was a fair or a cattle-market, going hungry in bad seasons, and in our luckier days attaching ourselves to some band of strolling posture-makers or comedians.

One day, after about a year of this life, I had the good fortune, in the market-place of Parma, to attract the notice of a rich English nobleman who was engaged in writing a book on the dances of the ancients. This gentleman, though no longer young, and afflicted with that strange English malady that obliges a man to wrap his feet in swaddling-clothes like new-born infants, was of a generous and paternal disposition, and offered, if I would accompany him to Florence, to give me a home and a genteel education. I remained with him about two years, during which time he had me carefully instructed in music, French and the art of the needle. In return for this, my principal duties were to perform in antique dances before the friends of my benefactor—whose name I could never learn to pronounce—and to read aloud to him the works of the modern historians and philosophers.

We lived in a large palace with exceedingly high-ceilinged rooms, which my friend would never have warmed on account of his plethoric habit, and as I had to dance at all seasons in the light draperies worn by the classical goddesses, I suffered terribly from chilblains and contracted a cruel cough. To this, however, I might have resigned myself; but when I learned from a young abate who frequented the house that the books I was compelled to read were condemned by the Church, and could not be perused without deadly peril to the soul, I at once resolved to fly from such contaminating influences. Knowing that his lordship would not consent to my leaving him, I took the matter out of his hands by slipping out one day during the carnival, carrying with me from that accursed house nothing but a few jewels that my benefactor had expressed the intention of leaving me in his will. At the nearest church I confessed my involuntary sin in reading the prohibited books, and having received absolution and the sacrament, I joined my friend the abate at Cafaggiolo, whence we travelled to Modena, where he was acquainted with a theatrical manager just then in search of a Columbine. My dancing and posturing at Florence had given me something of a name among the dilettanti, and I was at once engaged by the manager, who took me to Venice, where I subsequently joined the company of the excellent

Tartaglia with whom I am now acting. Since then I have been attended by continued success, which I cannot but ascribe to my virtuous resolve to face poverty and distress rather than profit a moment longer by the beneficence of an atheist.

All this I have related to show you how the poor ignorant girl you met at Chivasso was able to acquire something of the arts and usages of good company; but I will now pass on to the incident of my visit to Pianura. Our manager, then, had engaged some time since to give a series of performances at Pianura during the last carnival. The Bishop's nephew, Don Serafino, who has a pronounced taste for the theatre, had been instrumental in making the arrangement; but at the last moment he wrote us that, owing to the influence of the Duke's confessor, the Bishop had been obliged to prohibit the appearance of women on the stage of Pianura. This was a cruel blow, as we had prepared a number of comedies in which I was to act the leading part; and Don Serafino was equally vexed, since he did me the honor of regarding me as the chief ornament of the company. At length it was agreed that, to overcome the difficulty, it should be given out that the celebrated Tartaglia of Rimini would present himself at Pianura with his company of comedians, among whom was the popular favorite, Mirandolino of Chioggia, twin brother of the Signorina Miranda

Malmocco, and trained by that actress to play in all her principal parts.

This satisfied the scruples and interests of all concerned, and soon afterward I made my first appearance in Pianura. My success was greater than we had foreseen; for I threw myself into the part with such zest that every one was taken in, and even Don Serafino required the most categorical demonstration to convince him that I was not my own brother. The illusion I produced was, however, not without its inconveniences; for, among the ladies who thronged to see the young Mirandolino, were several who desired a closer acquaintance with him; and one of these, as it happened, was the Duke's mistress, the Countess Belverde. You will see the embarrassment of my situation. If I failed to respond to her advances, her influence was sufficient to drive us from the town at the opening of a prosperous season; if I discovered my sex to her, she might more cruelly avenge herself by throwing the whole company into prison, to be dealt with by the Holy Office. Under these circumstances, I decided to appeal to the Bishop, but without, of course, revealing to him that I was, so to speak, my own sister. His lordship, who is never sorry to do the Belverde a bad turn, received me with the utmost indulgence, and declared that, to protect my innocence from the designs of this new Potiphar's wife, he would not only give me a lodging in the

episcopal palace, but confer on me the additional protection of the minor orders. This was rather more than
I had bargained for, but he that wants the melon is a
fool to refuse the rind, and I thanked the Bishop for
his kindness and allowed him to give out that, my heart
having been touched by grace, I had resolved, at the
end of the season, to withdraw from the stage and prepare to enter the Church.

I now fancied myself safe; for I knew the Countess
could not attempt my removal without risk of having
her passion denounced to the Duke. I spent several
days very agreeably in the episcopal palace, entertained at his lordship's own table, and favored with
private conversations during which he told me many
curious and interesting things about the Duke and the
court, and delicately abstained from all allusion to my
coming change of vocation. The Countess, however, had
not been idle. One day I received notice that the Holy
Office disapproved of the appearance on the stage of a
young man about to enter the Church, and requested
me to withdraw at once to the Barnabite monastery,
where I was to remain till I received the minor orders.
Now the abbot of the Barnabites was the Belverde's
brother, and I saw at once that to obey this order
would place me in that lady's power. I again addressed
myself to the Bishop, but to my despair he declared
himself unable to aid me farther, saying that he dared

not offend the Holy Office, and that he had already run considerable risk in protecting me from the Countess.

I was accordingly transferred to the monastery, in spite of my own entreaties and those of the good Tartaglia, who moved heaven and earth to save his Columbine from sequestration. You may imagine my despair. My fear of doing Tartaglia an injury kept me from revealing my sex, and for twenty-four hours I languished in my cell, refusing food and air, and resisting the repeated attempts of the good monks to alleviate my distress. At length, however, I bethought me that the Countess would soon appear; and it flashed across me that the one person who could protect me from her was her brother. I at once sought an interview with the abbot, who received me with great indulgence. I explained to him that the distress I suffered was occasioned by the loss that my sequestration was causing my excellent manager, and begged him to use his influence to have me released from the monastery. The abbot listened attentively, and after a pause replied that there was but one person who could arrange the matter, and that was his sister the Countess Belverde, whose well-known piety gave her considerable influence in such matters. I now saw that no alternative remained but to confess the truth; and with tears of agitation I avowed my sex, and threw myself on his mercy.

I was not disappointed in the result. The abbot listened with the greatest benevolence to all the details of my adventure. He laughed heartily at his sister's delusion, but said I had done right in not undeceiving her, as her dread of ridicule might have led to unpleasant reprisals. He declared that for the present he could not on any account consent to let me out of his protection, but he promised, if I submitted myself implicitly to his guidance, not only to preserve me from the Belverde's machinations, but to ensure my reappearing on the stage within two days at the latest. Knowing him to be a very powerful personage I thought it best to accept these conditions, which in any case it would have been difficult to resist; and the next day he informed me that the Holy Office had consented to the Signorina Miranda Malmocco's appearing on the stage of Pianura during the remainder of the season, in consideration of the financial injury caused to the manager of the company by the edifying conversion of her twin-brother.

"In this way," the abbot was pleased to explain, "you will be quite safe from my sister, who is a woman of the most unexceptionable morals, and at the same time you will not expose our excellent Bishop to the charge of having been a party to a grave infraction of ecclesiastical discipline. — My only condition," he added with a truly paternal smile, "is that, after the Signorina

Miranda's performance at the theatre her twin-brother the Signor Mirandolino shall return every evening to the monastery: a condition which seems necessary to the preservation of our secret, and which I trust you will not regard as too onerous, in view of the service I have been happy enough to render you."

It would have ill become me to dispute the excellent ecclesiastic's wishes, and Tartaglia and the rest of the company having been sworn to secrecy, I reappeared that very evening in one of my favorite parts, and was afterward carried back to the monastery in the most private manner. The Signorina Malmocco's successes soon repaired the loss occasioned by her brother's withdrawal, and if any suspected their identity all were interested to conceal their suspicions.

Thus it came about that my visit to Pianura, having begun under the roof of a Bishop, ended in a monastery of Barnabites—nor have I any cause to complain of the hospitality of either of my hosts. . .

.   .   .   .

Odo, charmed by the vivacity with which this artless narrative was related, pressed Miranda to continue the history of her adventures. The actress laughingly protested that she must first refresh herself with one of the ices he had so handsomely provided; and meanwhile she begged the Count to favor them with a song.

This gentleman, who seemed glad of any pretext for

detaching himself from his elderly flame, rescued Mirandolina's lute from the inquisitive fingering of the monkey, and striking a few melancholy chords, sang the
following words, which he said he had learned from a
peasant of the Abruzzi:—

> *Flower of the thyme!*
> *She draws me as your fragrance draws the bees,*
> *She draws me as the cold moon draws the seas,*
> *And summer winter-time.*
>
> *Flower of the broom!*
> *Like you she blossoms over dark abysses,*
> *And close to ruin bloom her sweetest kisses,*
> *And on the brink of doom.*
>
> *Flower of the rue!*
> *She wore you on her breast when first we met.*
> *I begged your blossom and I wear it yet—*
> *Flower of regret!*

The song ended, the *prima amorosa*, overcome by
what she visibly deemed an appeal to her feelings, declared with some agitation that the hour was late and
she must withdraw. Miranda wished the actress an affec-
tionate good-night and asked the Count to light her to
her room, which was on the farther side of the gallery
surrounding the courtyard of the inn. Castelrovinato
complied with his usual air of resignation, and the door

[215]

closing on the couple, Odo and Miranda found themselves alone.

"And now," said the good-natured girl, placing herself on the sofa and turning to her guest with a smile, "if you will take a seat at my side I will gladly continue the history of my adventures.". .

IX

ODO woke with a start. He had been trying to break down a great gold-barred gate, behind which Fulvia, pale and disordered, struggled in the clutch of the blind beggar of the Corpus Domini. . . He sat up and looked about him. The gate was still there; but as he gazed it resolved itself into his shuttered window, barred with wide lines of sunlight. It was day, then! He sprang out of bed and flung open the shutters. Beneath him lay the piazza of Vercelli, bathed in the vertical brightness of a summer noon; and as he stared out on this inexorable scene, the clock over the Hospital struck twelve.

Twelve o'clock! And he had promised to meet Vivaldi at dawn behind the Umiliati! As the truth forced itself on Odo he dropped into a chair and hid his face with a groan. He had failed them again, then—and this time how cruelly and basely! He felt himself the victim of a conspiracy which in some occult manner was forever forcing him to outrage and betray the two beings he most longed to serve. The idea of a conspiracy flashed a sudden light on his evening's diversion and he sprang up with a cry. Yes! It was a plot, and any but a dolt must have traced the soprano's hand in this vulgar assault upon his senses. He choked with anger at the thought of having played the dupe when two lives he cherished were staked upon his vigilance...

To his furious summons Cantapresto presented a blank wall of ignorance. Yes, the cavaliere had given orders that the carriage should be ready before daybreak; but who was authorized to wake the cavaliere? After keeping the carriage two hours at the door Cantapresto had ventured to send it back to the stable; but the horses should instantly be put to, and within an hour they would be well forward on their journey. Meanwhile, should the barber be summoned at once? Or would the cavaliere first refresh himself with an excellent cup of chocolate, prepared under Cantapresto's own supervision?

Odo turned on him savagely. "Traitor—spy! In whose pay—?"

But the words roused him to a fresh sense of peril. Cantapresto, though he might have guessed Odo's intention, was not privy to his plan of rejoining Vivaldi and Fulvia; and it flashed across the young man that his self-betrayal must confirm the other's suspicions.

His one hope of protecting his friends was to affect indifference to what had happened; and this was made easier by the reflection that Cantapresto was after all but a tool in more powerful hands. To be spied on was so natural to an Italian of that day that the victim's instinct was rather to circumvent the spy than to denounce him.

Odo dismissed Cantapresto with the reply that he would give orders about the carriage later; desiring that meanwhile the soprano should purchase the handsomest set of filigree ornaments to be found in Vercelli, and carry them with the cavaliere Valsecca's compliments to the Signorina Malmocco.

Having thus rid himself of observation he dressed as rapidly as possible, trying the while to devise some means of tracing Vivaldi. But the longer he pondered the attempt the more plainly he saw its futility. Vivaldi, doubtless from motives of prudence, had not named the friend with whom he and Fulvia were to take shelter; nor did Odo even know in what quarter of the city to seek them. To question the police was to risk their last chance of safety; and for the same reason he dared not enquire of the posting-master whether any travellers had set out that morning for Lombardy. His natural activity of mind was hampered by a leaden sense of remissness. With what anguish of spirit must Vivaldi and Fulvia have awaited him in that hour of dawn behind the convent! What thoughts must have visited the girl's mind as day broadened, the city woke, and peril pressed on them with every voice and eye! And when at length they saw that he had failed them, which way did their hunted footsteps turn? Perhaps they dared not go back to the friend who had taken them in for the night. Perhaps even now they wandered through the streets, fearing arrest if they revealed themselves by venturing to engage a carriage. At every turn of his thoughts Odo was mocked by some vision of disaster; and an hour of perplexity yielded no happier expedient than that of repairing to the meeting-place behind the Umiliati. It was a deserted lane with few passers; and after vainly questioning the blank wall of the convent and the gates of a sinister-looking almshouse that faced it, he retraced his steps to the inn.

He spent a day of futile research and bitter thoughts, now straying abroad in the hope of meeting Vivaldi, now hastening back to the Three Crowns on the chance that some message might await him. He dared not let his mind rest on what might have befallen his friends; yet the alternative of contemplating his own course was one scarcely more endurable. Nightfall brought the conviction that the Professor and Fulvia had passed beyond his reach. It was clear that if they were still in Vercelli they did not mean to make their presence known to him, while in the event of their escape he was without means of tracing them farther. He knew indeed that their destination was Milan, but, should they reach there safely, what hope was there of finding them in a city of strangers? By a stroke of folly he had cut himself off from all communication with them, and his misery was enhanced by the discovery of his weakness. He who had fed his fancy on high visions, cherishing in himself the latent patriot and hero, had been driven by a girl's caprice to break the first law of manliness and honor! The event had already justified her; and in a flash of self-contempt he saw himself as she no doubt beheld him—the fribble preying like a summer insect on the slow growths of difficult years. . .

In bitterness of spirit he set out the next morning for Pianura. A half-melancholy interest drew him back to the scene of his first lonely years, and he had started early in order to push on that night to Pontesordo. At Valsecca, the regular posting-station between Vercelli and Pianura, he sent Cantapresto forward to the capital, and in a stormy yellow twilight drove alone across the waste land that dipped to the marshes. On his right the woods of the ducal chase hung black against the sky; and presently he saw ahead of him the old square keep, with a flight of swallows circling low about its walls.

In the muddy farm-yard a young man was belaboring a donkey laden with mulberry-shoots. The man stared for a moment at Odo's approach and then sullenly returned to his task.

Odo sprang out into the mud. "Why do you beat the brute?" said he indignantly. The other turned a dull face on him and he recognized his old enemy Giannozzo.

"Giannozzo," he cried, "don't you know me? I am the Cavaliere Valsecca, whose ears you used to box when you were a lad. Must you always be pummelling something, that you can't let that poor brute alone at the end of its day's work?"

Giannozzo, dropping his staff, stammered out that he craved his excellency's pardon for not knowing him, but that as for the ass it was a stubborn devil that would not have carried Jesus Christ without gibbing.

"The beast is tired and hungry," cried Odo, his old compassion for the sufferings of the farm-animals suddenly reviving. "How many hours have you worked it without rest or food?"

"No more than I have worked myself," said Giannozzo sulkily; "and as for its being hungry, why should it fare better than its masters?"

Their words had called out of the house a lean bent woman, whose shrivelled skin showed through the rents in her unbleached shift. At sight of Odo she pushed

Giannozzo aside and hurried forward to ask how she might serve the gentleman.

"With supper and a bed, my good Filomena," said Odo; and she flung herself at his feet with a cry.

"Saints of heaven, that I should not have known his excellency! But I am half-blind with the fever, and who could have dreamed of such an honor?" She clung to his knees in the mud, kissing his hands and calling down blessings on him. "And as for you, Giannozzo, you curd-faced fool, quick, see that his excellency's horses are stabled and go call your father from the cow-house, while I prepare his excellency's supper. And fetch me in a faggot to light the fire in the bailiff's parlor."

Odo followed her into the kitchen, where he had so often crouched in a corner to eat his polenta out of reach of her vigorous arm. The roof seemed lower and more smoke-blackened than ever, but the hearth was cold, and he noticed that no supper was laid. Filomena led him into the bailiff's parlor, where a mortal chill seized him. Cobwebs hung from the walls, the window-panes were broken and caked with grime, and the few green twigs which Giannozzo presently threw on the hearth poured a cloud of smoke into the heavy air.

There was a long delay while supper was preparing, and when at length Filomena appeared, it was only to produce, with many excuses, a loaf of vetch-bread, a bit of cheese and some dried quinces. There was nothing else in the house, she declared: not so much as a bit of lard to make soup with, a handful of *pasti* or a flask of wine. In the old days, as his excellency might remember, they had eaten a bit of meat on Sundays, and drunk *aquarolle* with their supper; but since the new taxes, it was as much as the farmers could do to feed their cattle, without having a scrap to spare for themselves. Jacopone, she continued, was bent double with the rheumatism, and had not been able to drive a plough or to work in the mulberries for over two years. He and the farm-lads sat in the cow-stables when their work was over, for the sake of the heat, and she carried their black bread out there to them: a cold supper tasted better in a warm place, and, as his excellency knew, all the windows in the house were unglazed save in the bailiff's parlor. Her man would be in presently to pay his duty to his excellency; but he had grown dull-witted since the rheumatism took him, and his excellency must not take it ill if his talk was a little childish.

Thereupon Filomena excused herself, that she might put a clean shirt on Jacopone, and Odo was left to his melancholy musings. His mind had of late run much on economic abuses; but what was any philandering with reform to this close contact with misery? It was as though white hungry faces had suddenly stared in at the windows of his brightly-lit life. What did these people care for education, enlightenment, the religion of humanity? What they wanted was fodder for their cattle, a bit of meat on Sundays and a faggot on the hearth.

Filomena presently returned with her husband; but Jacopone had shrunk into a crippled tremulous old man, who pulled a vague forelock at Odo without sign of recognition. Filomena, it was clear, was master at Pontesordo; for though Giannozzo was a man grown, and did a man's work, he still danced to the tune of his mother's tongue. It was from her that Odo, shivering over the smoky hearth, gathered the details of their wretched state. Pontesordo being a part of the ducal domain, they had led in the old days an easier life than their neighbors; but the new taxes had stripped them as bare as a mulberry-tree in June.

"How is a Christian to live, excellency, with the salt-tax doubled, so that the cows go dry for want of it; with half a *zecchin* on every pair of oxen, a *stajo* of wheat and two fowls to the parish, and not so much as a bite of grass allowed on the Duke's lands? In his late Highness's day the poor folk were allowed to graze their cattle on the borders of the chase; but now a man dare not pluck a handful of weeds there, or so much as pick up a fallen twig; though the deer may trample his young wheat, and feed off the patch of beans at his very door. They do say the Duchess has a kind heart, and

[224]

gives away money to the towns-folk; but we country-people who spend our lives raising fodder for her game never hear of her Highness but when one of her game-keepers comes down on us for poaching or stealing wood. — Yes, by the saints, and it was her Highness who sent a neighbor's lad to the galleys last year for felling a tree in the chase; a good lad as ever dug fur-row, but he lacked wood for a new ploughshare, and how in God's name was he to plough his field without it?"

So she went on, like a torrent after the spring rains; but when he named Momola she fell silent, and Gian-nozzo, looking sideways, drummed with his heel on the floor.

Odo glanced from one to the other. "She's dead, then?" he cried.

Filomena opened deprecating palms. "Can one tell, excellency? It may be she is off with the gypsies."

"The gypsies? How long since?"

"Giannozzo," cried his mother, as he stood glower-ing, "go see that the stable is locked and his excel-lency's horses bedded down." He slunk out and she began to gather up the remains of Odo's meagre supper.

"But you must remember when this happened."

"Holy Mother! It was the year we had frost in April and lost our hatching for want of leaves. But as for that child of ingratitude, one day she was here, the next she was gone — clean gone, as a nut drops from the tree—and I that had given the blood of my veins to nourish her! Since then, God is my witness, we have had nothing but misfortune. The next year it was the weevils in the wheat; and so it goes."

Odo was silent, seeing it was vain to press her. He fancied that the girl must have died—of neglect perhaps, or ill-usage—and that they feared to own it. His heart swelled, but not against them: they seemed to him no more accountable than cowed hunger-driven animals.

He tossed impatiently on the hard bed Filomena had made up for him in the bailiff's parlor, and was afoot again with the first light. Stepping out into the farm-yard he looked abroad over the flat gray face of the land. Around the keep stretched the new-ploughed fields and the pollarded mulberry-orchards; but these, with the hovels of the village, formed a mere islet in the surrounding waste of marsh and woodland. The scene symbolized fitly enough the social conditions of the country: the over-crowded peasantry huddled on their scant patches of arable ground, while miles of barren land represented the feudal rights that hemmed them in on every side.

Odo walked across the yard to the chapel. On the threshold he stumbled over a heap of mulberry-shoots and a broken ploughshare. Twilight held the place; but as he stood there the frescoes started out in the slant of the sunrise like dead faces floating to the surface of a river. Dead faces, yes: plaintive spectres of his childish fears and longings, lost in the harsh daylight of experience. He had forgotten the very dreams they stood for: Lethe flowed between and only one voice reached across the torrent. It was that of Saint Francis, lover of the poor.

The morning was hot as Odo drove toward Pianura, and limping ahead of him in the midday glare he presently saw the figure of a humpbacked man in a decent black dress and three-cornered hat. There was something familiar in the man's gait, and in the shape of his large head, poised on narrow stooping shoulders, and as the carriage drew abreast of him, Odo, leaning from the window, cried out, "Brutus—this must be Brutus!"

"Your excellency has the advantage of me," said the hunchback, turning on him a thin face lit by the keen eyes that had once searched his childish soul.

Odo met the rebuff with a smile. "Does that," said he, "prevent my suggesting that you might continue your way more comfortably in my carriage? The road is hot and dusty, and, as you see, I am in want of company."

The pedestrian, who seemed unprepared for this affable rejoinder, had the sheepish air of a man. whose rudeness has missed the mark.

"Why, sir," said he, recovering himself, "comfort is all a matter of habit, and I daresay the jolting of your carriage might seem to me more unpleasant than the heat and dust of the road, to which necessity has long since accustomed me."

"In that case," returned Odo with increasing amusement, "you will have the additional merit of sacrificing your pleasure to add to mine."

The hunchback stared. "And what have you or yours ever done for me," he retorted, "that I should sacrifice to your pleasure even the wretched privilege of being dusted by the wheels of your coach?"

"Why, that," replied Odo, "is a question I can scarce answer till you give me the opportunity of naming myself.—If you are indeed Carlo Gamba," he continued, "I am your old friend and companion Odo Valsecca."

The hunchback started. "The cavaliere Valsecca!" he cried. "I had heard that you were expected." He stood gazing at Odo. "Our next Duke!" he muttered.

Odo smiled. "I had rather," said he, "that my past commended me than my future. It is more than doubtful if I am ever able to offer you a seat in the Duke's carriage; but Odo Valsecca's is very much at your service."

Gamba bowed with a kind of awkward dignity. "I am grateful for a friend's kindness," he said, "but I do not ride in a nobleman's carriage."

"There," returned Odo with perfect good-humor, "you have the advantage of *me*; for I can no more escape doing so than you can escape spending your life in the company of an ill-tempered man." And courteously lifting his hat he called to the postilion to drive on.

The hunchback at this, flushing red, laid a hand on the carriage-door.

"Sir," said he, "I freely own myself in the wrong; but a smooth temper was not one of the blessings my unknown parents bequeathed to me; and I confess I had heard of you as one little concerned with your inferiors except as they might chance to serve your pleasure."

It was Odo's turn to color. "Look," said he, "at the fallibility of rumor; for I had heard of you as something of a philosopher, and here I find you not only taking a man's character on hearsay but denying him the chance to prove you mistaken!"

"I deny it no longer," said Gamba stepping into the coach; "but as to philosophy, the only claim I can make to it is that of being by birth a peripatetic."

His dignity appeased, the hunchback proved himself a most engaging companion, and as the carriage lumbered slowly toward Pianura he had time not only to recount his own history but to satisfy Odo as to many points of the life awaiting him.

Gamba, it appeared, owed his early schooling to a Jesuit priest who, visiting the foundling asylum, had been struck by the child's quickness, and had taken him home and bred him to be a clerk. The priest's death left his charge adrift, with a smattering of scholarship above his station, and none to whom he could turn for protection. For a while he had lived, as he said, like a street-cat, picking up a meal where he could, and sleeping in church-porches and under street-arcades, till one of the Duke's servants took pity on him and he was suffered to hang about the palace and earn his keep by doing the lacquey's errands. The Duke's attention having been called to him as a lad of parts, his Highness had given him to the Marquess of Cerveno, in whose service he remained till shortly before that young nobleman's death. The hunchback passed hastily over this period; but his reticence was lit by the angry flash of his eyes. After the Marquess's death he had lived for a while from hand to mouth, copying music, writing poetry for weddings and funerals, doing pen-and-ink portraits at a scudo apiece, and putting his hand to any honest job that came his way. Count Trescorre, who now and then showed a fitful recognition of the tie that was supposed to connect them, at length heard of the case to which he was come and offered him a trifling pension. This the hunchback refused, asking instead to be given some fixed employment. Trescorre then obtained his appointment as assistant to the Duke's librarian, a good old priest engrossed in compiling the early history of Pianura from the ducal archives; and this post Gamba had now filled for two years.

"It must," said Odo, "be one singularly congenial to you, if, as I have heard, you are of a studious habit. Though I suppose," he tentatively added, "the library is not likely to be rich in works of the new scientific and philosophic schools."

His companion received this observation in silence; and after a moment Odo continued: "I have a motive in asking, since I have been somewhat deeply engaged in the study of these writers, and my dearest wish is to continue while in Pianura my examination of their theories, and if possible to become acquainted with any who share their views."

He was not insensible of the risk of thus opening himself to a stranger; but the sense of peril made him the more eager to proclaim himself on the side of the cause he seemed to have deserted.

Gamba turned as he spoke, and their eyes met in one of those revealing glances that lay the foundations of friendship.

"I fear, cavaliere," said the hunchback with a smile, "that you will find both branches of investigation somewhat difficult to pursue in Pianura; for the Church takes care that neither the philosophers nor their books shall gain a footing in our most Christian state. Indeed," he

added, "not only must the library be free from heretical works, but the librarian clear of heretical leanings;
and since you have honored me with your confidence I
will own that, the court having got wind of my supposed tendency to liberalism, I live in daily expectation
of dismissal. For the moment they are content to keep
their spies on me; but were it not for the protection of
the good abate, my superior, I should long since have
been turned out."

"And why," asked Odo, "do you speak of the court
and the Church as one?"

"Because, sir, in our virtuous duchy the terms are
interchangeable. The Duke is in fact so zealous a son
of the Church that if the latter showed any leniency to
sinners the secular arm would promptly repair her negligence. His Highness, as you may have heard, is ruled
by his confessor, an adroit Dominican. The confessor,
it is true, has two rivals, the Countess Belverde, a lady
distinguished for her piety, and a German astrologer
or alchemist, lately come to Pianura, and calling himself a descendant of the Egyptian priesthood and an
adept of the higher or secret doctrines of Neoplatonism.
These three, however, though ostensibly rivals for the
Duke's favor, live on such good terms with one another
that they are suspected of having entered into a secret
partnership; while some regard them all as the emissa-
ries of the Jesuits, who, since the suppression of the So-

ciety, are known to have kept a footing in Pianura, as in most of the Italian states. As to the Duke, the death of the Marquess of Cerveno, the failing health of the little prince, and his own strange physical infirmities have so preyed on his mind that he is the victim of any who are unscrupulous enough to trade on the fears of a diseased imagination. His counsellors, however divided in doctrine, have at least one end in common; and that is, to keep the light of reason out of the darkened chamber in which they have confined him; and with such a ruler and such principles of government you may fancy that poor philosophy has not where to lay her head."

"And the people?" Odo pursued. "What of the fiscal administration? In some states where liberty of thought is forbidden the material welfare of the subject is nevertheless considered."

The hunchback shook his head. "It may be so," said he, "though I had thought the principle of moral tyranny must infect every branch of public administration. With us, at all events, where the Church party rules, the privileges and exemptions of the clergy are the chief source of suffering, and the state of passive ignorance in which they have kept the people has bred in the latter a dull resignation that is the surest obstacle to reform. Oh, sir," he cried, his eyes darkening with emotion, "if you could see, as I do, the blind brute

[233]

misery on which all the magnificence of rank and all the refinements of luxury are built, you would feel, as you drive along this road, that with every turn of the wheels you are passing over the bodies of those who have toiled without ceasing that you might ride in a gilt coach, and have gone hungry that you might feast in Kings' palaces!"

The touch of rhetoric in this adjuration did not discredit it with Odo, to whom the words were as caustic on an open wound. He turned to make some impulsive answer; but as he did so he caught sight of the towers of Pianura rising above the orchards and market-gardens of the suburbs. The sight started a new train of feeling, and Gamba, perceiving it, said quietly: "But this is no time to speak of such things."

A moment later the carriage had passed under the great battlemented gates, with their Etruscan bas-reliefs, and the motto of the house of Valsecca—*Humilitas*—surmounted by the ducal escutcheon.

Though the hour was close on noon the streets were as animated as at the angelus, and the carriage could hardly proceed for the crowd obstructing its passage. So unusual at that period was such a sight in one of the lesser Italian cities that Odo turned to Gamba for an explanation. At the same moment a roar rose from the crowd; and the coach turning into the Corso which led to the ducal palace and the centre of the town, Odo caught sight of a strange procession advancing from that direction. It was headed by a clerk or usher with a black cap and staff, behind whom marched two barefoot friars escorting between them a middle-aged man in the dress of an abate, his hands bound behind him and his head surmounted by a pasteboard mitre inscribed with the title: A Destroyer of Female Chastity. This man, who was of a simple and decent aspect, was so dazed by the buffeting of the crowd, so spattered by the mud and filth hurled at him from a hundred taunting hands, and his countenance distorted by so piteous a look of animal fear, that he seemed more like a madman being haled to Bedlam than a penitent making public amends for his offence.

"Are such failings always so severely punished in Pianura?" Odo asked, turning ironically to Gamba as the mob and its victim passed out of sight.

The hunchback smiled. "Not," said he, "if the offender be in a position to benefit by the admirable doctrines of probabilism, the direction of intention, or any one of the numerous expedients by which an indulgent Church has smoothed the way of the sinner; but as God does not give the crop unless man sows the seed, so His ministers bestow grace only when the penitent has enriched the treasury.—The fellow," he added, "is a man of some learning and of a retired and orderly way of living, and the charge was brought against him by a jeweller and his wife, who owed him a sum of money and are said to have chosen this way of evading payment. The priests are always glad to find a scapegoat of the sort, especially when there are murmurs against the private conduct of those in high places, and the woman, having denounced him, was immediately assured by her confessor that any debt incurred to a seducer was null and void, and that she was entitled to a hundred scudi of damages for having been led into sin."

X

AT the Duke's express wish, Odo was to lodge in the palace; and when he entered the courtyard he found Cantapresto waiting to lead him to his apartment.

The rooms assigned to him lay at the end of one of the wings overlooking the gardens; and as he mounted the great stairway and walked down the corridors with their frescoed walls and busts of Roman emperors he recalled the far-off night when he had passed through the same scenes as a frightened awestruck child. Where he had then beheld a supernatural fabric, peopled with divinities of bronze and marble, and glowing with light and color, he now saw a many-corridored palace, stately indeed, and full of a faded splendor, but dull and antiquated in comparison with the new-fangled elegance of the Sardinian court. Yet at every turn some object thrilled the fibres of old association or pride of race. Here he traversed a gallery hung with the portraits of his line; there caught a glimpse of the pages' antechamber through which he and his mother had been led when they waited on the Duke; and from the windows of his closet he overlooked the alleys and terraces where he had wandered with the hunchback.

One of the Duke's pages came to say that his Highness would receive the cavaliere when the court rose from dinner; and finding himself with two hours on his hands, Odo determined to await his kinsman's summons in the garden. Thither he presently repaired; and was soon, with a mournful pleasure, retracing the paths he had first explored in such an ecstasy of wonder. The pleached walks and parterres were in all the freshness of June. Roses and jasmine mingled on the terrace-walls, citron-trees ingeniously grafted with red and white carnations stood in Faenza jars before the lemonhouse, and marble nymphs and fauns peeped from thickets of flowering camellias. A noise of childish voices presently attracted Odo, and following a tunnel of clipped limes he came out on a theatre cut in the turf and set about with statues of Apollo and the Muses. A handful of boys in military dress were performing a series of evolutions in the centre of this space; and facing them stood a child of about ten years, in a Colonel's uniform covered with orders, his hair curled and powdered, a pasteboard sword in his hand, and his frail body supported on one side by a turbaned dwarf, on the other by an ecclesiastic who was evidently his governor. The child, as Odo approached, was calling out his orders to his regiment in a weak shrill voice, moving now here, now there, on his booted tottering legs, as his two supporters guided him, and painfully trying to flourish the paper weapon that was too heavy for his nerveless wrist. Behind this strange group stood another figure, that of a tall heavy man, richly dressed, with a curious Oriental-looking order on his breast and a veiled somnolent eye which he kept fixed on the little prince.

Odo had been about to advance and do homage to his cousin; but a sign from the man in the background arrested him. The manœuvres were soon over, the heir was lifted into a little gilded chariot drawn by white goats, his regiment formed in line and saluted him, and he disappeared down one of the alleys with his attendants.

This ceremony over, the tall man advanced to Odo with a bow and asked pardon for the liberty he had taken.

"You are doubtless," said he, "his Highness's cousin, the cavaliere Valsecca; and my excuse for intruding between yourself and the prince is that I am the Duke's physician, Count Heiligenstern, and that the heir is at present undergoing a course of treatment under my care. His health, as you probably know, has long been a cause of anxiety to his illustrious parents, and when I was summoned to Pianura the college of physicians had given up all hope of saving him. Since my coming, however, I flatter myself that a marked change is perceptible. My method is that of invigorating the blood by exciting the passions most likely to produce a generous vital ardor. Thus, by organizing these juvenile manœuvres, I arouse the prince's martial zeal; by encouraging him to study the history of his ancestors, I evoke his political ambition; by causing him to be led about the gardens on a pony, accompanied by a miniature pack of Maltese dogs in pursuit of a tame doe, I stimulate the passion of the chase; but it is essential to my system that one emotion should not violently counteract another, and I am therefore obliged to protect my noble patient from the sudden intrusion of new impressions."

This explanation, delivered in a sententious tone and with a strong German accent, seemed to Odo no more than a learned travesty of the familiar and pathetic expedient of distracting a sick child by the pretence of manly diversions. He was struck, however, by the physician's aspect, and would have engaged him in talk had not one of the Duke's gentlemen appeared with the announcement that his Highness would be pleased to receive the cavaliere Valsecca.

[239]

Like most dwellings of its kind in Italy, the palace of Pianura resembled one of those shells which reveal by their outer convolutions the gradual development of the creature housed within. For two or three generations after Bracciaforte, the terrible founder of the line, had made himself master of the republic, his descendants had clung to the old brick fortress or *roccà* which the great condottiere had held successfully against the burghers' arquebuses and the battering-rams of rival adventurers, and which still glassed its battlements in the slow waters of the Piana beside the city wall. It was Ascanio, the first Duke, the correspondent of Politian and Castiglione, who, finding the ancestral lair too cramped for the court of a humanist prince, had summoned Luciano da Laurana to build a palace better fitted to his state. Duke Ascanio, in bronze by Verrocchio, still looked up with pride from the palace-square at the brick and terra-cotta façade with its fruit-wreathed arches crowned by imperial profiles; but a later prince found the small rooms and intricate passages of Laurana's structure inadequate to the pomp of an ally of Leo X, and Vignola added the state apartments, the sculpture gallery and the libraries.

The palace now passed for one of the wonders of Italy. The Duke's guest, the witty and learned Aretino, celebrated it in verse, his friend Cardinal Bembo in prose; Correggio painted the walls of one room, Giulio Romano the ceiling of another. It seemed that magnificence could go no farther, till the seventeenth century brought to the throne a Duke who asked himself how a self-respecting prince could live without a theatre, a riding-school and an additional wing to lodge the ever-growing train of court officials who had by this time replaced the feudal men-at-arms. He answered the question by laying an extra tax on his people and inviting to Pianura the great Roman architect Carlo Borromini, who regretfully admitted that his illustrious patron was on the whole less royally housed than their Highnesses of Mantua and Parma. Within five years the "cavallerizza," the theatre and the gardens flung defiance at these aspiring potentates; and again Pianura took precedence of her rivals. The present Duke's father had expressed the most recent tendency of the race by the erection of a chapel in the florid Jesuit style; and the group of buildings thus chronicled in rich durable lines the varying passions and ambitions of three hundred years of power.

As Odo followed his guide toward the Duke's apartments he remarked a change in the aspect of the palace. Where formerly the corridors had been thronged with pages, lacqueys, and gaily-dressed cavaliers and ladies, only a few ecclesiastics now glided by: here a monsignore in ermine and lace rochet, attended by his chaplain and secretaries, there a cowled Dominican or a

sober-looking secular priest. The Duke was lodged in
the oldest portion of the palace, and Odo, who had
never visited these apartments, looked with interest at
the projecting sculptured chimney and vaulted ceiling
of the pages' antechamber, which had formerly been
the guard-room and was still hung with panoplies.
Thence he was led into a gallery lined with Scriptural
tapestries and furnished in the heavy style of the seventeenth century. Here he waited a few moments, hearing the sound of conversation in the room beyond;
then the door of this apartment opened, and a handsome Dominican passed out, followed by a page who
invited Odo to step into the Duke's cabinet.

This was a very small room, completely panelled in
delicate wood-carving touched with gold. Over this panelling, regardless of the beauty of its design, had been
hung a mass of reliquaries and small devotional bas-
reliefs and paintings, making the room appear more like
the chapel of a wonder-working saint than a prince's
closet. Here again Odo found himself alone; but the
page presently returned to say that his Highness was
not well and begged the cavaliere to wait on him in
his bed-chamber. The most conspicuous object in this
room was a great bedstead raised on a dais. The plumed
posts and sumptuous hangings of the bed gave it an
altar-like air, and the Duke himself, who lay between
the curtains, his wig replaced by a nightcap, a scapular

about his neck, and his shrivelled body wrapped in a brocaded dressing-gown, looked more like a relic than a man. His heavy under-lip trembled slightly as he offered his hand to Odo's salute.

"You find me, cousin," said he after a brief greeting, "much troubled by a question that has of late incessantly disturbed my rest—can the soul, after full intuition of God, be polluted by the sins of the body?" He clutched Odo's hand in his burning grasp. "Is it possible that there are human beings so heedless of their doom that they can go about their earthly pleasures with this awful problem unsolved? Oh, why has not some Pope decided it? Why has God left this hideous uncertainty hanging over us? You know the doctrine of Plotinus—'he who has access to God leaves the virtues behind him as the images of the gods are left in the outer temple.' Many of the Fathers believed that the Neoplatonists were permitted to foreshadow in their teachings the revelation of Christ; but on these occult points much doubt remains, and though certain of the great theologians have inclined to this interpretation, there are others who hold that it leans to the heresy of Quietism."

Odo, who had inferred in the Duke's opening words an allusion to the little prince's ill-health, or to some political anxiety, was at a loss how to reply to this strange appeal; but after a moment he said, "I have heard that your Highness's director is a man of great learning and discrimination. Can he not help your Highness to some decision on this point?"

The Duke glanced at him suspiciously. "Father Ignazio," said he, "is in fact well-versed in theology; but there are certain doctrines inaccessible to all but a few who have received the direct illumination of heaven, and on this point I cannot feel that his judgment is final." He wiped the dampness from his sallow forehead and pressed the scapular to his lips. "May you never know," he cried, "the agony of a father whose child is dying, of a sovereign who longs to labor for the welfare of his people, but who is racked by the thought that, in giving his mind to temporal duties and domestic affections while such spiritual difficulties are still unsolved, he may be preparing for himself an eternity of torture such as that—" and he pointed to an old and blackened picture of the Last Judgment that hung on the opposite wall.

Odo tried to frame a soothing rejoinder; but the Duke passionately interrupted him. "Alas, cousin, no rest is possible for one who has attained the rapture of the Beatific Vision, yet who trembles lest the mere mechanical indulgence of the senses may still subject him to the common penalty of sin! As a man who has devoted himself to the study of theology is privileged to argue on questions forbidden to the vulgar,

so surely fasting, maceration and ecstasy must liberate
the body from the bondage of prescribed morality.
Shall no distinction be recognized between my conduct
and that of the common sot or debauchee whose soul
lies in blind subjection to his lower instincts? I who
have labored early and late to remove temptation from
my people—who have punished offences against conduct as unsparingly as spiritual error—I who have not
scrupled to destroy every picture in my galleries that
contained a nude figure or a wanton attitude—I who
have been blessed from childhood by tokens of divine
favor and miraculous intervention—can I doubt that
I have earned the privileges of that higher state in
which the soul is no longer responsible for the failings
of the body? And yet—and yet—what if I were mistaken?" he moaned. "What if my advisers have deceived me? *Si autem et sic impius sum, quare frustra
laboravi?*" And he sank back on his pillows limp as an
empty glove.

Alarmed at his disorder, Odo stood irresolute whether
to call for help; but as he hesitated the Duke feebly
drew from his bosom a gold key attached to a slender
Venetian chain.

"This," said he, "unlocks the small tortoiseshell
cabinet yonder. In it you will find a phial of clear
liquor, a few drops of which will restore me. 'T is an
essence distilled by the Benedictine nuns of the Per-

petual Adoration, and peculiarly effective in accesses of spiritual disturbance."

Odo complied, and having poured the liquor into a glass, held it to his cousin's lips. In a moment the Duke's eye revived and he began to speak in a weak but composed voice, with an air of dignity in singular contrast to his previous self-abandonment. "I am," said he, "unhappily subject to such seizures after any prolonged exertion, and a conversation I have just had with my director has left me in no fit state to receive you. The cares of government sit heavy on one who has scarce health enough for the duties of a private station; and were it not for my son I should long since have withdrawn to the shelter of the monastic life." He paused and looked at Odo with a melancholy kindness. "In you," said he, "the native weakness of our complexion appears to have been tempered by the blood of your mother's house, and your countenance gives every promise of health and vivacity."

He broke off with a sigh and continued in a more authoritative tone: "You have learned from Count Trescorre my motive in summoning you to Pianura. My son's health causes me the liveliest concern, my own is subject to such seizures as you have just witnessed. I cannot think that, in this age of infidelity and disorder, God can design to deprive a Christian state of a line of sovereigns uniformly zealous in the defence of truth; but

the purposes of Heaven are inscrutable, as the recent
suppression of the Society of Jesus has most strangely
proved; and should our dynasty be extinguished I am
consoled by the thought that the rule will pass to one
of our house. Of this I shall have more to say to you in
future. Meanwhile your first business is to acquaint
yourself with your new surroundings. The Duchess
holds a circle this evening, where you will meet the
court; but I must advise you that the persons her
Highness favors with her intimacy are not those best
qualified to guide and instruct a young man in your
position. These you will meet at the house of the
Countess Belverde, one of the Duchess's ladies, a woman of sound judgment and scrupulous piety, who
gathers about her all our most learned men and saintly
ecclesiastics. Count Trescorre will instruct you in all
that becomes your position at court, and my director,
Father Ignazio, will aid you in the selection of a confessor. As to the Bishop, a most worthy and conver-
sable prelate, to whom I would have you show all due
regard, his zeal in spiritual matters is not as great as
I could wish, and in private talk he indulges in a laxity
of opinion against which I cannot too emphatically
warn you. Happily, however, Pianura offers other opportunities of edification. Father Ignazio is a man of
wide learning and inflexible doctrine, and in several
of our monasteries, notably that of the Barnabites, you

[247]

will find examples of sanctity and wisdom such as a
young man may well devoutly consider. Our convents
also are distinguished for the severity of their rule and
the spiritual privileges accorded them. The Carmelites
have every reason to hope for the beatification of their
aged Prioress, and among the nuns of the Perpetual
Adoration is one who has recently received the ineffable
grace of the *vulnus divinum*. In the conversation of
these saintly nuns, and of the holy abbot of the Barnabites, you will find the surest safeguard against
those errors and temptations that beset your age." He
leaned back with a gesture of dismissal; but added,
reddening slightly, as Odo prepared to withdraw:
"You will oblige me, cousin, when you meet my physician, Count Heiligenstern, by not touching on the
matter of the restorative you have seen me take."

Odo left his cousin's presence with a feeling of deep
discouragement. To a spirit aware of the new influences
abroad, and fresh from contact with evils rooted in the
very foundations of the existing system, there was a peculiar irony in being advised to seek guidance and instruction in the society of ecstatic nuns and cloistered
theologians. The Duke, with his sickly soul agrope in a
maze of Neoplatonism and probabilism, while his people
groaned under unjust taxes, while knowledge and intellectual liberty languished in a kind of moral pest-
house, seemed to Odo like a ruler who, in time of

famine, should keep the royal granaries locked and spend his days praying for the succor that his own hand might have dispensed.

In the tapestry room one of his Highness's gentlemen waited to reconduct Odo. Their way lay through the portrait gallery of which he had previously caught a glimpse, and here he begged his guide to leave him. He felt a sudden desire to meet his unknown ancestors face to face, and to trace the tendencies which, from the grim Bracciaforte and the stately sceptical humanist of Leo's age, had mysteriously forced the race into its ever-narrowing mould. The dusky canvases, hung high in tarnished escutcheoned frames, presented a continuous chronicle of the line, from Bracciaforte himself, with his predatory profile outlined by some early Tuscan hand against the turrets of his impregnable fortress. Odo lingered long on this image, but it was not till he stood beneath Piero della Francesca's portrait of the first Duke that he felt the thrill of kindred instincts. In this grave face, with its sensuous mouth and melancholy speculative eyes, he recognized the mingled strain of impressionability and unrest that had reached such diverse issues in his cousin and himself. The great Duke of the "Golden Age," in his Titianesque brocade, the statuette of a naked faun at his elbow, and a faun-like smile on his own ruddy lips, represented another aspect of the ancestral spirit: the rounded temperament of an age of Cyrenaicism, in which every moment was a ripe fruit sunned on all sides. A little farther on, the shadow of the Council of Trent began to fall on the ducal faces, as the uniform blackness of the Spanish habit replaced the sumptuous colors of the Renaissance. Here was the persecuting Bishop, Paul IV's ally against the Spaniards, painted by Caravaggio in hauberk and mailed gloves, with his motto—*Etiam cum gladio*—surmounting the episcopal chair; there the Duke who, after a life of hard warfare and stern piety, had resigned his office to his son and died in the "angelica vestis" of the tertiary order; and the "beatified" Duchess who had sold her jewels to buy corn for the poor during the famine of 1670, and had worn a hair-shirt under a corset that seemed stiff enough to serve all the purposes of bodily mortification. So the file descended, the colors fading, the shadows deepening, till it reached a baby *porporato* of the last century, who had donned the cardinal's habit at four, and stood rigid and a little pale in his red robes and lace, with a crucifix and a skull on the table to which the top of his berretta hardly reached.

It seemed to Odo as he gazed on the long line of faces as though their owners had entered one by one into a narrowing defile, where the sun rose later and set earlier on each successive traveller; and in every countenance from that of the first Duke to that of his own peruked

and cuirassed grandfather, he discerned the same symp-
tom of decadency: that duality of will which, in a deli-
cately-tempered race, is the fatal fruit of an undis-
turbed preëminence. They had ruled too long and
enjoyed too much; and the poor creature he had just
left to his dismal scruples and forebodings seemed the
mere empty husk of long-exhausted passions.

XI

THE Duchess was lodged in the Borromini wing
of the palace, and thither Odo was conducted
that evening.

To eyes accustomed to such ceremonial there was no
great novelty in the troop of powdered servants, the
major-domo in his short cloak and chain, and the florid
splendor of the long suite of rooms, decorated in a style
that already appeared over-charged to the more fastidious taste of the day. Odo's curiosity centred chiefly in
the persons peopling this scene, whose conflicting interests and passions formed, as it were, the framework
of the social structure of Pianura, so that there was not
a laborer in the mulberry-orchards or a weaver in the
silk-looms but depended for his crust of black bread
and the leaking roof over his head on the private whim
of some member of that brilliant company.

The Duchess, who soon entered, received Odo with

the flighty good-nature of a roving mind; but as her deep-blue gaze met his her color rose, her eyes lingered on his face, and she invited him to a seat at her side. Maria Clementina was of Austrian descent, and something in her free and noble port and the smiling arrogance of her manner recalled the aspect of her distant kinswoman, the young Queen of France. She plied Odo with a hundred questions, interrupting his answers with a playful abruptness, and to all appearances more engaged by his person than his discourse.

"Have you seen my son?" she asked. "I remember you a little boy scarce bigger than Ferrante, whom your mother brought to kiss my hand in the very year of my marriage. Yes—and you pinched my toy spaniel, sir, and I was so angry with you that I got up and turned my back on the company—do you remember? But how should you, being such a child at the time? Ah, cousin, how old you make me feel! I would to God my son looked as you did then; but the Duke is killing him with his nostrums. The child was healthy enough when he was born; but what with novenas and touching of relics and animal magnetism and electrical treatment, there's not a bone in his little body but the saints and the surgeons are fighting over its possession. Have you read 'Emile,' cousin, by the new French author—I forget his name? Well, I would have the child brought up like 'Emile,' allowed to run wild in the country and grow up sturdy and hard as a little peasant. But what heresies am I talking! The book is on the Index, I believe, and if my director knew I had it in my library I should be set up in the stocks on the market-place and all my court-gowns burnt at the Church door as a warning against the danger of importing the new fashions from France!—I hope you hunt, cousin?" she cried suddenly. "'T is my chief diversion and one I would have my friends enjoy with me. His Highness has lately seen fit to cut down my stables, so that I have scarce forty saddle-horses to my name, and the greater part but sorry nags at that; yet I can still find a mount for any friend that will ride with me and I hope to see you among the number if the Duke can spare you now and then from mass and benediction. His Highness complains that I am always surrounded by the same company; but is it my fault if there are not twenty persons at court that can survive a day in the saddle and a night at cards? Have you seen the Belverde, my mistress of the robes? She follows the hunt in a litter, cousin, and tells her beads at the death! I hope you like cards too, cousin? for I would have all my weaknesses shared by my friends, that they may be the less disposed to criticise them."

The impression produced on the Duchess by the cavaliere Valsecca was closely observed by several members of the group surrounding her Highness. One of these was Count Trescorre, who moved among the courtiers with an air of ease that seemed to establish without proclaiming the tie between himself and the Duchess. When Maria Clementina sat down at play, Trescorre joined Odo and with his usual friendliness pointed out the most conspicuous figures in the circle. The Duchess's society, as the Duke had implied, was composed of the livelier members of the court, chief among whom was the same Don Serafino who had figured so vividly in the reminiscences of Mirandolina and Cantapresto. This gentleman, a notorious loose liver and gamester, with some remains of good looks and a gay boisterous manner, played the leader of revels to her Highness's following; and at his heels came the flock of pretty women and dashing spendthrifts who compose the train of a young and pleasure-loving princess. On such occasions as the present, however, all the members of the court were obliged to pay their duty to her Highness; and conspicuous among these less frequent visitors was the Duke's director, the suave and handsome Dominican whom Odo had seen leaving his Highness's closet that afternoon. This ecclesiastic was engaged in conversation with the Prime-Minister, Count Pievepelago, a small feeble manikin covered with gold lace and orders. The deference with which the latter followed the Dominican's discourse excited Odo's attention; but it was soon diverted by the approach of a lady who joined herself to the group with an air of discreet familiarity. Though no longer young, she was still slender and graceful, and her languid eye and vaporish manner seemed to Odo to veil an uncommon alertness of perception. The rich sobriety of her dress, the jewelled rosary about her wrist, and most of all, perhaps, the murderous sweetness of the smile with which the Duchess addressed her, told him that here was the Countess Belverde; an inference which Trescorre confirmed.

"The Countess," said he, "or I should rather say, the Marchioness of Boscofolto, since the Duke has just bestowed on her the fief of that name, is impatient to make your acquaintance; and since you doubtless remember the saying of the Marquis de Montesquieu, that to know a ruler one must know his confessor and his mistress, you will perhaps be glad to seize both opportunities in one."

The Countess greeted Odo with a flattering deference and at once drew him into conversation with Pievepelago and the Dominican.

"We are discussing," said she, "the details of Prince Ferrante's approaching visit to the shrine of our Lady of the Mountain. This shrine lies about half an hour's ride beyond my villa of Boscofolto, where I hope to have the honor of receiving their Highnesses on their return from the pilgrimage. The Madonna del Monte,

as you doubtless know, has often preserved the ducal
house in seasons of peril, notably during the great
plague of 1630 and during the famine in the Duchess
Polixena's time, when her Highness, of blessed memory,
met our Lady in the streets distributing bread, in the
dress of a peasant-woman from the hills, but with a
necklace made of blood-drops instead of garnets. Father
Ignazio has lately counselled the little Prince's visiting
in state the protectress of his line, and his Highness's
physician, Count Heiligenstern, does not disapprove the
plan. In fact," she added, "I understand that he thinks
all special acts of piety beneficial, as symbolizing the
inward act by which the soul incessantly strives to re-
unite itself to the One."

The Dominican glanced at Odo with a smile. "The
Count's dialectics," said he, "might be dangerous were
they a little clearer; but we must hope he distinguishes
more accurately between his drugs than his dogmas."

"But I am told," the Prime-Minister here interposed
in a creaking rusty voice, "that her Highness is set
against the pilgrimage and will put every obstacle in
the way of its being performed."

The Countess sighed and cast down her eyes, the
Dominican remained silent, and Trescorre said quietly
to Odo, "Her Highness would be pleased to have you
join her in a game at basset." As they crossed the room
he added in a low tone: "The Duchess, in spite of her

remarkable strength of character, is still of an age to be readily open to new influences. I observed she was much taken by your conversation, and you would be doing her a service by engaging her not to oppose this pilgrimage to Boscofolto. We have Heiligenstern's word that it cannot harm the Prince, it will produce a good impression on the people, and it is of vital importance to her Highness not to side against the Duke in such matters." And he drew back with a smile as Odo approached the card-table.

Odo left the Duchess's circle with an increased desire to penetrate more deeply into the organization of the little world about him, to trace the operation of its various parts, and to put his hand on the mainspring about which they revolved; and he wondered whether Gamba, whose connection with the ducal library must give him some insight into the affairs of the court, might not prove as instructive a guide through this labyrinth as through the mazes of the ducal garden. With this object in mind he sought out the hunchback the next morning.

The Duke's library filled a series of rooms designed in the classical style of the cinque-cento. On the very threshold Odo was conscious of leaving behind the trivial activities of the palace, with the fantastic architecture which seemed their natural setting. Here all was based on a noble permanence of taste, a convergence of accumulated effort toward a chosen end, and the door was fittingly surmounted by Seneca's definition of the wise man's state:

Omnia illi secula ut deo serviunt.

Odo would gladly have lingered among the books which filled the rooms with an incense-like aroma of old leather. His imagination caressed in passing the yellowish vellum backs, the worn tooling of Aldine folios, the heavy silver clasps of ancient chronicles and psalters; but his first object was to find Gamba and renew the conversation of the previous day. In this he was disappointed. The only occupant of the library was the hunchback's friend and protector, the abate Crescenti, a tall white-haired priest with the roseate gravity and benevolent air of a donator in some Flemish triptych. The abate, courteously welcoming Odo, explained that he had despatched his assistant to the Benedictine monastery to copy certain ancient records of transactions between that order and the lords of Valsecca, and added that Gamba, on his return, should at once be apprised of the cavaliere's wish to see him.

The abate himself had been engaged, when his visitor entered, in collating manuscripts, but on Odo's begging him to return to his work, he said with a smile: "I do not suffer from an excess of interruptions, for the library is the least visited portion of the palace, and I am glad to welcome any who are disposed to inspect its

[258]

treasures. I know not, cavaliere," he added, "if the report of my humble labors has ever reached you;" and on Odo's affirmative gesture he went on, with the eagerness of a shy man who gathers assurance from the intelligence of his listener: "Such researches into the rude and uncivilized past seem to me as essential to the comprehension of the present as the mastering of the major premiss to the understanding of a syllogism; and to those who reproach me for wasting my life over the chronicles of barbarian invasions and the records of monkish litigations, instead of contemplating the illustrious deeds of Greek sages and Roman heroes, I confidently reply that it is more useful to a man to know his own father's character than that of a remote ancestor. Even in this quiet retreat," he went on, "I hear much talk of abuses and of the need for reform; and I often think that if they who rail so loudly against existing institutions would take the trouble to trace them to their source, and would, for instance, compare this state as it is to-day with its condition five hundred or a thousand years ago, instead of measuring it by the standard of some imaginary Platonic republic, they would find, if not less subject for complaint, yet fuller means of understanding and remedying the abuses they discover."

This view of history was one so new in the abate Crescenti's day that it surprised Odo with the revelation of unsuspected possibilities. How was it that among the philosophers whose works he had studied, none had thought of tracing in the social and political tendencies of the race the germ of wrongs so confidently ascribed to the cunning of priests and the rapacity of princes? Odo listened with growing interest while Crescenti, encouraged by his questions, pointed out how the abuses of feudalism had arisen from the small landowner's need of protection against the northern invader, as the concentration of royal prerogative had been the outcome of the King's intervention between his great vassals and the communes. The discouragement which had obscured Odo's outlook since his visit to Pontesordo was cleared away by the discovery that in a sympathetic study of the past might lie the secret of dealing with present evils. His imagination, taking the intervening obstacles at a bound, arrived at once at the general axiom to which such inductions pointed; and if he afterward learned that human development follows no such direct line of advance, but must painfully stumble across the wastes of error, prejudice and ignorance, while the theorizer traverses the same distance with a stroke of his speculative pinions; yet the influence of these teachings tempered his judgments with charity and dignified his very failures by a tragic sense of their inevitableness.

Crescenti suggested that Gamba should wait on Odo

that evening; but the latter being uncertain how far he might dispose of his time, enquired where the hunchback lodged, with a view of sending for him at a convenient moment. Having dined at the Duchess's table, and soon wearying of the vapid company of her associates, he yielded to the desire for contrast that so often guided his course, and set out toward sunset in search of Gamba's lodging.

It was his first opportunity of inspecting the town at leisure, and for a while he let his curiosity lead him as it would. The streets near the palace were full of noble residences, recording, in their sculptured doorways, in the wrought-iron work of torch-holders and window-grilles, and in every architectural detail, the gradual change of taste that had transformed the machicolations of the mediæval fighter into the open arcades and airy balconies of his descendant. Here and there, amid these inveterate records of dominion, rose the monuments of a mightier and more ancient power. Of these churches and monasteries, the greater number, dating only from the ascendancy of the Valseccas, showed an ordered and sumptuous architecture; but one or two buildings surviving from the period of the free city stood out among them with the austerity of desert saints in a throng of court ecclesiastics. The columns of the Cathedral porch were still supported on featureless porphyry lions worn smooth by generations of loungers;

and above the octagonal baptistery ran a fantastic bas-relief wherein the spirals of the vine framed an allegory of men and monsters, symbolizing, in their mysterious conflicts, the ever-recurring Manicheism of the middle ages. Fresh from his talk with Crescenti, Odo lingered curiously on these sculptures, which but the day before he might have passed by as the efforts of ignorant work-men, but which now seemed full of the significance that belongs to any incomplete expression of human thought or feeling. Of their relation to the growth of art he had as yet no clear notion; but as evidence of sensations that his forefathers had struggled to record, they touched him like the inarticulate stammerings in which childhood strives to convey its meaning.

He found Gamba's lodging on the upper floor of a decayed palace in one of the by-lanes near the Cathe-dral. The pointed arcades of this ancient building inclosed the remains of floriated mouldings, and the walls of the court showed traces of fresco-painting; but clothes-lines now hung between the arches, and about the well-head in the centre of the court sat a group of tattered women with half-naked children playing in the dirt at their feet. One of these women directed Odo to the staircase which ascended between damp stone walls to Gamba's door. This was opened by the hunchback himself, who, with an astonished exclamation, admitted his visitor to a scantily furnished room littered with books and papers. A child sprawled on the floor, and a young woman, who had been sewing in the fading light of the attic window, snatched him up as Odo entered. Her back being turned to the light, he caught only a slender youthful outline; but something in the turn of the head, the shrinking curve of the shoulders, carried him back to the little barefoot figure cowering in a corner of the kitchen at Pontesordo, while the farm-yard rang with Filomena's call—"Where are you then, child of iniquity?"

"Momola—don't you know me?" he exclaimed.

She hung back trembling, as though the sound of his voice roused an echo of fear; but Gamba, reddening slightly, took her hand and led her forward.

"It is, indeed," said he, "your excellency's old play-mate, the Momola of Pontesordo, who consents to share my poverty and who makes me forget it by the tender-ness of her devotion."

But Momola, at this, found voice. "Oh, sir," she cried, "it is he who took me in when I was half-dead and starving, who many a time went hungry to feed me, and who cares for the child as if it were his own!"

As she stood there, in her half-wild hollow-eyed beauty, which seemed a sickly efflorescence of the marshes, pressing to her breast another "child of in-iquity" as pale and elfish as her former self, she seemed to Odo the embodiment of ancient wrongs, risen from the wasted soil to haunt the dreams of its oppressors.

Gamba shrugged his shoulders. "Why," said he, "a child of my own is a luxury I am never likely to possess as long as I have wit to remember the fundamental axiom of philosophy: *entia non sunt multiplicanda præter necessitatem;* so it is natural enough fate should single me out to repair the negligence of those who have failed to observe that admirable principle.— And now," he added, turning gently to Momola, "it is time to put the boy to bed."

When the door had closed on her Odo turned to Gamba. "I could learn nothing at Pontesordo," he said. "They seemed unwilling to speak of her. What is her story and where did you first know her?"

Gamba's face darkened. "You will remember, cavaliere," he said, "that some time after your departure from Pianura I passed into the service of the Marquess of Cerveno, then a youth of about twenty, who combined with graceful manners and a fair exterior a nature so corrupt and cowardly that he seemed like some such noble edifice as this, designed to house great hopes and high ambitions, but fallen to base uses and become the shelter of thieves and prostitutes. Prince Ferrante being sickly from his birth, the Marquess was always looked on as the Duke's successor, and to Trescorre, who even then, as Master of the Horse, cherished the ambitions he has since realized, no prospect could have been more distasteful. My noble brother, to do him justice, has always hated the Jesuits, who, as you doubtless know, were all-powerful here before the recent suppression of the order. The Marquess of Cerveno was as completely under their control as the Duke is under that of the Dominicans, and Trescorre knew that with the Marquess's accession his own rule must end. He did his best to gain an influence over his future ruler, but failing in this resolved to ruin him.

"Cerveno, like all your house, was passionately addicted to the chase, and spent much of his time hunting in the forest of Pontesordo. One day the stag was brought to bay in the farm-yard of the old manor, and there Cerveno saw Momola, then a girl of sixteen, of a singular beauty which sickness and trouble have since effaced. The young Marquess was instantly taken; and though hitherto indifferent to women, yielded so completely to his infatuation that Trescorre, ever on the alert, saw in it an unexpected means to his end. He instantly married Momola to Giannozzo, whom she feared and hated; he schooled Giannozzo in the part of the jealous and vindictive husband, and by the liberal use of money contrived that Momola, while suffered to encourage the Marquess's addresses, should be kept so close that Cerveno could not see her save by coming to Pontesordo. This was the first step in the plan; the next was to arrange that Momola should lure her lover to the hunting-lodge on the edge of the chase. This lodge, as your excellency may remember, lies level with the marsh, and so open to noxious exhalations that a night's sojourn there may be fatal. The infernal scheme was carried out with the connivance of the scoundrels at the farm, who had no scruples about selling the girl for a few ducats; and as to Momola, can you wonder that her loathing of Giannozzo and of her wretched life at Pontesordo threw her defenceless into Trescorre's toils? All was cunningly planned to exasperate Cerveno's passion and Momola's longing to escape; and at length, pressed by his entreaties and innocently carrying out the designs of his foe, the poor girl promised to meet him after nightfall at the hunting-lodge. The secrecy of the adventure, and the peril to which it exposed him (for Trescorre had taken care to paint Giannozzo and his father in the darkest colors) were fuel to Cerveno's passion, and he went night after night to Pontesordo. The time was August, when the marsh breathes death, and the Duke, apprised of his favorite's imprudence, forbade his returning to the chase.

"Nothing could better have served Trescorre; for opposition spurred the Marquess's languid temper, and he had now the incredible folly to take up his residence in the lodge. Within three weeks the fever held him. He was at once carried to Pianura, and on recovering from his seizure was sent to take the mountain air at the baths of Lucca. But the poison was in his blood. He never regained more than a semblance of health, and his madness having run its course, his passion for Momola turned to hate of the poor girl to whom he ascribed his destruction. Giannozzo, meanwhile, terrified by the report that the Duke had winded the intrigue, and fearing to be charged with connivance, thought to prove his innocence by casting off his wife and disowning her child.

"What part I played in this grim business I leave your excellency to conceive. As the Marquess's creature I was forced to assist at the spectacle without power to stay its consequences; but when the child was born I carried the news to my master and begged him to come to the mother's aid. For answer, he had me beaten by his lacqueys and flung out of his house. I stomached the beating and addressed myself to Trescorre. My noble brother, whose insight is seldom at fault, saw that I knew enough to imperil him. The Marquess was dying and his enemy could afford to be generous. He gave me a little money and the following year obtained from the Duke my appointment as assistant librarian. In this way I was able to give Momola a home, and to save her child from the Innocenti. She and I, cavaliere, are the misshapen offspring of that cruel foster-parent, who rears more than half the malefactors in the state; but please heaven the boy shall have a better start in life, and perhaps grow up to destroy some of the evils on which that cursed charity thrives."

This narrative, and the sight of Momola and her child, followed so strangely on the spectacle of sordid misery he had witnessed at Pontesordo, that an inarticulate pity held Odo by the throat. Gamba's anger against the people at the farm seemed as senseless as their own cruelty to their animals. What were they all—Momola, her child, and her persecutors—but a sickly growth of the decaying social order? He felt an almost physical longing for fresh air, light, the rush of a purifying wind through the atmosphere of moral darkness that surrounded him.

XII

To relieve the tension of his thoughts he set forth to Gamba the purpose of his visit.

"I am," said he, "much like a stranger at a masked ball, where all the masks are acquainted with each other's disguises and concerted to mystify the visitor. Among the persons I have met at court several have shown themselves ready to guide me through this labyrinth; but, till they themselves unmask and declare their true characters, I am doubtful whither they may lead me; nor do I know of any so well fitted as yourself to give me a clue to my surroundings. As for my own disguise," he added with a smile, "I believe I removed it sufficiently on our first meeting to leave you no doubt as to the use to which your information will be put."

Gamba, who seemed touched by this appeal, nevertheless hesitated before replying. At length he said: "I have the fullest trust in your excellency's honor; but I must remind you that during your stay here you will be under the closest observation and that any opinions you express will at once be attributed to the persons you are known to frequent. I would not," he continued hastily, "say this for myself alone, but I have two mouths to feed and my views are already under suspicion."

Reassured by Odo's protestations, or rather, perhaps, by the more convincing warrant of his look and manner, Gamba proceeded to give him a detailed description of the little world in which chance had placed them.

"If you have seen the Duke," said he, "I need not tell you that it is not he who governs the duchy. We are ruled at present by a triumvirate consisting of the Belverde, the Dominican and Trescorre. Pievepelago, the Prime-Minister, is a dummy put in place by the Jesuits and kept there by the rivalries of the other three; but he is in his dotage and the courtiers are already laying wagers as to his successor. Many think Father Ignazio will replace him, but I stake my faith on Trescorre. The Duke dislikes him, but he is popular with the middle class, who, since they have shaken off the yoke of the Jesuits, would not willingly see an ecclesiastic at the head of the state. The Duchess's influence is also against the Dominican, for her Highness, being, as you know, connected with the Austrian court, is by tradition unfavorable to the Church party. The Duchess's preferences would weigh little with the Duke were it not that she is sole heiress to the old Duke of Monte Alloro, and that any attempt to bring that principality under the control of the Holy See might provoke the interference of Austria.

"In so ticklish a situation I see none but Trescorre to maintain the political balance. He has been adroit enough to make himself necessary to the Duchess without alienating the Duke; he has introduced one or two trifling reforms that have given him a name for liberality in spite of the heavy taxes with which he has loaded the peasantry; and has in short so played his cards as to profit by the foibles of both parties. — Her Highness," he continued, in reply to a question of Odo's, "was much taken by him when she first came to Pianura; and before her feelings had cooled he had contrived to make himself indispensable to her. The Duchess is always in debt; and Trescorre, as comptroller of finance, holds her by her besetting weakness. Before his appointment her extravagance was the scandal of the town. She borrowed from her ladies, her pages, her very lacqueys; when she went on a visit to her uncle of Monte Alloro she pocketed the money he bestowed on her servants; nay, she was even accused of robbing the Marchioness of Pievepelago, who, having worn one evening a diamond necklace which excited her Highness's admiration, was waylaid on the way home and the jewels torn from her neck by a crowd of masked ruffians among whom she is said to have recognized one of the ducal servants. These are doubtless idle reports; but it is certain that Trescorre's appointment engaged him still more to the Duchess by enabling him to protect her from such calumnies; while by increasing the land-taxes he has discharged the worst of her debts and thus made himself popular with the tradesmen she had ruined. Your excellency must excuse my attempting to paint the private character of her Highness. Such facts as I have reported are of public notoriety, but to exceed them would be an unwarranted presumption. I know she has the name of being affable to her dependents, capable of a fitful generosity, and easily moved by distress; and it is certain that her domestic situation has been one to excite pity and disarm criticism.

"With regard to his Highness, it is difficult either to detect his motives or to divine his preferences. His youth was spent in pious practices; and a curious reason is given for the origin of this habit. He was educated, as your excellency is doubtless aware, by a French philosopher of the school of Hobbes; and it is said that in the interval of his tasks the poor Duke, bewildered by his governor's distinctions between conception and cognition, and the object and the sentient, used to spend his time praying the saints to assist him in his atheistical studies; indeed a satire of the day describes him as making a novena to the Virgin to obtain a clearer understanding of the universality of matter. Others with more likelihood aver that he frequented the churches to escape from the tyranny of his pedagogue; and it is certain that from one cause or another his education threw him into the opposite extreme of a superstitious and mechanical piety. His marriage, his differences with the Duchess, and the evil influence of Cerveno, exposed him to new temptations, and for a time he led a life which seemed to justify the worst charges of the enemies of materialism. Recent events have flung him back on the exaggerated devotion of his youth, and now, when his health permits, he spends his time serving mass, singing in the choir at benediction and making pilgrimages to the relics of the saints in the different churches of the duchy.

"A few years since, at the instigation of his confessor, he destroyed every picture in the ducal gallery that contained any naked figure or represented any subject offensive to religion. Among them was Titian's famous portrait of Duke Ascanio's mistress, known as the goldsmith's daughter, and a Venus by the Venetian painter Giorgione, so highly esteemed in its day that Pope Leo X is said to have offered in exchange for it the gift of a papal benefice, and a Cardinal's hat for Duke Guidobaldo's younger son. His Highness, moreover, impedes the administration of justice by resisting all attempts to restrict the Church's right of sanctuary, upholds the Holy Office in its attacks on the press, and has recently issued a decree forbidding his subjects to study at the University of Pavia, where, as you know, the natural sciences are professed by the ablest scholars of Italy. He allows no public duties to interfere with his private devotions, and whatever the urgency of affairs, gives no audience to his ministers on holydays; and a Cardinal *a latere* recently passing through the duchy on his return to Rome was not received at the Duke's table because he chanced to arrive on a Friday.

"His Highness's fears for Prince Ferrante's health have drawn a swarm of quacks to Pianura, and the influence of the Church is sometimes counteracted by that of the physicians with whom the Duke surrounds himself. The latest of these, the famous Count Heiligenstern, who is said to have performed some remarkable cures by means of the electrical fluid and of animal magnetism, has gained such an ascendancy over the Duke that some suspect him of being an agent of the

Austrian court, while others declare that he is a Jesuit *en robe courte.* But just at present the people scent a Jesuit under every habit, and it is even rumored that the Belverde is secretly affiliated to a female branch of the Society. With such a sovereign and such ministers, your excellency need not be told how the state is governed. Trescorre, heaven save the mark! represents the liberal party; but his liberalism is like the generosity of the unarmed traveller who throws his purse to a foot-pad; and Father Ignazio is at hand to see that the people are not bettered at the expense of the Church.

"As to the Duke, having no settled policy, and being governed only through his fears, he leans first to one influence, then to another; but since the suppression of the Jesuits nothing can induce him to attack any ecclesiastical privileges. The diocese of Pianura holds a fief known as the Caccia del Vescovo, long noted as the most lawless district of the duchy. Before the death of the late Pope, Trescorre had prevailed on the Duke to annex it to the principality; but the dreadful fate of Ganganelli has checked bolder sovereigns than his Highness in their attempts on the immunities of the Church, and one of the fairest regions of our unhappy state remains a barren waste, the lair of outlaws and assassins, and a menace to the surrounding country. His Highness is not incapable of generous impulses and his occasional acts of humanity might endear him to his people, were it not that they despise him for being the creature of his favorites. Thus, the gift of Boscofolto to the Belverde has excited the bitterest discontent; for the Countess is notorious for her cruel exactions, and it is certain that at her death this rich fief will revert to the Church.—And now," Gamba ended with a smile, "I have made known to your excellency the chief characters in the masque, as rumor depicts them to the vulgar. As to the court, like the government, it is divided into two parties: the Duke's, headed by the Belverde, and containing the staider and more conservative members of the Church and the nobility; and the Duchess's, composed of every fribble and flatterer, every gamester and rake, every intriguing woman and vulgar parvenu that can worm a way into her favor. In such an atmosphere you may fancy how knowledge thrives. The Duke's library consists of a few volumes of theological casuistry, and her Highness never opens a book unless it be to scandalize her husband by reading some prohibited pamphlet from France. The University, since the fall of the Jesuits, has been in charge of the Barnabite order, and, for aught I know, the Ptolemaic system is still taught there, together with the dialectic of Aristotle. As to science, it is anathema; and the press being subject to the restrictions of the Holy Office, and the University closed to modern

[275]

thought, but few scholars are to be found in the duchy, save those who occupy themselves with belles-lettres, or, like the abate Crescenti, are engaged in historical research. Pianura, even in the late Duke's day, had its circle of lettered noblemen who patronized the arts and founded the local Arcadia; but such pursuits are out of fashion, the Arcadia languishes, and the Bishop of Pianura is the only dignitary that still plays the Mæcenas. His lordship, whose theological laxity and coolness toward the Holy Office have put him out of favor with the Duke, has, I am told, a fine cabinet of paintings (some of them, it is rumored, the very pictures that his Highness ordered to be burnt) and the episcopal palace swarms with rhyming *abatini*, fashionable playwrights and musicians, and the travelling archæologists who hawk their antiques about from one court to another. Here you may assist at interminable disputes as to the relative merits of Tasso and Ariosto, or listen to a learned dissertation on the verse engraved on a carnelian stone; but as to the questions now agitating the world, they are held of less account than a problem in counter-point or the construction of a doubtful line in Ovid. As long as Truth goes naked she can scarce hope to be received in good company; and her appearance would probably cause as much confusion among the Bishop's literati as in the councils of the Holy Office."

The old analogy likening the human mind to an imperfect mirror, which modifies the images it reflects, occurred more than once to Odo during the hunchback's lively delineation. It was impossible not to remember that the speaker owed his education to the charity of the order he denounced; and this fact suggested to Odo that the other lights and shadows in the picture might be disposed with more art than accuracy. Still, they doubtless embodied a negative truth, and Odo thought it probable that such intellectual diversion as he could hope for must be sought in the Bishop's circle.

It was two days later that he first beheld that prelate, heading the ducal pilgrimage to the shrine of the mountain Virgin. The day had opened with a confused flight of chimes from every bell-tower in Pianura, as though a migratory flock of notes had settled for a moment on the roofs and steeples of the city. The ducal party set forth early from the palace, but the streets were already spanned with arches and garlands of foliage, tapestries and religious paintings decked the façades of the wealthier houses, and at every street-shrine a cluster of candle-flames hovered like yellow butterflies above the freshly-gathered flowers. The windows were packed with spectators, and the crowds who intended to accompany the pilgrimage were already gathering, with their painted and gilt candles, from every corner of the town. Each church and monastery door poured forth its priests or friars to swell the line, and the various lay confraternities, issuing in their distinctive dress from their "lodges" or assembly-rooms, formed a link between the secular and religious divisions of the procession. The market-place was strewn with sand and sweet herbs; and here, on the doorsteps of the Cathedral, between the featureless porphyry lions, the Bishop waited with his red-robed chapter and the deacons carrying the painted banners of the diocese. Seen thus, with the cloth-of-gold dalmatic above his pontifical tunic, the mitre surmounting his clear-cut impassive face, and the crozier held aloft in his jewelled gloves, he might have stood for a chryselephantine divinity in the porch of some pagan temple.

Odo, riding beside the Duke's litter, had leisure to note not only the diverse features of the procession, but their varying effect on the spectators. It was plain that, as Trescorre had said, the pilgrimage was popular with the people. That imaginative sensuousness which has perpetually renewed the Latin Church by giving form and color to her dogmatic abstractions, by transmuting every successive phase of her belief into something to be seen and handled, found an irresistible outlet in a ceremony that seemed to combine with its devotional intent a secret element of expiation. The little prince

was dimly felt to be paying for the prodigality of his
fathers, to be in some way a link of suffering between
the tongue-tied misery of the fields and the insolent
splendor of the court; and a vague faith in the vicarious
efficacy of his devotion drew the crowd into momentary
sympathy with its rulers. Yet this was but an underlying element in the instinctive delight of the people
in the outward forms of their religion. Odo's late experiences had wakened him to the influences acting
on that obscure substratum of human life that still
seemed, to most men of his rank, of no more account
than the brick lining of their marble-coated palaces.
As he watched the mounting excitement of the throng,
and pictured to himself the lives suddenly lit up by
this pledge of unseen promises, he wondered that the
enemies of the Church should ascribe her predominance
to any cause but the natural needs of the heart. The
people lived in unlit hovels, for there was a tax on
mental as well as on material windows; but here was a
light that could pierce the narrowest crevice and scatter
the darkness with a single ray.

Odo noted with equal interest the impression produced by the various members of the court and the
Church dignitaries. The Duke's litter was coldly received, but a pitying murmur widened about the gilt
chair in which Prince Ferrante was seated at his governor's side, and the approach of Trescorre, mounted on

a fine horse and dressed with his usual sober elegance, woke a shout that made him for a moment the central figure of the procession. The Bishop was none too warmly welcomed; but when Crescenti appeared, white-haired and erect among the parish priests, the crowd swayed toward him like grasses in the suction of a current; and one of the Duke's gentlemen, seeing Odo's surprise, said with a smile: "No one does more good in Pianura than our learned librarian."

A different and still more striking welcome awaited the Duchess, who presently appeared on her favorite white hackney, surrounded by the members of her household. Her reluctance to take part in the pilgrimage had been overcome by the exhilaration of showing herself to the public, and as she rode along in her gold-embroidered habit and plumed hat she was just such an image of radiant and indulgent sovereignty as turns enforced submission into a romantic allegiance. Her flushing cheek and kindled eye showed the reaction of the effect she produced, and if her subjects forgot her debts, her violences and follies, she was perhaps momentarily transformed into the being their enthusiasm created. She was at any rate keenly alive to the admiration she excited and eager to enhance it by those showy impulses of benevolence that catch the public eye; as when, at the city gates, she stopped her horse to intervene in behalf of a soldier who had been put

under arrest for some slight infraction of duty, and
then rode on enveloped in the passionate shouting of
the crowd.

The shrine at which the young prince was to pay his
devotions stood just beyond the city, on the summit of
one of the low knolls which pass for hills in the level
landscape of Pianura. The white-columned church with
its classical dome and portico had been erected as a
thank-offering after the plague of 1630, and the nave
was lined with life-sized votive figures of Dukes and
Duchesses clad in the actual wigs and robes that had
dressed their transient grandeur. As the procession
wound into the church, to the ringing of bells and
the chanting of the choir, Odo was struck by the spectacle of that line of witnesses, watching in glassy-eyed
irony the pomp and display to which their mouldering
robes and tarnished insignia seemed to fix so brief a
term. Once or twice already he had felt the shows of
human power as no more than vanishing reflections
on the tide of being; and now, as he knelt near the
shrine, with its central glitter of jewels and its nimbus
of wavering lights, and listened to the reiterated ancient wail:

> *Mater inviolata, ora pro nobis!*
> *Virgo veneranda, ora pro nobis!*
> *Speculum justitiæ, ora pro nobis!*

it seemed to him as though the bounds of life and

[281]

death were merged, and the sumptuous group of which he formed a part already dusted over with oblivion.

XIII

SPITE of the mountain Madonna's much-vaunted powers, the first effect of the pilgrimage was to provoke a serious indisposition in the Duke. Exhausted by fasting and emotion, he withdrew to his apartments and for several days denied himself to all but Heiligenstern, who was suspected by some of suffering his patient's disorder to run its course with a view to proving the futility of such remedies. This break in his intercourse with his kinsman left Odo free to take the measure of his new surroundings. The company most naturally engaging him was that which surrounded the Duchess; but he soon wearied of the trivial diversions it offered. It had ever been necessary to him that his pleasures should touch the imagination as well as the senses; and with such refinements of enjoyment the gallants of Pianura were unacquainted. Odo indeed perceived with a touch of amusement that, in a society where Don Serafino set the pace, he must needs lag behind his own lacquey. Cantapresto had, in fact, been hailed by the Bishop's nephew with a cordiality that proclaimed them old associates in folly; and the soprano's manner seemed to declare that, if ever he had

held the candle for Don Serafino, he did not grudge
the grease that might have dropped on his cassock.
He was soon prime favorite and court buffoon in the
Duchess's circle, organizing pleasure-parties, composing
scenarios for her Highness's private theatre, and producing at court any comedian or juggler the report of
whose ability reached him from the market-place. Indefatigable in the contriving of such diversions, he soon
virtually passed out of Odo's service into that of her
Highness: a circumstance which the young man the
less regretted as it left him freer to cultivate the acquaintance of Gamba and his friends without exposing
them to Cantapresto's espionage.

Odo had felt himself specially drawn toward the
abate Crescenti; and the afternoon after their first
meeting he had repaired to the librarian's dwelling.
Crescenti was the priest of an ancient parish lying near
the fortress; and his tiny house was wedged in an angle
of the city walls, like a bird's nest in the mouth of a
disused cannon. A long flight of steps led up to his
study, which on the farther side opened level with a
vine-shaded patch of herbs and damask roses in the
projection of a ruined bastion. This interior, the home
of studious peace, was as cheerful and well-ordered as
its inmate's mind; and Odo, seated under the vine per-
gola in the late summer light, and tasting the abate's
Val Pulicella, while he turned over the warped pages of

old codes and chronicles, felt the stealing charm of a
sequestered life.

He had learned from Gamba that Crescenti was a
faithful parish priest as well as an assiduous scholar,
but he saw that the librarian's beneficence took that
purely personal form which may coexist with a serene
acceptance of the general evils underlying particular
hardships. His charities were performed in the old un-
questioning spirit of the Roman distribution of corn;
and doubtless the good man who carries his loaf of
bread and his word of hope into his neighbor's hovel
reaps a more tangible return than the lonely thinker
who schemes to undermine the strongholds of injustice.
Still there was a perplexing contrast between the super-
ficiality of Crescenti's moral judgments and the breadth
and penetration of his historic conceptions. Odo was
too inexperienced to reflect that a man's sense of the
urgency of improvement lies mainly in the line of his
talent: as the merchant is persuaded that the roads
most in need of mending are those on which his business makes him travel. Odo himself was already conscious of living in a many-windowed house, with out-
looks diverse enough to justify more than one view of
the universe; but he had no conception of that concentration of purpose that may make the mind's flight to
its goal as direct and unvarying as the course of a
homing bird.

The talk turning on Gamba, Crescenti spoke of the help which the hunchback gave him in his work among the poor. "His early hardships," said he, "have given him an insight into character that my happier circumstances have denied me; and he has more than once been the means of reclaiming some wretch that I despaired of. Unhappily, his parts and learning are beyond his station, and will not let him rest in the performance of his duties. His mind, I often tell him, is like one of those inn parlors hung with elaborate maps of the three Heretical Cities; whereas the only topography with which the virtuous traveller need be acquainted is that of the Heavenly City to which all our journeyings should tend. The soundness of his heart reassures me as to this distemper of the reason; but others are less familiar with his good qualities, and I tremble for the risks to which his rashness may expose him."

The librarian went on to say that Gamba had a pretty poetical gift, which he was suspected of employing in the composition of anonymous satires on the court, the government, and the Church. At that period every Italian town was as full of lampoons as a marsh of mosquitoes, and it was as difficult in the one case as the other for the sufferer to detect the specific cause of his sting. The moment in Italy was a strange one. The tide of reform had been turned back by the very act devised to hasten it: the suppression of the Society of Jesus. The shout of liberation that rose over the downfall of the order had sunk to a guarded whisper. The dark legend already forming around Ganganelli's death, the hint of that secret liquor distilled for the order's use in a certain convent of Perugia, hung like a menace on the political horizon; and the disbanded Society seemed to have tightened its hold on the public conscience as a dying man's clutch closes on his victorious enemy.

So profoundly had the Jesuits impressed the world with the sense of their mysterious power that they were felt to be like one of those animal organisms which, when torn apart, carry on a separate existence in every fragment. Ganganelli's bull had provided against their exercising any political influence, or directing opinion as confessors or as public educators; but they were known to be everywhere in Italy, either hidden in other orders, or acting as lay agents of foreign powers, as tutors in private families, or simply as secular priests. Even the confiscation of their wealth did not seem to diminish the popular sense of their strength. Perhaps because that strength had never been completely explained, even by their immense temporal advantages, it was felt to be latent in themselves, and somehow capable of withstanding every kind of external pressure. They had moreover benefited by the reaction which always follows on the breaking-up of any great organization. Their detractors were already beginning to forget their faults and remember their merits. The people had been taught to hate the Society as the possessor of wealth and privileges which should have been theirs; but when the Society fell its possessions were absorbed by the other powers, and in many cases the people suffered from abuses and mal-administration which they had not known under their Jesuit land-lords. The aristocracy had always been in sympathy with the order, and in many states the Jesuits had been banished simply as a measure of political expediency, a sop to the restless masses. In these cases the latent power of the order was concealed rather than diminished by the pretence of a more liberal government, and everywhere, in one form or another, the unseen influence was felt to be on the watch for those who dared to triumph over it too soon.

Such conditions fostered the growth of social satire. Constructive ambition was forced back into its old disguises, and ridicule of individual weaknesses replaced the general attack on beliefs and institutions. Satirical poems in manuscript passed from hand to hand in coffee-houses, casinos and drawing-rooms, and every conspicuous incident in social or political life was borne on a biting quatrain to the confines of the state. The Duke's gift of Boscofolto to the Countess Belverde had stirred up a swarm of epigrams, and the most malignant among them, Crescenti averred, were openly ascribed to Gamba.

"A few more imprudences," he added, "must cost him his post; and if your excellency has any influence with him I would urge its being used to restrain him from such excesses."

Odo, on taking leave of the librarian, ran across Gamba at the first street-corner; and they had not proceeded a dozen yards together when the eye of the Duke's kinsman fell on a snatch of doggerel scrawled in chalk on an adjacent wall.

> *Beware* (the quatrain ran) *O virtuous wife or maid,*
> *Our ruler's fondness for the shade,*
> *Lest first he woo thee to the leafy glade*
> *And then into the deeper wood persuade.*

This crude play on the Belverde's former title and the one she had recently acquired was signed *Carlo Gamba*.

Odo glanced curiously at the hunchback, who met the look with a composed smile. "My enemies don't do me justice," said he; "I could do better than that if I tried;" and he effaced the words with a sweep of his shabby sleeve.

Other lampoons of the same quality were continually cropping up on the walls of Pianura, and the ducal police were kept as busy rubbing them out as a band of weeders digging docks out of a garden. The Duchess's debts, the Duke's devotions, the Belverde's extortions, Heiligenstern's mummery, and the political rivalry between Trescorre and the Dominican, were sauce to the citizen's daily bread; but there was nothing in these popular satires to suggest the hunchback's trenchant irony.

It was in the Bishop's palace that Odo read the first lampoon in which he recognized his friend's touch. In this society of polished dilettanti such documents were valued rather for their literary merits than for their political significance; and the pungent lines in which the Duke's panaceas were hit off (the Belverde figuring among them as a Lenten diet, a dinner of herbs and a wonder-working bone) caused a flutter of professional envy in the episcopal circle.

The Bishop received company every evening; and Odo soon found that, as Gamba had said, it was the best company in Pianura. His lordship lived in great state in the Gothic palace adjoining the Cathedral. The gloomy vaulted rooms of the original structure had been abandoned to the small fry of the episcopal retinue. In the chambers around the courtyard his lordship drove a thriving trade in wines from his vineyards, while his clients awaited his pleasure in the armory, where the panoplies of his fighting predecessors

still rusted on the walls. Behind this façade a later
prelate had built a vast wing overlooking a garden
which descended by easy terraces to the Piana. In the
high-studded apartments of this wing the Bishop held
his court and lived the life of a wealthy secular nobleman. His days were agreeably divided between hunting,
inspecting his estates, receiving the visits of antiqua-
rians, artists and literati, and superintending the em-
bellishments of his gardens, then the most famous in
North Italy; while his evenings were given to the more
private diversions which his age and looks still justified.
In religious ceremonies or in formal intercourse with
his clergy he was the most imposing and sacerdotal of
bishops; but in private life none knew better how to
disguise his cloth. He was moreover a man of parts,
and from the construction of a Latin hexameter to the
growing of a Holland bulb, had a word worth hearing
on all subjects likely to engage the dilettante. A liking
soon sprang up between Odo and this versatile prelate; and in the retirement of his lordship's cabinet,
or pacing with him the garden-alleys set with ancient
marbles, the young man gathered many precepts of
that philosophy of pleasure which the great church-
men of the eighteenth century practised with such rare
completeness.

The Bishop had not, indeed, given much thought
to the problems which most deeply engaged his com-

panion. His theory of life took no account of the future and concerned itself little with social conditions outside his own class; but he was acquainted with the classical schools of thought, and, having once acted as the late Duke's agent at the French court, had frequented the Baron d'Holbach's drawing-room and familiarized himself with the views of the Encyclopædists; though it was clear that he valued their teachings chiefly as an argument against asceticism.

"Life," said he to Odo, as they sat one afternoon in a garden-pavilion above the river, a marble Mercury confronting them at the end of a vista of clipped myrtle, "life, cavaliere, is a stock on which we may graft what fruit or flower we choose. See the orange-tree in that Capo di Monte jar: in a week or two it will be covered with red roses. Here again is a citron set with carnations; and but yesterday my gardener sent me word that he had at last succeeded in flowering a pomegranate with jasmine. In such cases the gardener chooses as his graft the flower which, by its color and fragrance, shall most agreeably contrast with the original stock; and he who orders his life on the same principle, grafting it with pleasures that form a refreshing offset to the obligations of his rank and calling, may regard himself as justified by Nature, who, as you see, smiles on such abnormal unions among her children.—Not long ago," he went on, with a reminiscent smile, "I had here un-

der my roof a young person who practised to perfection
this art of engrafting life with the unexpected. Though
she was only a player in a strolling company—a sweet-
heart of my wild nephew's, as you may guess—I have
met few of her sex whose conversation was so instructive
or who so completely justified the Scriptural adage, *the
sweetness of the lips increaseth learning. . .*" He broke
off to sip his chocolate. "But why," he continued, "do
I talk thus to a young man whose path is lined with
such opportunities? The secret of happiness is to say
with the great Emperor, 'Everything is fruit to me
which thy seasons bring, O Nature.'"

"Such a creed, monsignore," Odo ventured to return,
"is as flattering to the intelligence as to the senses; for
surely it better becomes a reasoning being to face fate
as an equal than to cower before it like a slave; but,
since you have opened yourself so freely on the subject,
may I carry your argument a point farther and ask how
you reconcile your conception of man's destiny with the
authorized teachings of the Church?"

The Bishop raised his head with a guarded glance.

"Cavaliere," said he, "the ancients did not admit the
rabble to their sacred mysteries; nor dare we permit the
unlettered to enter the hallowed precincts of the temple
of reason."

"True," Odo acquiesced; "but if the teachings of
Christianity are the best safeguard of the people, should

not those teachings at least be stripped of the grotesque excrescences with which the superstition of the people and—perhaps—the greed and craft of the priesthood have smothered the simple precepts of Jesus?"

The Bishop shrugged his shoulders. "As long," said he, "as the people need the restraint of a dogmatic religion so long must we do our utmost to maintain its outward forms. In our market-place on feast-days there appears the strange figure of a man who carries a banner painted with an image of Saint Paul surrounded by a mass of writhing serpents. This man calls himself a descendant of the apostle and sells to our peasants the miraculous powder with which he killed the great serpent at Malta. If it were not for the banner, the legend, the descent from Saint Paul, how much efficacy do you think those powders would have? And how long do you think the precepts of an invisible divinity would restrain the evil passions of an ignorant peasant? It is because he is afraid of the plaster God in his parish church, and of the priest who represents that God, that he still pays his tithes and forfeitures and keeps his hands from our throats. By Diana," cried the Bishop, taking snuff, "I have no patience with those of my calling who go about whining for apostolic simplicity, and would rob the churches of their ornaments and the faithful of their ceremonies.

"For my part," he added, glancing with a smile about

the delicately-stuccoed walls of the pavilion, through the windows of which climbing roses shed their petals on the rich mosaics transferred from a Roman bath, "for my part, when I remember that 'tis to Jesus of Nazareth I owe the good roof over my head and the good nags in my stable; nay, the very venison and pheasants from my preserves, with the gold plate I eat them off, and above all the leisure to enjoy as they deserve these excellent gifts of the Creator—when I consider this, I say, I stand amazed at those who would rob so beneficent a deity of the least of his privileges!—But why," he continued again after a moment, as Odo remained silent, "should we vex ourselves with such questions, when Providence has given us so fair a world to enjoy and such varied faculties with which to apprehend its beauties? I think you have not yet seen the Venus Callipyge in bronze that I have lately received from Rome?" And he rose and led the way to the house.

This conversation revealed to Odo a third conception of the religious idea. In Piedmont religion imposed itself as a military discipline, the enforced duty of the Christian citizen to the heavenly state; to the Duke it was a means of purchasing spiritual immunity from the consequences of bodily weakness; to the Bishop, it replaced the *panem et circenses* of ancient Rome. Where, in all this, was the share of those whom Christ had come to save? Where was Saint Francis's devotion to his heavenly bride, the Lady Poverty? Though here and there a good parish priest like Crescenti ministered to the temporary wants of the peasantry, it was only the free-thinker and the atheist who, at the risk of life and fortune, labored for their moral liberation. Odo listened with a saddened heart, thinking, as he followed his host through the perfumed shade of the gardens, and down the long saloon at the end of which the Venus stood, of those who for the love of man had denied themselves such delicate emotions and gone forth cheerfully to exile or imprisonment. These were the true lovers of the Lady Poverty, the band in which he longed to be enrolled; yet how restrain a thrill of delight as the slender dusky goddess detached herself against the cool marble of her niche, looking, in the sun-rippled green penumbra of the saloon, with a sound of water falling somewhere out of sight, as though she had just stepped dripping from the wave?

In the Duchess's company life struck another gait. Here was no waiting on subtle pleasures, but a headlong gallop after the cruder sort. Hunting, gaming and masquerading filled her Highness's days; and Odo had felt small inclination to keep pace with the cavalcade, but for the flying huntress at its head. To the Duchess's *view halloo* every drop of blood in him responded; but a vigilant image kept his bosom barred. So they rode, danced, diced together, but like strangers who cross hands at a veglione. Once or twice he fancied the Duchess was for unmasking; but her impulses came and went like fireflies in the dusk, and it suited his humor to remain a looker-on.

So life piped to him during his first days at Pianura: a merry tune in the Bishop's company, a mad one in the Duchess's; but always with the same sad undertone, like the cry of the wind on a warm threshold.

XIV

TRESCORRE too kept open house, and here Odo found a warmer welcome than he had expected. Though Trescorre was still the Duchess's accredited lover, it was clear that the tie between them was no longer such as to make him resent her kindness to her young kinsman. He seemed indeed anxious to draw Odo into her Highness's circle, and surprised him by a frankness and affability of which his demeanor at Turin had given no promise. As leader of the anti-clericals he stood for such liberalism as dared show its head in Pianura; and he seemed disposed to invite Odo's confidence in political matters. The latter was, however, too much the child of his race not to hang back from such an invitation. He did not distrust Trescorre more than the other courtiers; but it was a time when every ear was alert for the foot-fall of treachery, and the rashest man did not care to taste first of any cup that was offered him.

These scruples Trescorre made it his business to dispel. He was the only person at court who was willing to discuss politics, and his clear view of affairs excited Odo's admiration if not his concurrence. Odo's was in fact one of those dual visions which instinctively see both sides of a case and take the defence of the less popular. Gamba's principles were dear to him; but he did not therefore believe in the personal baseness of every opponent of the cause. He had refrained from mentioning the hunchback to his supposed brother; but the latter, in one of their talks, brought forward Gamba's name, without reference to the relationship, but with high praise for the young librarian's parts. This, at the moment, put Odo on his guard; but Trescorre having one day begged him to give Gamba warning of some petty danger that threatened him from the clerical side, it became difficult not to believe in an interest so attested; the more so as Trescorre let it be seen that Gamba's political views were not such as to detract from his sympathy.

"The fellow's brains," said he, "would be of infinite use to me; but perhaps he serves us best at a distance. All I ask is that he shall not risk himself too near Father Ignazio's talons, for he would be a pretty morsel to throw to the Holy Office, and the weak point of such a man's position is that, however dangerous in life, he can threaten no one from the grave."

Odo reported this to Gamba, who heard with a two-edged smile. "Yes," was his comment, "he fears me enough to want to see me safe in his fold."

Odo flushed at the implication. "And why not?" said he. "Could you not serve the cause better by attaching yourself openly to the liberals than by lurking in the ditch to throw mud at both parties?"

"The liberals!" sneered Gamba. "Where are they? And what have they done? It was they who drove out the Jesuits; but to whom did the Society's lands go? To the Duke, every acre of them! And the peasantry suffered far less under the fathers, who were good agriculturists, than under the Duke, who is too busy with monks and astrologers to give his mind to irrigation or the reclaiming of waste land. As to the University, who replaced the Jesuits there? Professors from Padua or Pavia? Heaven forbid! But holy Barnabites that have scarce Latin enough to spell out the Lives of the Saints! The Jesuits at least gave a good education to the upper classes; but now the young noblemen are as ignorant as peasants."

Trescorre received at his house, besides the court functionaries, all the liberal faction and the Duchess's personal friends. He kept a lavish state, but lacking the Bishop's social gifts, was less successful in fusing the different elements of his circle. The Duke, for the first few weeks after his kinsman's arrival, received no company, and did not even appear in the Belverde's drawing-rooms; but Odo deemed it none the less politic to show himself there without delay.

The new Marchioness of Boscofolto lived in one of the finest palaces of Pianura, but prodigality was the least of her failings, and the meagreness of her hospitality was an unfailing source of epigram to the drawing-rooms of the opposition. True, she kept open table for half the clergy in the town (omitting, of course, those worldly ecclesiastics who frequented the episcopal palace), but it was whispered that she had persuaded her cook to take half wages in return for the privilege of victualling such holy men, and that the same argument enabled her to obtain her provisions below the market price. In her outer antechamber the servants yawned dismally over a cold brazier, without so much as a game of cards to divert them, and the long enfilade of saloons leading to her drawing-room was so scantily lit that her guests could scarce recognize each other in passing. In the room where she sat, a tall crucifix of ebony and gold stood at her elbow and a holy-water cup encrusted with jewels hung on the wall at her side. A dozen or more ecclesiastics were always gathered in stiff seats about the hearth; and the aspect of the apartment, and the Marchioness's semi-monastic costume, justified the nickname of "the sacristy," which the Duchess had bestowed on her rival's drawing-room.

Around the small fire on this cheerless hearth the fortunes of the state were discussed and directed, benefices disposed of, court appointments debated, and reputations made and unmade in tones that suggested the low drone of a group of canons intoning the psalter in an empty cathedral. The Marchioness, who appeared as eager as the others to win Odo to her party, received him with every mark of consideration and pressed him to accompany her on a visit to her brother, the Abbot of the Barnabites: an invitation which he accepted with the more readiness as he had not forgotten the part played by that religious in the adventure of Mirandolina of Chioggia.

He found the Abbot a man with a bland intriguing eye and centuries of pious leisure in his voice. He received his visitors in a room hung with smoky pictures of the Spanish school, showing Saint Jerome in the wilderness, the death of Saint Peter Martyr, and other sanguinary passages in the lives of the saints; and Odo, seated among such surroundings, and hearing the Abbot deplore the loose lives and religious negligence of certain members of the court, could scarce repress a smile as the thought of Mirandolina flitted through his mind.

"She must," he reflected, "have found this a sad

change from the Bishop's palace;" and admired with
what philosophy she had passed from one protector to
the other.

Life in Pianura, after the first few weeks, seemed on
the whole a tame business to a youth of his appetite;
and he secretly longed for a pretext to resume his
travels. None, however, seemed likely to offer; for it
was clear that the Duke, in the interval of more pressing concerns, wished to study and observe his kinsman.
When sufficiently recovered from the effects of the
pilgrimage, he sent for Odo and questioned him closely
as to the way in which he had spent his time since
coming to Pianura, the acquaintances he had formed
and the churches he had frequented. Odo prudently
dwelt on the lofty tone of the Belverde's circle, and on
the privilege he had enjoyed in attending her on a visit
to the holy Abbot of the Barnabites; touching more
lightly on his connection with the Bishop, and omitting
all mention of Gamba and Crescenti. The Duke assumed
a listening air, but it was clear that he could not put
off his private thoughts long enough to give an open
mind to other matters; and Odo felt that he was nowhere so secure as in his cousin's company. He remembered, however, that the Duke had plenty of eyes to
replace his own, and that a secret which was safe in
his actual presence might be in mortal danger on
his threshold.

His Highness on this occasion was pleased to inform his kinsman that he had ordered Count Trescorre to place at the young man's disposal an income enabling him to keep a carriage and pair, four saddle-horses and five servants. It was scant measure for an heir-presumptive, and Odo wondered if the Belverde had had a hand in the apportionment; but his indifference to such matters (for though personally fastidious he cared little for display) enabled him to show such gratitude that the Duke, fancying he might have been content with less, had nearly withdrawn two of the saddle-horses. This becoming behavior greatly advanced the young man in the esteem of his Highness, who accorded him on the spot the *petites entrées* of the ducal apartments. It was a privilege Odo had no mind to abuse; for if life moved slowly in the Belverde's circle it was at a standstill in the Duke's. His Highness never went abroad but to serve mass in some church (his almost daily practice) or to visit one of the numerous monasteries within the city. From Ash Wednesday to Easter Monday it was his custom to transact no public or private business. During this time he received none of his ministers, and saw his son but for a few moments once a day; while in Holy Week he made a retreat with the Barnabites, the Belverde withdrawing for the same period to the convent of the Perpetual Adoration.

Odo, as his new life took shape, found his chief interest in the society of Crescenti and Gamba. In the Duchess's company he might have lost all taste for soberer pleasures, but that his political sympathies wore a girl's reproachful shape. Ever at his side, more vividly than in the body, Fulvia Vivaldi became the symbol of his best aims and deepest failure. Sometimes, indeed, her look drove him forth in the Duchess's train, but more often, drawing him from the crowd of pleasure-seekers, beckoned the way to solitude and study. Under Crescenti's tuition he began the reading of Dante, who just then, after generations of neglect, was once more lifting his voice above the crowd of minor singers. The mighty verse swept Odo out to open seas of thought, and from his vision of that earlier Italy, hapless, bleeding, but alive and breast to breast with the foe, he drew the presage of his country's resurrection.

Passing from this high music to the company of Gamba and his friends was like leaving a church where the penitential psalms are being sung for the market-place where mud and eggs are flying. The change was not agreeable to a fastidious taste; but, as Gamba said, you cannot clean out a stable by waving incense over it. After some hesitation, he had agreed to make Odo acquainted with those who, like himself, were secretly working in the cause of progress. These were mostly of the middle-class, physicians, lawyers, and such men of letters as could subsist on the scant wants of an unliterary town. Ablest among them was the bookseller, Andreoni, whose shop was the meeting-place of all the literati of Pianura. Andreoni, famous throughout Italy for his editions of the classics, was a man of liberal views and considerable learning, and in his private room were to be found many prohibited volumes, such as Beccaria's Crime and Punishment, Gravina's Hydra Mystica, Concini's History of Probabilism and the Amsterdam editions of the French philosophical works.

The reformers met at various places, and their meetings were conducted with as much secrecy as those of the Honey-Bees. Odo was at first surprised that they should admit him to their conferences; but he soon divined that the gatherings he attended were not those at which the private designs of the party were discussed. It was plain that they belonged to some kind of secret association; and before he had been long in Pianura he learned that the society of the Illuminati, that bugbear of priests and princes, was supposed to have agents at work in the duchy. Odo had heard little of this execrated league, but that it was said to preach atheism, tyrannicide and the complete abolition of territorial rights; but this, being the report of the enemy, was to be received with a measure of doubt. He tried to learn from Gamba whether the Illuminati actually had a lodge in the city; but on this point he could extract no information. Meanwhile he listened with interest to discussions on taxation, irrigation, and such economic problems as might safely be aired in his presence.

These talks brought vividly before him the political corruption of the state and the misery of the unprivileged classes. All the land in the duchy was farmed on the métayer system, and with such ill results that the peasants were always in debt to their landlords. The weight of the evil lay chiefly on the country-people, who had to pay on every pig they killed, on all the produce they carried to market, on their farm-implements, their mulberry-orchards and their silk-worms, to say nothing of the tithes to the parish. So oppressive were these obligations that many of the peasants, forsaking their farms, enrolled themselves in the mendicant orders, thus actually strengthening the hand of their oppressors. Of legislative redress there was no hope, and the Duke was inaccessible to all but his favorites. The previous year, as Odo learned, eight hundred poor laborers, exasperated by want, had petitioned his Highness to relieve them of the corvée; but though they had raised fifteen hundred *scudi* to bribe the court official who was to present their address, no reply had ever been received. In the city itself, the monopoly of corn and tobacco weighed heavily on the merchants, and the strict censorship of the press made the open ventilation of wrongs impossible, while the

Duke's *sbirri* and the agents of the Holy Office could drag a man's thoughts from his bosom and search his midnight dreams. The Church party, in the interest of their order, fostered the Duke's fears of sedition and branded every innovator as an atheist; the Holy Office having even cast grave doubts on the orthodoxy of a nobleman who had tried to introduce the English system of ploughing on his estates. It was evident to Odo that the secret hopes of the reformers centred in him, and the consciousness of their belief was sweeter than love in his bosom. It diverted him from the follies of his class, fixed his thoughts at an age when they are apt to range, and thus slowly shaped and tempered him for high uses.

In this fashion the weeks passed and summer came. It was the Duchess's habit to escape the August heats by retiring to the dower-house on the Piana, a league beyond the gates; but the little prince being still under the care of the German physician, who would not consent to his removal, her Highness reluctantly lingered in Pianura. With the first leafing of the oaks Odo's old love for the budding earth awoke, and he rode out daily in the forest toward Pontesordo. It was but a flat stretch of shade, lacking the voice of streams and the cold breath of mountain-gorges: a wood without humors or surprises; but the mere spring of the turf was delightful as he cantered down the grass alleys roofed with level boughs, the outer sunlight just gilding the lip of the long green tunnel.

Sometimes he attended the Duchess, but oftener chose to ride alone, setting forth early after a night at cards or a late vigil in Crescenti's study. One of these solitary rides brought him without premeditation to a low building on the fenny edge of the wood. It was a small house, added, it appeared, to an ancient brick front adorned with pilasters, perhaps a fragment of some woodland temple. The door-step was overgrown with a stealthy green moss and tufted with giant fennel; and a shutter swinging loose on its hinge gave a glimpse of inner dimness. Odo guessed at once that this was the hunting-lodge where Cerveno had found his death; and as he stood looking out across the oozy secrets of the marsh, the fever seemed to hang on his steps. He turned away with a shiver; but whether it were the sullen aspect of the house, or the close way in which the wood embraced it, the place suddenly laid a detaining hand upon him. It was as though he had reached the heart of solitude. Even the faint woodland noises seemed to recede from that dense circle of shade, and the marsh turned a dead eye to heaven.

Odo tethered his horse to a bough and seated himself on the door-step; but presently his musings were disturbed by the sound of voices, and the Duchess, attended by her gentlemen, swept by at the end of a long glade. He fancied she waved her hand to him; but being in no humor to join the cavalcade, he remained seated, and the riders soon passed out of sight. As he sat there sombre thoughts came to him, stealing up like exhalations from the fen. He saw his life stretched out before him, full of broken purposes and ineffectual effort. Public affairs were in so perplexed a case that consistent action seemed impossible to either party, and their chief efforts were bent toward directing the choice of a regent. It was this, rather than the possibility of his accession, which fixed the general attention on Odo, and pledged him to circumspection. While not concealing that in economic questions his sympathies were with the liberals, he had carefully abstained from political action, and had hoped, by the strict observance of his religious duties, to avoid the enmity of the Church party. Trescorre's undisguised sympathy seemed the pledge of liberal support, and it could hardly be doubted that the choice of a regent in the Church party would be unpopular enough to imperil the dynasty. With Austria hovering on the horizon the Church herself was not likely to take such risks; and thus all interests seemed to centre in Odo's appointment.

New elements of uncertainty were however perpetually disturbing the prospect. Among these was Heiligenstern's growing influence over the Duke. Odo had seen little of the German physician since their first meeting. Hearsay had it that he was close-pressed by the spies of the Holy Office, and perhaps for this reason he remained withdrawn in the Duke's private apartments and rarely showed himself abroad. The little prince, his patient, was as seldom seen, and the accounts of the German's treatment were as conflicting as the other rumors of the court. It was noised on all sides, however, that the Duke was ill-satisfied with the results of the pilgrimage, and resolved upon less hallowed measures to assure his heir's recovery. Hitherto, it was believed, the German had conformed to the ordinary medical treatment; but the clergy now diligently spread among the people the report that supernatural agencies were to be employed. This rumor caused such general agitation that it was said both parties had made secret advances to the Duchess in the hope of inducing her to stay the scandal. Though Maria Clementina felt little real concern for the public welfare, her stirring temper had more than once roused her to active opposition of the government, and her kinship with the old Duke of Monte Alloro made her a strong factor in the political game. Of late, however, she seemed to have wearied of this sport, throwing herself entirely into the private diversions of her station, and alluding with laughing indifference to her husband's necromantic researches.

Such was the conflicting gossip of the hour; but it was in fact idle to forecast the fortunes of a state dependent on a valetudinary's whims; and rumor was driven to feed upon her own conjectures. To Odo the state of affairs seemed a satire on his secret aspirations. In a private station or as a ruling prince he might have served his fellows: as a princeling on the edge of power he was no more than the cardboard sword in a toy armory.

Suddenly he heard his name pronounced and starting up saw Maria Clementina at his side. She rode alone, and held out her hand as he approached.

"I have had an accident," said she, breathing quickly. "My girth is broke and I have lost the rest of my company."

She was glowing with her quick ride, and as Odo lifted her from the saddle her loosened hair brushed his face like a kiss. For a moment she seemed like life's answer to the dreary riddle of his fate.

"Ah," she sighed, leaning on him, "I am glad I found you, cousin; I hardly knew how weary I was;" and she dropped languidly to the door-step.

Odo's heart was beating hard. He knew it was only the stir of the spring sap in his veins, but Maria Clementina wore a look of morning brightness that might have made a soberer judgment blink. He turned away to examine her saddle. As he did so, he observed that

her girth was not torn, but clean cut, as with sharp
scissors. He glanced up in surprise, but she sat with
drooping lids, her head thrown back against the lintel;
and repressing the question on his lips he busied himself with the adjustment of the saddle. When it was in
place he turned to give her a hand; but she only smiled
up at him through her lashes.

"What!" said she with an air of lovely lassitude,
"are you so impatient to be rid of me? I should have
been so glad to linger here a little." She put her hand
in his and let him lift her to her feet. "How cool and
still it is! Look at that little spring bubbling through
the moss. Could you not fetch me a drink from it?"

She tossed aside her riding-hat and pushed back the
hair from her warm forehead.

"Your Highness must not drink of the water here,"
said Odo, releasing her hand.

She gave him a quick derisive glance. "Ah, true,"
she cried; "this is the house to which that abandoned
wretch used to lure poor Cerveno." She drew back to
look at the lodge. "Were you ever in it?" she asked
curiously. "I should like to see how the place looks."

She laid her hand on the door-latch, and to Odo's
surprise it yielded to her touch. "We're in luck, I vow,"
she declared with a laugh. "Come, cousin, let us visit
the temple of romance together."

The allusion to Cerveno jarred on Odo, and he followed her in silence. Within doors, the lodge was seen to consist of a single room, gaily painted with hunting-scenes framed in garlands of stucco. In the dusk they could just discern the outlines of carved and gilded furniture, and a Venice mirror gave back their faces like phantoms in a magic crystal.

"This is stifling," said Odo impatiently. "Would your Highness not be better in the open?"

"No, no," she persisted. "Unbar the shutters and we shall have air enough. I love a deserted house: I have always fancied that if one came in noiselessly enough one might catch the ghosts of the people who used to live in it."

He obeyed in silence, and the green-filtered forest noon filled the room with a quiver of light. A chill stole upon Odo as he looked at the dust-shrouded furniture, the painted harpsichord with green mould creeping over its keyboard, the consoles set with empty wine flagons and goblets of Venice glass. The place was like the abandoned corpse of pleasure.

But Maria Clementina laughed and clapped her hands. "This is enchanting," she cried, throwing herself into an arm-chair of threadbare damask, "and I shall rest here while you refresh me with a glass of Lacrima Christi from one of those dusty flagons.— They are empty, you say? Never mind, for I have a flask of cordial in my saddle-bag. Fetch it, cousin, and wash these two glasses in the spring, that we may toast all the dead lovers that have drunk out of them."

When Odo returned with the flask and glasses, she had brushed the dust from a slender table of inlaid wood, and drawn a seat near her own. She filled the two goblets with cordial and signed to Odo to seat himself beside her.

"Why do you pull such a glum face?" she cried, leaning over to touch his glass before she emptied hers. "Is it that you are thinking of poor Cerveno? On my soul, I question if he needs your pity! He had his hour of folly, and was too gallant a gentleman not to pay the shot. For my part I would rather drink a poisoned draught than die of thirst."

The wine was rising in waves of color over her throat and brow, and setting her glass down she suddenly laid her ungloved hand on Odo's.

"Cousin," she said in a low voice, "I could help you if you would let me."

"Help me?" he said, only half-aware of her words in the warm surprise of her touch.

She drew back, but with a look that seemed to leave her hand in his.

"Are you mad," she murmured, "or do you despise your danger?"

"Am I in danger?" he echoed smiling. He was thinking how easily a man might go under in that deep blue

[313]

gaze of hers. She dropped her lids as though aware of his thought.

"Why do you concern yourself with politics?" she went on with a new note in her voice. "Can you find no diversion more suited to your rank and age? Our court is a dull one, I own—but surely even here a man might find a better use for his time."

Odo's self-possession returned in a flash. "I am not," cried he gaily, "in a position to dispute it at this moment;" and he leaned over to recapture her hand. To his surprise she freed herself with an affronted air.

"Ah," she said, "you think this a device to provoke a gallant conversation." She faced him nobly now. "Look," said she, drawing a folded paper from the breast of her riding-coat. "Have you not frequented these houses?"

Suddenly sobered, he ran his eye over the paper. It contained the dates of the meetings he had attended at the houses of Gamba's friends, with the designation of each house. He turned pale.

"I had no notion," said he, with a smile, "that my movements were of interest in such high places; but why does your Highness speak of danger in this connection?"

"Because it is rumored that the lodge of the Illuminati, which is known to exist in Pianura, meets secretly at the houses on this list."

Odo hesitated a moment. "Of that," said he, "I have no report. I am acquainted with the houses only as the residence of certain learned and reputable men, who devote their leisure to scientific studies."

"Oh," she interrupted, "call them by what name you please! It is all one to your enemies."

"My enemies?" said he lightly. "And who are they?"

"Who are they?" she repeated impatiently. "Who are they not? Who is there at court that has such cause to love you? The Holy Office? The Duke's party?"

Odo smiled. "I am perhaps not in the best odor with the Church party," said he, "but Count Trescorre has shown himself my friend, and I think my character is safe in his keeping. Nor will it be any news to him that I frequent the company you name."

She threw back her head with a laugh. "Boy," she cried, "you are blinder even than I fancied! Do you know why it was that the Duke summoned you to Pianura? Because he wished his party to mould you to their shape, in case the regency should fall into your hands. And what has Trescorre done? Shown himself your friend, as you say — won your confidence, encouraged you to air your liberal views, allowed you to show yourself continually in the Bishop's company, and to frequent the secret assemblies of free-thinkers and conspirators — and all that the Duke may turn against you and perhaps name him regent in your stead! Believe

[315]

me, cousin," she cried with a mounting urgency, "you never stood in greater need of a friend than now. If you continue on your present course you are undone. The Church party is resolved to hunt down the Illuminati, and both sides would rejoice to see you made the scapegoat of the Holy Office." She sprang up and laid her hand on his arm. "What can I do to convince you?" she said passionately. "Will you believe me if I ask you to go away—to leave Pianura on the instant?"

Odo had risen also, and they faced each other in silence. There was an unmistakable meaning in her tone: a self-revelation so simple and ennobling that she seemed to give herself as hostage for her words.

"Ask me to stay, cousin—not to go," he whispered, her yielding hand in his.

"Ah, madman," she cried, "not to believe me *now!* But it is not too late if you will still be guided."

"I will be guided—but not away from you."

She broke away, but with a glance that drew him after. "It is late now and we must set forward," she said abruptly. "Come to me to-morrow early. I have much more to say to you."

The words seemed to be driven out on her quick breathing, and the blood came and went in her cheek like a hurried messenger. She caught up her riding-hat and turned to put it on before the Venice mirror.

[316]

Odo, stepping up behind her, looked over her shoulder to catch the reflection of her blush. Their eyes met for a laughing instant; then he drew back deadly pale, for in the depths of the dim mirror he had seen another face.

The Duchess cried out and glanced behind her. "Who was it? Did you see her?" she said, trembling.

Odo mastered himself instantly.

"I saw nothing," he returned quietly. "What can your Highness mean?"

She covered her eyes with her hands. "A girl's face," she shuddered—"there in the mirror—behind mine— a pale face with a black travelling-hood over it—"

He gathered up her gloves and riding-whip and threw open the door of the pavilion.

"Your Highness is weary and the air here insalubrious. Shall we not ride?" he said.

Maria Clementina heard him with a blank stare. Suddenly she roused herself and made as though to pass out; but on the threshold she snatched her whip from him and, turning, flung it full at the mirror. Her aim was good and the chiselled handle of the whip shattered the glass to fragments.

She caught up her long skirt and stepped into the open.

"I brook no rivals!" said she with a white-lipped smile. "And now, cousin," she added gaily, "to horse!"

[317]

XV

ODO, as in duty bound, waited the next morning on the Duchess; but word was brought that her Highness was indisposed, and could not receive him till evening.

He passed a drifting and distracted day. The fear lay much upon him that danger threatened Gamba and his associates; yet to seek them out in the present conjuncture might be to play the stalking-horse to their enemies. Moreover, he fancied the Duchess not incapable of using political rumors to further her private caprice; and scenting no immediate danger he resolved to wait upon events.

On rising from dinner he was surprised by a summons from the Duke. The message, an unusual one at that hour, was brought by a slender pale lad, not in his Highness's service, but in that of the German physician Heiligenstern. The boy, who was said to be a Georgian rescued from the Grand Signior's galleys, and whose small oval face was as smooth as a girl's, accosted Odo in one of the remoter garden alleys with the request to follow him at once to the Duke's apartment. Odo complied, and his guide loitered ahead with an air of unconcern, as though not wishing to have his errand guessed. As they passed through the tapestry gallery preceding the gentlemen's antechamber, footsteps and voices were heard within. Instantly the boy was by Odo's side and had drawn him into the embrasure of a window. A moment later Trescorre left the ante-chamber and walked rapidly past their hiding-place. As soon as he was out of sight the Georgian led Odo from his concealment and introduced him by a private way to the Duke's closet.

His Highness was in his bed-chamber; and Odo, on being admitted, found him, still in dressing-gown and nightcap, kneeling with a disordered countenance before the ancient picture of the Last Judgment that hung on the wall facing his bed. He seemed to have forgotten that he had asked for his kinsman; for on the latter's entrance he started up with a suspicious glance and hastily closed the panels of the picture, which (as Odo now noticed) appeared to conceal an inner paint-ing. Then, gathering his dressing-gown about him, he led the way to his closet and bade his visitor be seated.

"I have," said he, speaking in a low voice, and glanc-ing apprehensively about him, "summoned you hither privately to speak on a subject which concerns none but ourselves.—You met no one on your way?" he broke off to enquire.

Odo told him that Count Trescorre had passed, but without perceiving him.

The Duke seemed relieved. "My private actions," said he querulously, "are too jealously spied upon by my ministers. Such surveillance is an offence to my authority, and my subjects shall learn that it will not frighten me from my course." He straightened his bent shoulders and tried to put on the majestic look of his official effigy. "It appears," he continued, with one of his sudden changes of manner, "that the Duchess's uncle, the Duke of Monte Alloro, has heard favorable reports of your wit and accomplishments, and is desirous of receiving you at his court." He paused, and Odo concealed his surprise behind a profound bow.

"I own," the Duke went on, "that the invitation comes unseasonably, since I should have preferred to keep you at my side; but his Highness's great age, and his close kinship to my wife, through whom the request is conveyed, make it impossible for me to refuse." The Duke again paused, as though uncertain how to proceed. At length he resumed:—"I will not conceal from you that his Highness is subject to the fantastical humors of his age. He makes it a condition that the length of your stay shall not be limited; but should you fail to suit his mood you may find yourself out of favor in a week. He writes of wishing to send you on a private mission to the court of Naples; but this may be no more than a passing whim. I see no way, however, but to let you go, and to hope for a favorable welcome for you. The Duchess is determined upon giving her uncle this pleasure, and in fact has consented in return to

oblige me in an important matter." He flushed and
averted his eyes. "I name this," he added with an
effort, "only that her Highness may be aware that it
depends on herself whether I hold to my side of the
bargain. Your papers are already prepared and you
have my permission to set out at your convenience.
Meanwhile it were well that you should keep your
preparations private, at least till you are ready to
take leave." And with the air of dignity he could still
assume on occasion, he rose and handed Odo his passport.

Odo left the closet with a beating heart. It was clear
that his departure from Pianura was as strongly opposed by some one in high authority as it was favored
by the Duchess; and why opposed and by whom he
could not so much as hazard a guess. In the web of
court intrigues it was difficult for the wariest to grope
his way; and Odo was still new to such entanglements.
His first sensation was one of release, of a future suddenly enlarged and cleared. The door was open again
to opportunity, and he was of an age to greet the unexpected like a bride. Only one thought disturbed him.
It was clear that Maria Clementina had paid high for
his security; and did not her sacrifice, whatever its nature, constitute a claim upon his future? In sending
him to her uncle, whose known favorite she was, she
did not let him out of her hand. If he accepted this

chance of escape he must hereafter come and go as she bade. At the thought, his bounding fancy slunk back humbled. He saw himself as Trescorre's successor, his sovereign's official lover, taking up again, under more difficult circumstances, and without the zest of inexperience, the dull routine of his former bondage. No, a thousand times no; he would fetter himself to no woman's fancy! Better find a pretext for staying in Pianura, affront the Duchess by refusing her aid, risk his prospects, his life even, than bow his neck twice to the same yoke. All her charm vanished in this vision of unwilling subjection. . .

Disturbed by these considerations, and anxious to compose his spirits, Odo bethought himself of taking refuge in the Bishop's company. Here at least the atmosphere was clear of mystery: the Bishop held aloof from political intrigue and breathed an air untainted by the *odium theologicum*. Odo found his lordship seated in the cool tessellated saloon which contained his chiefest treasures—marble busts ranged on pedestals between the windows, the bronze Venus Callipyge, and various tables of *pietra commessa* set out with vases and tazzas of antique pattern. A knot of virtuosi gathered about one of these tables were engaged in examining a collection of engraved gems displayed by a lapidary of Florence; while others inspected a Greek manuscript which the Bishop had lately received from Syria. Beyond the

windows, a *cedrario* or orange-walk stretched its sunlit
vista to the terrace above the river; and the black cas-
socks of one or two priests who were strolling in the
clear green shade of a pleached alley made pleasant
spots of dimness in the scene.

Even here, however, Odo was aware of a certain disquietude. The Bishop's visitors, instead of engaging
in animated disputations over his lordship's treasures,
showed a disposition to walk apart, conversing in low
tones; and he himself, presently complaining of the
heat, invited Odo to accompany him to the grot beneath the terrace. In this shaded retreat, studded with
shells and coral and cooled by an artificial wind forced
through the conchs of marble Tritons, his lordship at
once began to speak of the rumors of public disaffection.

"As you know," said he, "my duties and tastes alike
seclude me from political intrigue, and the scandal of
the day seldom travels beyond my kitchens. But as
creaking signboards announce a storm, the hints and
whispers of my household tell me there is mischief
abroad. My position protects me from personal risk,
and my lack of ambition from political enmity; for it
is notorious I would barter the highest honors in the
state for a Greek vase or a bronze of Herculaneum—
not to mention the famous Venus of Giorgione, which,
if report be true, his Highness has burned at Father
Ignazio's instigation. But yours, cavaliere, is a less

sheltered walk, and perhaps a friendly warning may be of service. Yet," he added after a pause, "a warning I can scarce call it, since I know not from what quarter the danger impends. *Proximus ardet Ucalegon;* but there is no telling which way the flames may spread. I can only advise you that the Duke's growing infatuation for his German magician has bred the most violent discontent among his subjects, and that both parties appear resolved to use this disaffection to their advantage. It is said his Highness intends to subject the little prince to some mysterious treatment connected with the rites of the Egyptian priesthood, of whose secret doctrine Heiligenstern pretends to be an adept. Yesterday it was bruited that the Duchess loudly opposed the experiment; this afternoon it is given out that she has yielded. What the result may be, none can foresee; but whichever way the storm blows, the chief danger probably threatens those who have had any connection with the secret societies known to exist in the duchy."

Odo listened attentively, but without betraying any great surprise; and the Bishop, evidently reassured by his composure, suggested that, the heat of the day having declined, they should visit the new Indian pheasants in his volary.

The Bishop's hints had not helped his listener to a decision. Odo indeed gave Cantapresto orders to prepare as privately as possible for their departure; but rather to appear to be carrying out the Duke's instructions than with any fixed intention of so doing. How to find a pretext for remaining he was yet uncertain. To disobey the Duke was impossible; but in the general state of tension it seemed likely enough that both his Highness and the Duchess might change their minds within the next twenty-four hours. He was reluctant to appear that evening in the Duchess's circle; but the command was not to be evaded, and he went thither resolved to excuse himself early.

He found her Highness surrounded by the usual rout that attended her. She was herself in a mood of wild mirth, occasioned by the drolleries of an automatic female figure which a travelling showman introduced by Cantapresto had obtained leave to display at court. This lively puppet performed with surprising skill on the harpsichord, giving the company, among other novelties, selections from the maestro Piccini's latest opera and a concerto of the German composer Glück.

Maria Clementina seemed at first unaware of her kinsman's presence, and he began to hope he might avoid any private talk with her; but when the automaton had been dismissed and the card-tables were preparing, one of her gentlemen summoned him to her side. As usual, she was highly rouged in the French fashion, and her cold blue eyes had a light which set off the extraordinary fairness of her skin.

"Cousin," said she at once, "have you your papers?" Her tone was haughty and yet eager, as though she scorned to show herself concerned, yet would not have had him believe in her indifference. Odo bowed without speaking.

"And when do you set out?" she continued. "My good uncle is impatient to receive you."

"At the earliest moment, madam," he replied with some hesitation.

The hesitation was not lost on her and he saw her flush through her rouge.

"Ah," said she in a low voice, "the earliest moment is none too early!—Do you go to-morrow?" she persisted; but just then Trescorre advanced toward them, and under a burst of assumed merriment she privately signed to Odo to withdraw.

He was glad to make his escape, for the sense of walking among hidden pitfalls was growing on him. That he had acquitted himself awkwardly with the Duchess he was well aware; but Trescorre's interruption had at least enabled him to gain time. An increasing unwillingness to leave Pianura had replaced his former impatience to be gone. The reluctance to desert his friends was coupled with a boyish desire to stay and see the game out; and behind all his other impulses lurked the instinctive resistance to any feminine influence save one.

The next morning he half-expected another message from the Duchess; but none came, and he judged her to be gravely offended. Cantapresto appeared early with the rumor that some kind of magical ceremony was to be performed that evening in the palace; and toward noon the Georgian boy again privately came to Odo and requested him to wait on the Duke when his Highness rose from supper. This increased Odo's fears for Gamba, Andreoni and the other reformers; yet he dared neither seek them out in person nor entrust a message to Cantapresto. As the day passed, however, he began to throw off his apprehensions. It was not the first time since he had come to Pianura that there had been ominous talk of political disturbances, and he knew that Gamba and his friends were not without means of getting under shelter. As to his own risk, he did not give it a thought. He was not of an age or a temper to weigh personal danger against the excitement of conflict; and as evening drew on he found himself wondering with some impatience if after all nothing unusual would happen.

He supped alone, and at the appointed hour proceeded to the Duke's apartments, taking no farther precaution than to carry his passport about him. The palace seemed deserted. Everywhere an air of apprehension and mystery hung over the long corridors and dimly-lit antechambers. The day had been sultry, with a low sky foreboding great heat, and not a breath of air entered at the windows. There were few persons about, but one or two beggars lurked as usual on the landings of the great staircase, and Odo, in passing, felt his sleeve touched by a woman cowering under the marble ramp in the shadow thrown by a colossal Cæsar. Looking down, he heard a voice beg for alms, and as he gave it the woman pressed a paper into his hand and slipped away through the darkness.

Odo hastened on till he could assure himself of being unobserved; then he unfolded the paper and read these words in Gamba's hand: "Have no fear for any one's safety but your own." With a sense of relief he hid the message and entered the Duke's antechamber.

Here he was received by Heiligenstern's Oriental servant, who, with a mute salutation, led him into a large room where the Duke's pages usually waited. The walls of this apartment had been concealed under hangings of black silk worked with cabalistic devices. Oil-lamps set on tripods of antique design shed a faint light over the company seated at one end of the room, among whom Odo recognized the chief dignitaries of the court. The ladies looked pale but curious, the men for the most part indifferent or disapproving. Intense quietness prevailed, broken only by the soft opening and closing of the door through which the guests were admitted. Presently the Duke and Duchess emerged from his Highness's closet. They were followed by Prince Ferrante, supported by his governor and his dwarf, and robed in a silken dressing-gown which hung in voluminous folds about his little shrunken body. Their Highnesses seated themselves in two arm-chairs in front of the court, and the little prince reclined beside his mother.

No sooner had they taken their places than Heiligenstern stepped forth, wearing a doctor's gown and a quaintly-shaped bonnet or mitre. In his long robes and strange headdress he looked extraordinarily tall and pale, and his features had the glassy-eyed fixity of an ancient mask. He was followed by his two attendants, the Oriental carrying a frame-work of polished metal, not unlike a low narrow bed, which he set down in the middle of the room; while the Georgian lad, who had exchanged his *fustanella* and embroidered jacket for a flowing white robe, bore in his hands a crystal globe set in a gold stand. Having reverently placed it on a small table, the boy, at a signal from his master, drew forth a phial and dropped its contents into a bronze vat or brazier which stood at the far end of the room. Instantly clouds of perfumed vapor filled the air, and as these dispersed it was seen that the black hangings of the walls had vanished with them, and the spectators found themselves seated in a kind of open temple through which the eye travelled down colonnaded vistas set with statues and fountains. This magical prospect was bathed in sunlight, and Odo observed that, though the lamps had gone out, the same brightness suffused the room and illuminated the wondering faces of the audience. The little prince uttered a cry of delight, and the magician stepped forward, raising a long white wand in his hand.

"This," said he, in measured accents, "is an evocation of the Temple of Health, into whose blissful precincts the wisdom of the ancients was able to lead the sufferer who put his trust in them. This *deceptio visûs*, or product of rhabdomancy, easily effected by an adept of the Egyptian mysteries, is designed but to prefigure the reality which awaits those who seek health through the ministry of the disciples of Iamblichus. It is no longer denied among men of learning that those who have been instructed in the secret doctrine of the ancients are able, by certain correspondences of nature, revealed only to the initiated, to act on the inanimate world about them, and on the animal economy, by means beyond the common capabilities of man." He paused a moment, and then, turning with a low bow to the Duke, enquired whether his Highness desired the rites to proceed.

The Duke signed his assent, and Heiligenstern, raising his wand, evoked another volume of mist. This time it was shot through with green flames, and as the wild light subsided the room was once more revealed with its black hangings, and the lamps flickered into life again.

After another pause, doubtless intended to increase the tension of the spectators, the magician bade his servant place the crystal before him. He then raised his hands as if in prayer, speaking in a strange chanting jargon, in which Odo detected fragments of Greek and Latin, and the recurring names of the Judaic demons and angels. As this ceased Heiligenstern beckoned to the Georgian boy, who approached him with bowed head and reverently folded hands.

"Your Highness," said Heiligenstern, "and this distinguished company, are doubtless familiar with the magic crystal of the ancients, in which the future may be deciphered by the pure in heart. This lad, whom I rescued from slavery and have bred to my service in the solemn rites of the priesthood of Isis, is as clear in spirit as the crystal which stands before you. The future lies open to him in this translucent sphere and he is prepared to disclose it at your bidding."

There was a moment's silence; but on the magician's repeating his enquiry the Duke said: "Let the boy tell me what he sees."

Heiligenstern at once laid his hands on his acolyte's head and murmured a few words over him; then the boy advanced and bent devoutly above the crystal. Almost immediately the globe was seen to cloud, as though suffused with milk; the cloud gradually faded and the boy began to speak in a low hesitating tone.

"I see," he said, "I see a face . . . a fair face . . ." he faltered and glanced up almost apprehensively at Heiligenstern, whose gaze remained impenetrable. The boy began to tremble. "I see nothing," he said in a whisper. "There is one here purer than I . . . the crystal will not speak for me in that other's presence. . ."

"Who is that other?" Heiligenstern asked.

The boy fixed his eyes on the little prince. An excited murmur ran through the company and Heiligenstern again advanced to the Duke. "Will your Highness," he asked, "permit the prince to look into the sacred sphere?"

Odo saw the Duchess extend her hand impulsively toward the child; but at a signal from the Duke the little prince's chair was carried to the table on which the crystal stood. Instantly the former phenomenon was repeated, the globe clouding and then clearing itself like a pool after rain.

"Speak, my son," said the Duke. "Tell us what the heavenly powers reveal to you."

The little prince continued to pore over the globe without speaking. Suddenly his thin face reddened and he clung more closely to his companion's arm.

"I see a beautiful place," he began, his small fluting voice rising like a bird's pipe in the stillness, "a place a thousand times more beautiful than this . . . like a garden . . . full of golden-haired children . . . with beautiful strange toys in their hands . . . they have wings like birds . . . they *are* birds . . . ah! they are flying away from me . . . I see them no more . . . they vanish through the trees . . ." He broke off sadly.

Heiligenstern smiled. "That, your Highness, is a vision of the prince's own future, when, restored to health, he is able to disport himself with his playmates in the gardens of the palace."

"But they were not the gardens of the palace!" the little boy exclaimed. "They were much more beautiful than our gardens."

Heiligenstern bowed. "They appeared so to your Highness," he deferentially suggested, "because all the world seems more beautiful to those who have regained their health."

"Enough, my son!" exclaimed the Duchess with a shaken voice. "Why will you weary the child?" she continued, turning to the Duke; and the latter, with evident reluctance, signed to Heiligenstern to cover the crystal. To the general surprise, however, Prince Ferrante pushed back the black velvet covering which the Georgian boy was preparing to throw over it.

"No, no," he exclaimed, in the high obstinate voice

of the spoiled child, "let me look again ... let me see some more beautiful things ... I have never seen anything so beautiful, even in my sleep!" It was the plaintive cry of the child whose happiest hours are those spent in unconsciousness.

"Look again, then," said the Duke, "and ask the heavenly powers what more they have to show you."

The boy gazed in silence; then he broke out: "Ah, now we are in the palace ... I see your Highness's cabinet ... no, it is the bed-chamber ... it is night ... and I see your Highness lying asleep ... very still ... very still ... your Highness wears the scapular received last Easter from his Holiness ... It is very dark ... Oh, now a light begins to shine ... where does it come from? Through the door? No, there is no door on that side of the room ... It shines through the wall at the foot of the bed ... ah! I see—" his voice mounted to a cry—"The old picture at the foot of the bed ... the picture with the wicked people burning in it ... has opened like a door ... the light is shining through it ... and now a lady steps out from the wall behind the picture ... oh, so beautiful ... she has yellow hair, as yellow as my mother's, but longer ... oh, much longer ... she carries a rose in her hand ... and there are white doves flying about her shoulders ... she is naked, quite naked, poor lady! but she does not seem to mind ...

she seems to be laughing about it . . . and your Highness . . ."

The Duke started up violently. "Enough—enough!" he stammered. "The fever is on the child . . . this agitation is . . . most pernicious . . . Cover the crystal, I say!"

He sank back, his forehead damp with perspiration. In an instant the crystal had been removed, and Prince Ferrante carried back to his mother's side. The boy seemed in no wise affected by his father's commotion. His eyes burned with excitement, and he sat up eagerly, as though not to miss a detail of what was going forward. Maria Clementina leaned over and clasped his hand, but he hardly noticed her. "I want to see some more beautiful things!" he insisted.

The Duke sat speechless, a fallen heap in his chair, and the courtiers looked at each other, their faces shifting spectrally in the faint light, like phantom travellers waiting to be ferried across some mysterious river. At length Heiligenstern advanced and with every mark of deference addressed himself to the Duke.

"Your Highness," said he quietly, "need be under no apprehension as to the effect produced upon the prince. The magic crystal, as your Highness is aware, is under the protection of the blessed spirits, and its revelations cannot harm those who are pure-minded enough to receive them. But the chief purpose of this assemblage was to witness the communication of vital force to the prince, by means of the electrical current. The crystal, by revealing its secrets to the prince, has testified to his perfect purity of mind, and thus declared him to be in a peculiarly fit state to receive what may be designated as the Sacrament of the new faith."

A murmur ran through the room, but Heiligenstern continued without wavering: "I mean thereby to describe that natural religion which, by instructing its adepts in the use of the hidden potencies of earth and air, testifies afresh to the power of the unseen Maker of the Universe."

The murmur subsided, and the Duke, regaining his voice, said with an assumption of authority: "Let the treatment begin."

Heiligenstern immediately spoke a word to the Oriental, who bent over the metal bed which had been set up in the middle of the room. As he did so the air again darkened and the figures of the magician and his assistants were discernible only as flitting shades in the obscurity. Suddenly a soft pure light overflowed the room, the perfume of flowers filled the air, and music seemed to steal out of the very walls. Heiligenstern whispered to the governor and between them they lifted the little prince from his chair and laid him gently on the bed. The magician then leaned over the boy with a slow weaving motion of the hands.

"If your Highness will be pleased to sleep," he said, "I promise your Highness the most beautiful dreams."

The boy smiled back at him and he continued to bend above the bed with flitting hands. Suddenly the little prince began to laugh.

"What does your Highness feel?" the magician asked.

"A prickling . . . such a soft warm prickling . . . as if my blood were sunshine with motes dancing in it . . . or as if that sparkling wine of France were running all over my body."

"It is an agreeable sensation, your Highness?"

The boy nodded.

"It is well with your Highness?"

"Very well."

Heiligenstern began a low rhythmic chant, and gradually the air darkened, but with the mild dimness of a summer twilight, through which sparks could be seen flickering like fireflies about the reclining prince. The hush grew deeper; but in the stillness Odo became aware of some unseen influence that seemed to envelop him in waves of exquisite sensation. It was as though the vast silence of the night had poured into the room and like a dark tepid sea were lapping about his body and rising to his lips. His thoughts, dissolved into emotion, seemed to waver and float on the stillness like seaweed on the lift of the tide. He stood spell-bound, lulled, yielding himself to a blissful dissolution.

Suddenly he became aware that the hush was too intense, too complete; and a moment later, as though stretched to the cracking-point, it burst terrifically into sound. A huge uproar shook the room, crashing through it like a tangible mass. The sparks whirled in a menacing dance round the little prince's body, and, abruptly blotted, left a deeper darkness, in which the confused herding movements of startled figures were indistinguishably merged. A flash of silence followed; then the liberated forces of the night broke in rain and thunder on the rocking walls of the room.

"Light—light!" some one stammered; and at the same moment a door was flung open, admitting a burst of candle-light and a group of figures in ecclesiastical dress, against which the white gown and black hood of Father Ignazio detached themselves. The Dominican stepped toward the Duke.

"Your Highness," said he in a tone of quiet resolution, "must pardon this interruption; I act at the bidding of the Holy Office."

Even in that moment of profound disarray the name sent a deeper shudder through his hearers. The Duke, who stood grasping the arms of his chair, raised his head and tried to stare down the intruders; but no one heeded his look. At a signal from the Dominican a servant had brought in a pair of candelabra, and in their commonplace light the cabalistic hangings, the magician's appliances and his fantastically-dressed attendants looked as tawdry as the paraphernalia of a village quack. Heiligenstern alone survived the test. Erect, at bay as it were, his black robe falling in hieratic folds, the white wand raised in his hands, he might have personified the Prince of darkness drawn up undaunted against the hosts of the Lord. Some one had snatched the little prince from his stretcher, and Maria Clementina, holding him to her breast, sat palely confronting the sorcerer. She alone seemed to measure her strength against his in some mysterious conflict of the will. But meanwhile the Duke had regained his voice.

"My father," said he, "on what information does the Holy Office act?"

The Dominican drew a parchment from his breast. "On that of the Inquisitor General, your Highness," he replied, handing the paper to the Duke, who unfolded it with trembling hands but was plainly unable to master its contents. Father Ignazio beckoned to an ecclesiastic who had entered the room in his train.

"This, your Highness," said he, "is the abate de Crucis of Innsbruck, who was lately commissioned by the Holy Office to enquire into the practices and doctrine of the order of the Illuminati, that corrupt and atheistical sect which has been the cause of so much scandal among the German principalities. In the course of his investigations he became aware that the order

[339]

had secretly established a lodge in Pianura; and hastening hither from Rome to advise your Highness of the
fact, has discovered in the so-called Count Heiligenstern one of the most notorious apostles of the order."
He turned to the priest. "Signor abate," he said, "you
confirm these facts?"

The abate de Crucis quietly advanced. He was a slight
pale man of about thirty, with a thoughtful and indulgent cast of countenance.

"In every particular," said he, bowing profoundly to
the Duke, and speaking in a low voice of singular sweetness. "It has been my duty to track this man's career
from its ignoble beginning to its infamous culmination,
and I have been able to place in the hands of the Holy
Office the most complete proofs of his guilt. The so-
called Count Heiligenstern is the son of a tailor in a
small village of Pomerania. After passing through various vicissitudes with which I need not trouble your
Highness, he obtained the confidence of the notorious
Dr. Weishaupt, the founder of the German order of the
Illuminati, and together this precious couple have in-
defatigably propagated their obscene and blasphemous
doctrines. That they preach atheism and tyrannicide I
need not tell your Highness; but it is less generally
known that they have made these infamous doctrines
the cloak of private vices from which even paganism
would have recoiled. The man now before me, among

other open offences against society, is known to have
seduced a young girl of a noble family in Ratisbon and
to have murdered her child. His own wife and children
he long since abandoned and disowned; and the youth
yonder, whom he describes as a Georgian slave rescued
from the Grand Signior's galleys, is in fact the wife of
a Greek juggler of Ravenna, and has forsaken her husband to live in criminal intercourse with an atheist and
assassin."

This indictment, pronounced with an absence of emotion which made each word cut the air like the separate
stroke of a lash, was followed by a prolonged silence;
then one of the Duchess's ladies cried out suddenly and
burst into tears. This was the signal for a general out-
break. The room was filled with a confusion of voices,
and among the groups surging about him Odo noticed
a number of the Duke's *sbirri* making their way quietly
through the crowd. The notary of the Holy Office advanced toward Heiligenstern, who had placed himself
against the wall, with one arm flung about his trembling acolyte. The Duchess, her boy still clasped against
her, remained proudly seated; but her eyes met Odo's
in a glance of terrified entreaty, and at the same instant
he felt a clutch on his sleeve and heard Cantapresto's
whisper.

"Cavaliere, a boat waits at the landing below the
tanners' lane. The shortest way to it is through the

gardens and your excellency will find the gate beyond the Chinese pavilion unlocked."

He had vanished before Odo could look round. The latter still wavered; but as he did so he caught Trescorre's face through the crowd. The minister's eye was fixed on him; and the discovery was enough to make him plunge through the narrow wake left by Cantapresto's retreat.

Odo made his way unhindered to the anteroom, which was also thronged, ecclesiastics, servants and even beggars from the courtyard jostling each other in their struggle to see what was going forward. The confusion favored his escape, and a moment later he was hastening down the tapestry gallery and through the vacant corridors of the palace. He was familiar with half-a-dozen short-cuts across this network of passages; but in his bewilderment he pressed on down the great stairs and across the echoing guard-room that opened on the terrace. A drowsy sentinel challenged him; and on Odo's explaining that he sought to leave, and not to enter, the palace, replied that he had his Highness's orders to let no one out that night. For a moment Odo was at a loss; then he remembered his passport. It seemed to him an interminable time before the sentinel had scrutinized it by the light of a guttering candle, and to his surprise he found himself in a cold sweat of fear. The rattle of the storm simulated footsteps at his heels and he felt the blind rage of a man within shot of invisible foes.

The passport restored, he plunged out into the night. It was pitch-black in the gardens and the rain drove down with the guttural rush of a midsummer storm. So fierce was its fall that it seemed to suck up the earth in its black eddies, and he felt himself swept along over a heaving hissing surface, with wet boughs lashing out at him as he fled. From one terrace to another he dropped to lower depths of buffeting dripping darkness, till he found his hand on the gate-latch and swung to the black lane below the wall. Thence on a run he wound to the tanners' quarter by the river: a district commonly as foul-tongued as it was ill-flavored, but to-night clean-purged of both evils by the vehement sweep of the storm. Here he groped his way among slippery places and past huddled out-buildings to the piles of the wharf. The rain was now subdued to a noiseless vertical descent, through which he could hear the tap of the river against the piles. Scarce knowing what he fled or whither he was flying, he let himself down the steps and found the flat of a boat's bottom underfoot. A boatman, distinguishable only as a black bulk in the stern, steadied his descent with outstretched hand; then the bow swung round, and after a laboring stroke or two they caught the current and were swept down through the rushing darkness.

END OF VOL. I